# A Good Man

## FATHERS AND SONS IN POETRY AND PROSE

Edited by
Irv Broughton

FAWCETT COLUMBINE • NEW YORK

A Fawcett Columbine Book
Published by Ballantine Books
Introduction and compilation copyright © 1993 Irv Broughton

Owing to limitations of space, permissions acknowledgments
appear at the back of this book.

Library of Congress Cataloging-in-Publication Data
A Good man : fathers and sons in poetry and prose/
[edited by] Irv Broughton.—1st ed.
    p. cm.
  ISBN 0-449-90747-3
    1. Fathers and sons—Literary collections. I. Broughton, Irv.
PN6071.F3G66 1993
808.8'03520431—dc20                          92-54994
                                              CIP

Designed by Ann Gold
Manufactured in the United States of America
First Edition: June 1993
10 9 8 7 6 5 4 3 2 1

ACKNOWLEDGMENTS

Special thanks to my editor, Sam Vaughan, for his generous assistance and to Ginny Faber and Phebe Kirkham for their help. Thanks also to my wife, Connie, for her support and encouragement, not to mention the part she played in making me a father. Thanks, too, to Bob Zeller for the assist early on in the project as well as to Marge and Bill Walker.

# Contents

# Introduction

In recent years I have thought a lot about how you sum up a man's life—a father's life: I am here, his son. So are his four other sons. His sweet wife. My children. Perhaps you also sum it up by saying quite simply what he liked, for he liked many things. He liked Rye Krisp; most anything approved by the Pennsylvania Department of Agriculture—which he thought was definitive; he liked prunes—before he needed them and natural foods before they were on everybody's shopping list; he liked tall pines; he liked Ronnie's pumpernickel; he liked Swiss chard, saying it in a lingering Massachusetts accent—that's with the harrdd sound to the charrdd; he liked the rich dark earth of Zellwood; he liked to take his white Buick bounding into the fields and pastures of Florida; he loved Harris tweed—though he seldom wore it in the warmer climate where he had lived on and off for more than fifty years; years ago he liked to plunge into Rock Springs in his boxer shorts, which he preferred because he swore no one could tell them from a swimsuit; he loved blackstrap molasses processed with the help of Otis Balcolm's daddy's mule; he loved Scotch broom from the East Dennis countryside of his youth; he loved "prime locations"; he liked Ritter relish on anything; he liked the ripple of the North Carolina mountains; and he liked the clouds—they were the mountains of Florida.

In a world of expediency, he wasn't expedient; in a world of fluff and posturing, he was genuine. If the measure of man is his parlance—how he speaks—my dad was special. Things and life were "wonderful." There were "wonderful people," "wonderful friends"—we had "wonderful brothers." In his college years they called him "Smiling Dick Broughton." Through his life, he smiled a lot; he appreciated a lot. He especially appreciated his friends, the people who hung with him in the tough times. They were his heroes. And in his own, doggedly persistent way, he hung with them. He was often generous to a fault.

This book is an outgrowth of my feelings for my father. He was a good man—difficult, complex, and good. I started by writing a eulogy on his death in 1990. This book is perhaps a check delivered late.

I learned from my father a great many lessons. I learned, for example, that the best thing to do is frequently the hardest; that conformity is not altogether a virtue; that truth is the measure of the man; and that giddy popularity is a surface we can only expect to slide on. I didn't, I suppose, as is true of many men, learn much about tears. I did learn something about caring and responsibility, some of it humorous. I wrote once about him running beside me in a track meet, trying to feed his son a small Dixie cup of water as water sloshed and spilled over his business suit. But in serious times, when a neighbor fell sick or into hardship, when a trauma reached deep into someone's life, my father (and my mother) faced it off with a sympathy as absolute and bright as morning prayer. He was that way to the end, dying of cancer, concerned more for his family than himself.

I find my own father everywhere across the pages of this book. In reading John Hall Wheelock's poem of his father's magnificent gardens, I think of our father's prized gardens where huge fists of zinnias pulled themselves up the retaining wall and find his presence. Indeed he was obsessed with details—and with doing things his way—as in Bill Henderson's "Ceremonies" from *His Son: A Child of the Fifties*. I also find him in an interesting and unusual story by Sherwood Anderson where his bellowing, powerful presence at times, growing up, embarrassed, even enlivened, me and at times taught me, I believe, about what an "original" was, and maybe about creativity.

His sudden anger exists some in Andrew Hudgins's poem, "My Father's Rage." And I see myself, to a degree, in Robert Hayden's poem, "Those Winter Sundays," where the consuming world of youth knows only its own dire priorities. Though my father was not a brutal man—a taskmaster maybe, but not a brutal man—I find him, as I read, in the duality of the excerpt from Massimo Taparelli A'Azeglio's *A Happy Childhood*. I see him in a peculiar, general way in the conviction of these well-chosen words—though he was not a writer and could be imprecise or misfire, as we all can when it comes to the difficult task of communication. Mostly, however, when he loved something and spoke of it, be it the resplendent, white sandy bottom of a Florida lake, a sunset, or the way live oaks gathered almost religiously in a field, he made you love it too. Finally, I measure his loss in Greg Kuzma's stunning poem about carrying on when a father is gone.

But I should stop, for the book is not really about me, or my father—though we both are in these pages in the sum of the work, and I am here in the choices made. This book is about what a father is and what the role of father means—father from a man's perspective. It is my hope that fathers and sons everywhere will find themselves in this wide tidal wave of stories, poems, and reminiscences as I did over and over, and that the women who share their lives, the mothers, wives, and daughters will find something herein, too.

Walt Disney pointed out once how few songs were written about fathers. The number of songs today on the subject probably hasn't increased, and certainly there is not a surplus of books that focus on fathers—especially by men exploring the lives of fathers. That is another reason that I have chosen to explore exclusively the father–son relationship: to examine fathers with their unpopular decisions, bold moves, sudden anger, ofttimes inchoate love, absences, silences, and wild caprice. Fathers represent many good things that go beyond the tabloid details of endless talk shows, or deadbeat ledgers of divorce courts, or the children's shows that have dad as unredeemed buffoon.

My friend, the late T. W. Murray, Sr., inventor, industrialist, wonderful man, said, "Men are more vulnerable." The comment startled me. "Because they never give up," he continued. Of course, some do, but more than a few do not. This book mostly deals with fathers who put themselves on the line, failing, falling, striving, and rising up. It also deals with the age-old battles and decisions men—and fathers—must take on: the security, safety, and unerring care of family; the struggle to balance livelihood with other claims; the need to express love, to communicate, to maintain a complex relationship with a woman; as well as the indefatigable need to be strong and tender, open and direct, in the full knowledge of the world's odds and realities.

This book is memories warm and tough, father with moles and wrinkles too, father foot-sore from the march. It is about forgiveness, at times, about loss and regeneration—a form of birth; about who we got to walk with us and teach us after we were born. There is also the kind of love that transcends differences—that highlights the perfections from the too-easy-to-see imperfections, and binds human beings to one another, fathers to sons—and whole families together.

*A Good Man* is a portrait in words of fathers and sons, the shapes of their lives and the sometimes fog-shrouded inlets of their own feelings. It is an amalgam of what they love. Above all, it is a glimpse of a subject important in this and any time and, as I hold fast to my own father's memory, a celebration of fathers everywhere and in all times.

*James Wright*

# Father

In paradise I poised my foot above the boat and said:
Who prayed for me?
                              But only the dip of an oar
In water sounded; slowly fog from some cold shore
Circled in wreaths around my head.

But who is waiting?
                              And the wind began,
Transfiguring my face from nothingness
To tiny weeping eyes. And when my voice
Grew real, there was a place
Far, far below on earth. There was a tiny man—

It was my father wandering round the waters at the wharf
Irritably he circled and he called
Out to the marine currents up and down,
But heard only a cold unmeaning cough,
And saw the oarsman in the mist enshawled.

He drew me from the boat. I was asleep.
And we went home together.

# I
# Their Sides,
# Their Earthly
# Shapes

*Life all around me here in the village:*
*Tragedy, comedy, valor and truth,*
*Courage, constancy, heroism, failure—*
*All in the loom, and oh what patterns!*
                                    Edgar Lee Masters

Matthew J. Spireng

# The Snake

I was to follow my father that day
into the woods beyond the field to walk
where hemlock and oak kept grass away, but
I stayed far, far back intending to stalk
him, follow his tracks and leap out *Surprise!*
*Surprise!* and watch his face to see the shock
in his eyes. Before I left the field, he
disappeared and I came across a snake
coiled on a rock, a snake as big and black
as any on TV, waiting to strike
if only I'd come close. I screamed for help
and ran for the house as if every dark
thing that had ever lurked under my bed
was at my heels the whole hellish way back
to where my mother was. *Momma, a snake,*
*a snake!* I cried, the hot tears on my cheek
burning where a branch had whipped, and father
came running, brushed tears with his fingers like
dew on a window. *Surprised you, did he?*
*I'm sorry,* he said. He would never look
the same again, never seem so simple.

*Jerome Weidman*
# My Father Sits in the Dark

y father has a peculiar habit. He is fond of sitting in the dark, alone. Sometimes I come home very late. The house is dark. I let myself in quietly because I do not want to disturb my mother. She is a light sleeper. I tiptoe into my room and undress in the dark. I go to the kitchen for a drink of water. My bare feet make no noise. I step into the room and almost trip over my father. He is sitting in a kitchen chair, in his pajamas, smoking his pipe.

"Hello, Pop," I say.

"Hello, son."

"Why don't you go to bed, Pa?"

"I will," he says.

But he remains there. Long after I am asleep I feel sure that he is still sitting there, smoking.

Many times I am reading in my room. I hear my mother get the house ready for the night. I hear my kid brother go to bed. I hear my sister come in. I hear her do things with jars and combs until she, too, is quiet. I know she has gone to sleep. In a little while I hear my mother say good night to my father. I continue to read. Soon I become thirsty. (I drink a lot of water.) I go to the kitchen for a drink. Again I almost stumble across my father. Many times it startles me. I forget about him. And there he is—smoking, sitting, thinking.

"Why don't you go to bed, Pop?"

"I will, son."

But he doesn't. He just sits there and smokes and thinks. It worries me. I can't understand it. What can he be thinking about? Once I asked him.

"What are you thinking, Pa?"

"Nothing," he said.

Once I left him there and went to bed. I awoke several hours later.

I was thirsty. I went to the kitchen. There he was. His pipe was out. But he sat there, staring into a corner of the kitchen. After a moment I became accustomed to the darkness. I took my drink. He still sat and stared. His eyes did not blink. I thought he was not even aware of me. I was afraid.

"Why don't you go to bed, Pop?"

"I will, son," he said. "Don't wait up for me."

"But," I said, "you've been sitting here for hours. What's wrong? What are you thinking about?"

"Nothing, son," he said. "Nothing. It's just restful. That's all."

The way he said it was convincing. He did not seem worried. His voice was even and pleasant. It always is. But I could not understand it. How could it be restful to sit alone in an uncomfortable chair far into the night, in darkness?

What can it be?

I review all the possibilities. It can't be money. I know that. We haven't much, but when he is worried about money he makes no secret of it. It can't be his health. He is not reticent about that either. It can't be the health of anyone in the family. We are a bit short on money, but we are long on health. (Knock wood, my mother would say.) What can it be? I am afraid I do not know. But that does not stop me from worrying.

Maybe he is thinking of his brothers in the old country. Or of his mother and his two stepmothers. Or of his father. But they are all dead. And he would not brood about them like that. I say brood, but it is not really true. He does not brood. He does not even seem to be thinking. He looks too peaceful, too, well not contented, just too peaceful, to be brooding. Perhaps it is as he says. Perhaps it is restful. But it does not seem possible. It worries me.

If I only knew what he thinks about. If I only knew that he thinks at all. I might not be able to help him. He might not even need help. It may be as he says. It may be restful. But at least I would not worry about it.

Why does he just sit there, in the dark? Is his mind failing? No, it can't be. He is only fifty-three. And he is just as keen-witted as ever. In fact, he is the same in every respect. He still likes beet soup. He still reads the second section of the *Times* first. He still wears wing collars. He still believes that Debs could have saved the country and that T.R. was a tool of moneyed interests. He is the same in every way. He does not even look older than he did five years ago. Everybody remarks about that. Well-preserved, they say. But he sits in the dark, alone, smoking, staring straight ahead of him, unblinking, into the small hours of the night.

If it is as he says, if it is restful, I will let it go at that. But suppose it is not. Suppose it is something I cannot fathom. Perhaps he needs help. Why doesn't he speak? Why doesn't he frown or laugh or cry? Why doesn't he do something? Why does he just sit there?

Finally I become angry. Maybe it is just my unsatisfied curiosity. Maybe I am a bit worried. Anyway, I become angry.

"Is something wrong, Pop?"

"Nothing, son. Nothing at all."

But this time I am determined not to be put off. I am angry.

"Then why do you sit here all alone, thinking, till late?"

"It's restful son. I like it."

I am getting nowhere. Tomorrow he will be sitting there again. I will be puzzled. I will be worried. I will not stop now. I am angry.

"Well, what do you think about, Pa? Why do you just sit here? What's worrying you? What do you think about?"

"Nothing's worrying me, son. I'm all right. It's just restful. That's all. Go to bed, son."

My anger has left me. But the feeling of worry is still there. I must get an answer. It seems so silly. Why doesn't he tell me? I have a funny feeling that unless I get an answer I will go crazy. I am insistent.

"But what do you think about, Pa? What is it?"

"Nothing, son. Just things in general. Nothing special. Just things."

I can get no answer.

It is very late. The street is quiet and the house is dark. I climb the steps softly, skipping the ones that creak. I let myself in with my key and tiptoe into my room. I remove my clothes and remember that I am thirsty. In my bare feet I walk to the kitchen. Before I reach it I know he is there.

I can see the deeper darkness of his hunched shape. He is sitting in the same chair, his elbows on his knees, his cold pipe in his teeth, his unblinking eyes staring straight ahead. He does not seem to know I am there. He did not hear me come in. I stand quietly in the doorway and watch him.

Everything is quiet, but the night is full of little sounds. As I stand there motionless I begin to notice them. The ticking of the alarm clock on the icebox. The low hum of an automobile passing many blocks away. The swish of papers moved along the street by a breeze. A whispering rise and fall of sound, like low breathing. It is strangely pleasant.

The dryness in my throat reminds me. I step briskly into the kitchen.

"Hello, Pop," I say.

"Hello, son," he says. His voice is low and dreamlike. He does not change his position or shift his gaze.

I cannot find the faucet. The dim shadow of light that comes through the window from the streetlamp only makes the room seem darker. I reach for the short chain in the center of the room. I snap on the light.

He straightens up with a jerk, as though he has been struck. "What's the matter, Pop?" I ask.

"Nothing," he says. "I don't like the light."

I snap the light off. I drink my water slowly. I must take it easy, I say to myself. I must get to the bottom of this.

"Why don't you go to bed? Why do you sit here so late in the dark?"

"It's nice," he says. "I can't get used to lights. We didn't have lights when I was a boy in Europe."

My heart skips a beat and I catch my breath happily. I begin to think I understand. I remember the stories of his boyhood in Austria. I see the wide-beamed *kretchma,* with my grandfather behind the bar. It is late, the customers are gone, and he is dozing. I see the bed of glowing coals, the last of the roaring fire. The room is already dark, and growing darker. I see a small boy, crouched on a pile of twigs at one side of the huge fireplace, his starry gaze fixed on the dull remains of the dead flames. The boy is my father.

I remember the pleasure of those few moments while I stood quietly in the doorway watching him.

"You mean there's nothing wrong? You just sit in the dark because you like it, Pop?" I find it hard to keep my voice from rising in a happy shout.

"Sure," he says. "I can't think with the light on."

I set my glass down and turn to go back to my room. "Good night, Pop," I say.

"Good night," he says.

Then I remember. I turn back. "What do you think about, Pop?" I ask.

His voice seems to come from far away. It is quiet and even again. "Nothing," he says softly. "Nothing special."

*Massimo Taparelli A'Azeglio*

## *from* A Happy Childhood

W hilst living at this villa, our father was accustomed to take us out for long walks, which were the subjects of special regulations. We were strictly forbidden to ask, "Have we far to go?"—"What time is it?" or to say, "I am thirsty; I am hungry; I am tired," but in everything else we had full liberty of speech and action. Returning from one of these excursions, we one day found ourselves below Castel di Poggio, a rugged stony path leading towards Vincigliata. In one hand I had a nosegay of wild flowers, gathered by the way, and in the other a stick, when I happened to stumble, and fell awkwardly. My father sprang forward to pick me up, and seeing that one arm pained me, he examined it and found that in fact the arm was broken below the elbow. At this time my eyes were fixed upon him, and I could see his countenance change, and assume such an expression of tenderness and anxiety that he no longer appeared to be the same man. He bound up my arm as well as he could, and we then continued our way homewards. After a few moments, during which my father had resumed his usual calmness, he said to me—

"Listen, Mammolino: your mother is not well. If she knows you are hurt it will hurt her worse. You must be brave, my boy: tomorrow morning we will go to Florence, where all that is needed can be done for you; but this evening you must not show you are in pain. Do you understand?"

All this was said with his usual firmness and authority, but also with the greatest affection. I was only too glad to have so important and difficult a task entrusted to me. The whole evening I sat quietly in a corner, supporting my poor little broken arm as best I could, and my mother only thought me tired by the long walk, and had no suspicion of the truth.

The next day I was taken to Florence, and my arm was set, but to complete the cure I had to be sent to the Baths of Vinadio a few years afterward. Some people may, in this instance, think my father was cruel. I remember the fact as if it were but yesterday, and I am sure such an idea never for one minute entered my mind. The expression of ineffable tenderness which I had read in his eyes had so delighted me, it seemed so reasonable to avoid alarming my mother, that I looked on the hard task allotted me as a fine opportunity of displaying my courage. I did so because I had not been spoilt, and good principles had been implanted early within me; and now that I am an old man and have known the world, I bless the severity of my father; and I could wish every Italian child might have one like him, and derive more profit than I did—in thirty years' time Italy would then be the first of nations.

Moreover, it is a fact that children are much more observant than is commonly supposed, and never regard as hostile a just but affectionate severity. I have always seen them disposed to prefer persons who keep them in order to those who constantly yield to their caprices; and soldiers are just the same in this respect.

The following is another example to prove that my father did not deserve to be called cruel:

He thought it a bad practice to awaken children suddenly, or to let their sleep be abruptly disturbed. If we had to rise early for a journey, he would come to my bedside and softly hum a popular song, two lines of which still ring in my ears:

> *Chi vuol veder l'aurora*
> *Lasci le molli piume.*
> *(He who the early dawn would view*
> *Down pillows must eschew.)*

And by gradually raising his voice, he awoke me without the slightest start. In truth, with all his severity, Heaven knows I loved him.

*Peter Meinke*
# Father

My father's eyes rolled upward in Paul's Diner,
not in fine frenzy but diabetic coma

and we thought when they refocused two weeks
later it was time to make amends. We

had circled one another for fifty years,
he round as a sumo wrestler, I blind

as a blinkered horse: we couldn't get a grip.
I remember now the smell of his sweat

as we dug boulders for the fence out back
and how later in the ball game he stuck

out his arm at home plate and my tall friend
folded across it like laundry on a line

and let me tell you, old man, I was proud
at having the strongest father on the block.

*David Bottoms*
# The Desk

Under the fire escape, crouched, on knee in cinders,
I pulled the ball-peen hammer from my belt,
cracked a square of window pane,
the gummed latch, and swung the window,
crawled through that stone hole into the boiler room
of Canton Elementary School, once Canton High,
where my father served three extra years
as star halfback and sprinter.
Behind a flashlight's
cane of light, I climbed a staircase almost a ladder
and found a door. On the second nudge of my shoulder,
it broke into a hallway dark as history,
at whose end lay the classroom I had studied
over and over in the deep obsession of memory.

I swept that room with my light—an empty blackboard,
a metal table, a half-globe lying on the floor
like a punctured basketball—then followed
that beam across the rows of desks,
the various catalogs of lovers, the lists
of all those who would and would not do what,
until it stopped on the corner desk of the back row,
and I saw again, after many years, the name
of my father, my name, carved deep into the oak top.

To gauge the depth I ran my finger across that scar,
and wondered at the dreams he must have lived
as his eyes ran back and forth
from the cinder yard below the window
to the empty practice field

to the blade of his pocket knife etching carefully
the long, angular lines of his name,
the dreams he must have laid out one behind another
like yard lines, in the dull, pre-practice afternoons
of geography and civics, before he ever dreamed
of Savo Sound or Guadalcanal.
                              In honor of dreams
I sank to my knees on the smooth, oiled floor,
and stood my flashlight on its end.
Half the yellow circle lit the underedge of the desk,
and in that split light I tapped the hammer
easy up the overhang of the desk top. Nothing gave
but the walls' sharp echo, so I swung again,
and again harder, and harder still in half anger
rising to anger at the stubborn joint, losing all fear
of my first crime against the city, the county;
the state, whatever government claimed domination,
until I had hammered up in the ringing dark
a salvo of crossfire, and on a frantic recoil glanced
the flashlight, the classroom spinning black
as a coma.
                  I've often pictured the face of the teacher
whose student first pointed to that topless desk,
the shock of a slow hand rising from the back row,
their eyes meeting over the question of absence.
I've wondered too if some low authority of the system
discovered that shattered window
and finding no typewriters, no business machines,
no audiovisual gear missing, failed to account for it,
so let it pass as minor vandalism.
                              I've heard nothing.
And rarely do I fret when I see that oak scar leaning
against my basement wall, though I wonder what it means
to own my father's name.

*Jonathan Schwartz*
# Over the Purple Hills

N orman Savitt drove up to visit his son in the school's dormitory. It was a difficult trip from the city to the small west Connecticut town where Norman had found a place for his ten-year-old: a dorm with private rooms and clean hallways, a school with a bit of a reputation. Jesse had told his father that he understood why he had to live at school—that his mother was sick, that his mother was in bed all the time, and that his dad was in California a lot of the time, that it was "the very best thing to do."

"The only thing, for now," Norman had said. "For now," Norman had repeated.

He was making his second trip since the beginning of school. This time, Sunday morning of Thanksgiving weekend, the going was tough. A light snow was falling, windblown and tricky in the gray November light. Norman had an early Christmas gift for Jesse, a baseball glove from F A O Schwarz. Jesse had told him on the phone that all he wanted to do for the rest of his life was to have a catch with someone, "all day every day right through the winter and spring and next summer and all next year."

At the school's gate Norman had to get out of the car and use the phone on the brick wall to reach the front office and announce his arrival.

It was one o'clock as Norman inched along the pebbled driveway for the three-quarters of a mile to the parking area near the dorm. How distant this was from seven that morning when he had put Carol on a train to North Carolina, where she would join an experimental diet program for hypertension.

Norman was forty-eight, with both members of his immediate family under guard, miles from home, miles from the hotel in which they lived. He was visiting one of them today, and the other next week in Durham. He imagined sadly that he would visit them forever, that it would go on and on, like Jesse's idea of a catch. He got out of the car and walked through the snow without realizing that he was wearing Jesse's glove.

The dorm, with its long dimly lit halls and cubbyhole rooms and clamoring radiators, served as a headquarters for the disengaged, boys who were far too young for vigorous schoolwork, boys from Latin America and Japan and Germany and Texas, who showered centrally under fluorescent lights and brushed their teeth with Calox powder, and, barefoot on the cold stone floor, returned to their rooms for lights out at nine.

Norman knew what Jesse believed; his son had leaked it all out in bits and pieces. Jesse believed that his parents were right. He was different from all the other boys he knew, and deserved to be in a dormitory with foreign-exchange students because he himself was a foreigner. He didn't know how to behave. He was so unusually improper that both his mother and father, as loving as they were, as famous as they were, with famous friends to whose houses they would go, in whose houses special meals would be prepared for Jesse's mother because of her illness—that's how *loved* his parents were—couldn't have a life worth living if Jesse was actually around. And, besides, they lived in a hotel with just one bedroom and a living room and a kitchen and a hallway to the back door where they threw out the garbage, and there wasn't any room for him, even if he were a perfect boy, a perfect son. So they did what they had to do, which was to find a dormitory *and* a school in the very same place, so that he could have everything all at once and not be a bother in a hotel.

Jo Stafford was singing behind Jesse's closed door. Before knocking, Norman listened for a moment. "In the night, though we're apart, there's a ghost of you within my haunted heart."

"Daddy!" Jesse said, with a hug and face kisses and another big hug.

Jesse's window overlooked the woods in which the school was set. His mother had sent up a bright orange rug, a porcelain desk lamp, a lithograph of a sailboat on a winter lake, a thick brown quilt, a small record player, and blue curtains with teddy bears and flowers that Jesse had stored under the bed. He had thumbtacked baseball cards to a bulletin board of his own, and to a calendar with Disney characters in the corners. He had put a line through each passing day. Norman, sitting on the bed, noticed that April 14 of the next year, 1949, was circled. He asked about it.

"Baseball begins," Jesse said.

"Is this the right glove?" Norman asked.

"It's *absolutely* great. It's just like my old glove."

Norman knew where Jesse had picked up "absolutely." He heard himself along the way: "The show was *absolutely* great." "I've written an absolutely great song." He saw himself as exaggerated and false, the pretensions of the theater seeping out, and into his son.

Jesse had stacks of records on the floor. Norman's own songs, Kern, Rachmaninoff, Rodgers. Jesse wanted his father to hear some of them. He played Nat Cole, Frankie Laine, Peggy Lee.

Norman had brought a picnic lunch he had left in the car.

"Could we have a catch?" Jesse asked excitedly.

"It's snowing," Norman said.

"Just on the way to the car?"

"But it's *really* snowing," Norman said.

"It doesn't matter, there's no one on the field."

"I don't have a glove," Norman said.

"I have two, the old one and the new one."

"But I need a lefty glove."

"Raphael has one," Jesse said. "Please, Daddy."

Raphael, an eleven-year-old Cuban, didn't reply to Jesse's knock. Jesse opened his door.

The room was a warehouse of comic books and Mr. Goodbars. Small crucifixes were nailed to all four walls. A pile of clothes lay in the middle of the floor; Jesse found the baseball glove beneath them.

The wind had subsided a bit, but the snow had not. They made their way slowly through it to the deserted playing field.

"Get out there!" Jesse shouted to his father.

Norman felt the sting of Jesse's throw through Raphael's flimsy mitt. At first his returns were wild, making Jesse run. Jesse dug the ball out of the snow time and again, until his father became more accurate.

"You're great at this!" Jesse shouted, after a time.

Norman was exhilarated. "Make me run for one!" he shouted.

Jesse tossed one high.

Norman, on the run, even through the snow, even in his long overcoat, caught up with it.

*"Great!"* Jesse yelled. "Absolutely great!"

"One more!" Norman shouted into a gust of wind and blowing snow.

Jesse threw another that was harder to play.

Norman reached for it at the last moment.

"Norman DiMaggio!" Jesse yelled, his voice cracking up there so high.

"Could we eat in the car?" Jesse asked, on the way to the parking area.

"It's too cold," Norman said.

"We could leave the engine running so it'll be warm," Jesse said.

"You really want to?" Norman said, giving in.

"We just sit in the back like passengers."

"We're bundled up."

"It'll make me feel like we're going on a trip together. It's like somebody's driving us."

"Where?" Norman asked as they reached the car.

"I don't know. Maybe home, for a visit or something. I mean, I wouldn't *stay,* or anything."

Norman had roast beef sandwiches, Cokes and Oreos.

They sat in the back of the car in their overcoats, dropping crumbs into the cloth napkins that Carol had insisted Norman take. "Do you have the napkins?" she had asked, standing by the train that morning.

While Jesse talked about baseball, Norman imagined his drive back home, back to the Volney Hotel, up the elevator to the sixteenth floor, the suite immaculate, vacuumed and dusted by the noontime maids.

He would arrive to face Carol's absence. He would call her in Durham. He saw himself sitting on her side of the bed, his elbows resting on his knees, Carol being called to what Norman imagined as a phone booth in a hall, a long-distance hiss making it difficult to hear. How was the trip? he would ask. What kind of room do you have. When do you see Dr. Klempner. What is a good time to call. It's snowing here. Is it snowing there. I love you. Do you love me.

"Did Mommy leave this morning?" Jesse asked, shifting out of baseball.

Norman hoped that Jesse hadn't noticed that his father had been miles away.

"Early this morning," Norman said, sipping a Coke. "Everything was right on time, everything was just fine. The regimen down there will help her. People from all over the world go down there."

"Will it cure her?" Jesse asked.

"We just don't know," Norman said.

Jesse had never been told how seriously ill his mother was, how frightened his father was of any ringing telephone. "Mr. Savitt, it's for you." And the news, handed out by a stranger, or a doctor, or a concierge with an accent. "Mr. Savitt, the woman you married on July twelfth, 1934, the mother of your son, Jesse, has died."

"What's the worst that can happen?" Jesse asked.

"Your mother is the strongest woman I know," Norman said.

When they were finished eating, they got out of the car to face another gust of wind that blew the snow around, forcing them to hurry back to the dorm. Inside, they took seats across from each other in the leisure room, while Raphael lay on his stomach reading comic books.

Norman told Jesse about the show he was writing. Jesse already knew some of his father's new melodies. He had memorized them on first hearing, and many times after lights out he had sung them quietly to himself.

"What's the road schedule?" Jesse asked.

"New Haven, April first. Then the Wilbur in Boston, April nineteenth. Then the Majestic, May something, probably the ninth. And I've got an absolutely *great* Western kind of song. Is there a piano here?" Norman asked.

"There is an upright on the stage in the gym. The doors might be locked because of the holidays," Jesse said.

"Let's try," Norman said. "Raphael, do you want to come?"

"Where," Raphael said.

"No he doesn't," Jesse said impatiently. "Let's do it alone. *Please.*"

"Certainly," Norman said, recognizing his error.

"Stay here," Jesse said to Raphael.

"Where," Raphael said.

Jesse led his father across the playing field, their old footprints vanished in the fresh white snow.

They entered the school's main building through the kitchen, and walked in single file down a dark corridor to an indoor playroom, through two locker rooms and up a flight of stairs.

The gym was open, the largest room in the school, used for chapel in the morning, and basketball, and for theatrical productions on a stage at the far end.

A hundred metal chairs faced the stage, left in place through the holidays after the Thanksgiving service Wednesday afternoon.

Jesse took a seat in the fourth row.

"You're my *best* audience," Norman shouted, going to the stage, his voice ringing out in the strange, unaccommodating acoustics of the gymnasium.

"This is a *Western* song," Norman told Jesse again. "A sort of cowboy song. I think it's absolutely one of the *best* melodies I've ever written."

"Does it have a title?" Jesse asked.

"It's called 'Over the Purple Hills.' Isn't that a nice title? The lyric, when I write it, will say something like, over the purple hills on the other side of somewhere, there's magic and peace. And only people with determination can get there. Do you know what *serene* means? It means a lack of trouble in your heart. Well, that's over the purple hills. Do you understand?"

"Sure," Jesse said, from the fourth row. "Is everything purple there?"

"No. It's very light. It's filled with sun. Like the day on Long Island when you said you could see France. That kind of real sun and clarity. The purple is deep in the mountains."

"I see," Jesse said.

"I have only one line of the lyric, and then I'll just play the rest of the melody."

Norman sat formally at the piano for a moment or two, gathering in Jesse's complete attention.

"Over the purple hills, far away, far far away," he sang in his clear, familiar baritone, the piano woefully out of tune.

Blowing snow swirled outside the windows. The gym, unlit, was bathed in white, Jesse felt himself rising into the air, still seated on his metal chair. His father's melody held him high above everyone.

John N. Morris

# Bringing Up Father

For too long he has followed too much
The devices of his own heart.
It falls to you to restrain him.
The family is not a democracy. Rely
On instinct and your immense
Power to terrify. *Out of his exhausted sleep*
*You bring him bolt-upright in a moment.*
At first this discipline is almost total.

He has illusions, and you are one of them.
Every day he brings you
Himself for your approbation.
Though his belief in you is unbounded,
Tutor him in disappointment.
Like you he will have to learn
To live with your limitations. (You, too,
Must modify your expectations:
Nothing you can do
Will make him always just and kind,
Though he aches for your admiration.)

At times you will have wondered
What was in it for you. Indulge yourself.
Run screaming from the house.
For hours he will understand you.
He, too, has his despairs. Like you
He will cry out
Against the world that it has wronged him.
"The best is not to be born,"
He will say, the enormous baby!

In time you will leave him alone.
This is the school of kindness.
You say goodbye to him,
This imperfection.
You have made a life for him.
He shares your disappointment.
This is what you both embrace,
Meeting and parting. You cleave to this.
At last he will leave you
The empty nest, abandon
You to the care of your children.
At last he will have learned
Everything they have to teach you.

*Sherwood Anderson*
# Discovery of a Father

O ne of the strangest relationships in the world is that between father and son. I know it now from having sons of my own.

A boy wants something very special from his father. You hear it said that fathers want their sons to be what they feel they cannot themselves be, but I tell you it also works the other way. I know that as a small boy I wanted my father to be a certain thing he was not. I wanted him to be a proud, silent, dignified father. When I was with other boys and he passed along the street, I wanted to feel a glow of pride: "There he is. That is my father."

But he wasn't such a one. He couldn't be. It seemed to me then that he was always showing off. Let's say someone in our town had got up a show. They were always doing it. The druggist would be in it, the shoestore clerk, the horse doctor, and a lot of women and girls. My father would manage to get the chief comedy part. It was, let's say, a Civil War play and he was a comic Irish soldier. He had to do the most absurd things. They thought he was funny, but I didn't.

I thought he was terrible. I didn't see how Mother could stand it. She even laughed with the others. Maybe I would have laughed if it hadn't been my father.

Or there was a parade, the Fourth of July or Decoration Day. He'd be in that, too, right at the front of it, as Grand Marshal or something, on a white horse hired from a livery stable.

He couldn't ride for shucks. He fell off the horse and everyone hooted with laughter, but he didn't care. He even seemed to like it. I remember once when he had done something ridiculous, and right out on Main Street, too. I was with some other boys and they were laughing and shouting at him and he was shouting back and having as good a time as they were. I ran down an alley back of some store and there in the Presbyterian Church sheds I had a good long cry.

Or I would be in bed at night and Father would come home a little lit up and bring some men with him. He was a man who was never alone. Before he went broke, running a harness shop, there were always a lot of men loafing in the shop. He went broke, of course, because he gave too much credit. He couldn't refuse it and I thought he was a fool. I had got to hating him.

There'd be men I didn't think would want to be fooling around with him. There might even be the superintendent of our schools and a quiet man who ran the hardware store. Once, I remember, there was a white-haired man who was a cashier of the bank. It was a wonder to me they'd want to be seen with such a windbag. That's what I thought he was. I know now what it was that attracted them. It was because life in our town, as in all small towns, was at times pretty dull and he livened it up. He made them laugh. He could tell stories. He'd even get them to singing.

If they didn't come to my house they'd go off, say at night, to where there was a grassy place by a creek. They'd cook food there and drink beer and sit about listening to his stories.

He was always telling stories about himself. He'd say this or that wonderful thing happened to him. It might be something that made him look like a fool. He didn't care.

If an Irishman came to our house, right away Father would say he was Irish. He'd tell what county in Ireland he was born in. He'd tell things that happened there when he was a boy. He'd make it seem so real that, if I hadn't known he was born in southern Ohio, I'd have believed him myself.

If it was a Scotchman, the same thing happened. He'd get a burr into his speech. Or he was a German or a Swede. He'd be anything the other man was. I think they all knew he was lying, but they seemed to like him just the same. As a boy that was what I couldn't understand.

And there was Mother. How could she stand it? I wanted to ask but never did. She was not the kind you asked such questions.

I'd be upstairs in my bed, in my room above the porch, and Father would be telling some of his tales. A lot of Father's stories were about the Civil War. To hear him tell it he'd been in about every battle. He'd known Grant, Sherman, Sheridan, and I don't know how many others. He'd been particularly intimate with General Grant so that when Grant went East, to take charge of all the armies, he took Father along.

"I was an orderly at headquarters and Sam Grant said to me, 'Irve,' he said, 'I'm going to take you along with me."

It seems he and Grant used to slip off sometimes and have a quiet drink together. That's what my father said. He'd tell about the day Lee surrendered and how, when the great moment came, they couldn't find Grant.

"You know," my father said, "about General Grant's book, his memoirs. You've read of how he said he had a headache and how, when he got word that Lee was ready to call it quits, he was suddenly and miraculously cured.

"Huh," said Father, "He was in the woods with me.

"I was in there with my back against a tree. I was pretty well cornered. I had got hold of a bottle of pretty good stuff.

"They were looking for Grant. He had got off his horse and come into the woods. He found me. He was covered with mud.

"I had the bottle in my hand. What'd I care? The war was over. I knew we had them licked."

My father said that he was the one who told Grant about Lee. An orderly riding by had told him, because the orderly knew how thick he was with Grant. Grant was embarrassed.

"But, Irve, look at me. I'm all covered with mud," he said to Father.

And then, my father said, he and Grant decided to have a drink together. They took a couple of shots and then, because he didn't want Grant to show up potted before the immaculate Lee, he smashed the bottle against the tree.

"Sam Grant's dead now and I wouldn't want it to get out on him," my father said.

That's just one of the kind of things he'd tell. Of course, the men knew he was lying, but they seemed to like it just the same.

When we got broke, down and out, do you think he ever brought anything home? Not he. If there wasn't anything to eat in the house, he'd go off visiting around at farm houses. They all wanted him. Sometimes he'd stay away for weeks. Mother working to keep us fed, and then home he'd come bringing, let's say, a ham. He'd got it from some farmer friend. He'd slap it on the table in the kitchen. "You bet I'm going to see that my kids have something to eat," he'd say, and Mother would just stand smiling at him. She'd never say a word about all the weeks and months he'd been away, not leaving us a cent for food. Once I heard her speaking to a woman in our street. Maybe the woman had dared to sympathize with her. "Oh," she said, "it's all right. He isn't ever dull like most of the men in this street. Life is never dull when my man is about."

But often I was filled with bitterness and sometimes I wished he wasn't my father. I'd even invent another man as my father. To protect my mother I'd make up stories of a secret marriage that for some strange reason never got known. As though some man, say the president of a railroad company or maybe a congressman, had married my mother, thinking his wife was dead and then it turned out she wasn't.

So they had to hush it up but I got born just the same. I wasn't really the son of my father. Somewhere in the world there was a very dignified, quite wonderful man who was really my father. I even made myself half believe these fancies.

And then there came a certain night. Mother was away from home. Maybe there was church that night. Father came in. He'd been off somewhere for two or three weeks. He found me alone in the house, reading by the kitchen table.

It had been raining and he was very wet. He sat and looked at me for a long time, not saying a word. I was startled, for there was on his face the saddest look I had ever seen. He sat for a time, his clothes, dripping. Then he got up.

"Come on with me," he said.

I got up and went with him out of the house. I was filled with wonder but I wasn't afraid. We went along a dirt road that led down into a valley, about a mile out of town, where there was a pond. We walked in silence. The man who was always talking had stopped his talking.

I didn't know what was up and had the queer feeling that I was with a stranger. I don't know whether my father intended it so. I don't think he did.

The pond was quite large. It was still raining hard and there were flashes of lightning followed by thunder. We were on a grassy bank at the pond's edge when my father spoke, and in the darkness and rain his voice sounded strange.

"Take off your clothes," he said. Still filled with wonder, I began to undress. There was a flash of lightning and I saw that he was already naked.

Naked, we went into the pond. Taking my hand, he pulled me in. It may be that I was too frightened, too full of a feeling of strangeness, to speak. Before that night my father had never seemed to pay any attention to me.

"And what is he up to now?" I kept asking myself. I did not swim very well, but he put my hand on his shoulder and struck out into the darkness.

He was a man with big shoulders, a powerful swimmer. In the darkness I could feel the movements of his muscles. We swam to the far edge of the pond and then back to where we had left our clothes. The rain continued and the wind blew. Sometimes my father swam on his back, and when he did he took my hand in his large powerful one and moved it over so it rested always on his shoulder. Sometimes there would be a flash of lightning, and I could see his face quite clearly.

It was as it was earlier, in the kitchen, a face filled with sadness. There would be the momentary glimpse of his face, and then again the darkness, the wind and the rain. In me there was a feeling I had never known before.

It was a feeling of closeness. It was something strange. It was as though there were only we two in the world. It was as though I had been jerked suddenly out of myself, out of my world of the schoolboy, out of a world in which I was ashamed of my father.

He had become blood of my blood; he the strong swimmer and I the boy clinging to him in the darkness. We swam in silence, and in silence we dressed in our wet clothes and went home.

There was a lamp lighted in the kitchen, and when we came in, the water dripping from us, there was my mother. She smiled at us. I remember that she called us "boys." "What have you boys been up to?" she asked, but my father did not answer. As he had begun the evening's experience with me in silence, so he ended it. He turned and looked at me. Then he went, I thought, with a new and strange dignity, out of the room.

I climbed the stairs to my room, undressed in darkness and got into bed. I couldn't sleep and did not want to sleep. For the first time I knew that I was the son of my father. He was a storyteller as I was to be. It may be that I even laughed a little softly there in the darkness. If I did, I laughed knowing that I would never again be wanting another father.

*Gamble Rogers*
# *from* My Father Was a Voyager

When he was forty-three years of age and I was six, my father and I stood alone in the early evening on a boardwalk at Cape Hatteras and watched an Atlantic Northeaster looming. A thunderhead nosed down along the horizon from the north as smooth and ominous as the snout of a macaw. A single star strove above a thunderous chaos of sky, a shivering of timbers underfoot.

"Buckshot, did you ever think about what would become of you if you were out there by yourself, in something like this?"

He faced the raging ocean and he radiated strange power.

"What I mean is," he went on, "do you have any idea where you would go?"

I was terrified and felt I had been caught desperately wanting. I imagined I might be swallowed up. I feared even his power. But his voice was soft, his hand so meek upon my shoulder that I held to his leg as those words came back over me: "Do you have any idea where you would go?"

Suddenly, he seemed to be asking the question for himself and, in that scant instant, I went from the fear of strange powers to the most perfect love a man can share with another man: the love a son feels for a father who wholly declares his own confusion in the face of that dull mystification which is the levee of all mankind.

And so, my father was a voyager. I think of him now as on that ocean and shall ever see him in that striding star. I sense his elbow at the tiller, his hand on the lifeline, his finger on the string.

My father was a voyager.

*James Wright*
# Youth

Strange bird,
His song remains secret.
He worked too hard to read books.
He never heard how Sherwood Anderson
Got out of it, and fled to Chicago, furious to free himself
From his hatred of factories.
My father toiled fifty years
At Hazel-Atlas Glass,
Caught among girders that smash the kneecaps
Of dumb honyaks.
Did he shudder with hatred in the cold shadow of grease?
Maybe. But my brother and I do know
He came home as quiet as the evening.

He will be getting dark, soon,
And loom through new snow.
I know his ghost will drift home
To the Ohio River, and sit down, alone,
Whittling a root.
He will say nothing.
The waters flow past, older, younger
Than he is, or I am.

*Guy de Maupassant*
## *from* Solitude

EDITOR'S NOTE: *Men and fathers are sometimes characterized as—even criticized for—hiding their feelings and concealing themselves in work and interpersonal relationships, in life. In the following piece about two men who are taking a walk after a party, de Maupassant explores this age-old complexity:*

"As for me, now, I have closed my soul. I no longer tell anyone what I think, what I believe and what I love. Knowing myself condemned to this appalling loneliness, I observe these things, without ever giving my opinion. What do I care for opinions, pleasures, creeds! Not being able to share anything with anyone, I have lost interest in everything. My hidden thoughts remain an eternal secret. I have commonplace answers for everyday questions, and a smile which says 'yes' when I do not even wish to take the trouble to answer.

"Do you understand me?"

We had gone up the long avenue to the Arc de Triomphe, and back again to the Place de la Concorde, for he had said all this very slowly, adding many details which I cannot remember at present.

He stopped, and, suddenly stretching his arm towards the great granite obelisk, standing like a sentinel in the center of Paris, this exiled monument, bearing on its sides the history of its country written in strange characters, he cried:

"There! We are all like that!"

Then he left me without another word.

Was he intoxicated, crazy or very wise? I have not yet found out. At times it seems to me that he was right, and then, again, I think he must have lost his mind.

*Thomas Wolfe*
# His Father's Hands

Gant lay in the splendid coffin, with his great hands folded quietly on his breast. Later, the boy could not forget his father's hands. They were the largest, most powerful, and somehow the most shapely hands he had ever seen. And even though his great right hand had been so crippled and stiffened by an attack of inflammatory rheumatism, ten years before, that he had never regained the full use of it, and since that time could only hold the great wooden mallet that the stonecutters use in the painful and clumsy half-clasp between the thumb and the big stiffened fingers, his hands never lost their character of life, strength, and powerful shapeliness.

The hands had given to the interminable protraction of his living death a kind of concrete horror that it otherwise would not have had. For as his powerful gaunt figure waned and wasted under the ravages of the cancer that was consuming him until he had become only the enfeebled shadow of his former self, his gaunt hands, on which there was so little which death could consume, lost none of their former rock-like heaviness, strength and shapely power. Thus, even when the giant figure of the man had become nothing but a spectral remnant of itself, sunk in a sorrow of time, awaiting death, those great, still-living hands of power and strength hung incredibly, horribly, from that spectral form of death to which they were attached.

And for this reason those powerful hands of life evoked, as nothing else could have done, in an instant searing flash of memory and recognition, the lost world of his father's life of manual power, hunger, fury, savage abundance and wild joy, the whole enchanted structure of that lost life of magic he had made for them. Constantly, those great hands of life joined, with an almost grotesque incongruity, to that scarecrow form of wasting death would awake for them, as nothing else on earth could do, all of the sorrowful ghosts of time, the dream-like spell and terror of the years between, the years of phantom death, the horror of unreality, strangeness, disbelief, and memory, that haunted them.

So it was now, even in death, with his father's hands. In their powerful, gaunt, and shapely clasp, as he lay dead in his coffin, there seemed to be held and gathered, somehow, all of his life that could never die—a living image of the essential quality of his whole life with its fury and unrest, desire and hunger, the tremendous sweep and relish of his enormous appetites and the huge endowment of its physical and sensual powers.

. . . .

And just as poet, prophet, priest and conqueror might each retain in death some living and fitting image of his whole life's truth, so would the strength, the skill, all of the hope, hunger, fury, and unrest that had lashed and driven on through life the gaunt figure of a stone-cutter, be marvellously preserved in the granite power and symmetry of those undying hands.

*James J. McAuley*

# My Father's Mistress

I met Nellie Conroy, my father's mistress of twenty years or more, in the lounge of the Wicklow Hotel a few days after I got back to Dublin from Beirut, where I had gone to settle my father's affairs after his death in a plane crash.

On March 15th, 1963, he was flying a De Havilland York, a twenty-year-old World War II bomber converted to freighter, from Teheran to Beirut. An engine caught fire after take-off and caused the crash. There were 1,200 pounds of fuel on board, so when the plane went in from only 400 feet, nine miles from the Teheran runway, it was a kind of Viking funeral for my father, Noel McAuley, after thirty-five years of flying.

His coffin returned to Ireland a few weeks later, and he was buried in the family grave in Naas, in the green heart of Kildare. It was decided that I should go out to Beirut, where he had been living for four years, as the representative of the family.

Before I left, contact was made with Nellie Conroy. She was the woman who—according to my mother's side of the story—had ruined my mother's life. My beautiful Aunt Tess loved plots and schemes, and spent many hours and many bottles of Power's whiskey plotting with my mother how to make my father pay for his infidelity. At any rate, that's how I interpreted those whispered sessions behind closed doors in those days.

There was a brief traumatic separation at one point; but mostly the campaign to shake my Old Man loose from his alluring, mysterious Nellie was fought in sly underhanded ways I knew little or nothing about after I was sent away to Clongowes, the Jesuit boarding-school—another of Aunt Tess's schemes, or so I thought at the time. There were counter-plots from my father's side of the family. My grandmother fed us children dire hints of unmentionable wickedness on my mother's side of the family, for which *she* would have to pay.

So my contact with Nellie Conroy was, emotionally, a very complex one. Resentment was overridden by a shared grief, and mixed with the excitement of encountering someone who in the imagination of my youth had been as sinfully glamorous as Ingrid Bergman or Marlene Dietrich. She had learned that I was going to Beirut, and somehow got word to me that she would be grateful if I could return the briefcase she had given my father a long time before. And any letters, photos, etc., I might find.

I had glimpsed her in the church at my father's funeral; at least, I assumed the veiled woman in black at the back of the church, half-obscured by a pillar, was Nellie. She was gone when we carried the coffin from the church to the hearse, and the cortege of over a hundred cars began the slow journey to the grave in Naas. Whether or not it was Nellie, I was affected later when I got the message about the briefcase. How hard it must have been for her, not being family, still the object of much hostility, her husband having left her and emigrated to Canada years before. She and my father had been lovers for over twenty years.

At the time of my father's death I had been married for five years, with two small sons, but with many incidents of the kind which my ironic Da would refer to as "a rift in the lute." My unhappy marriage made me perhaps a little more sympathetic to Nellie's situation, so I was glad to do her a good turn, even at the risk of appearing disloyal to my mother— who was so devastated by "poor Noel's" death that she had a serious nervous breakdown and was in hospital when the funeral took place.

Among her four children, I was her "pet" for a fair number of years. All four of us strove to make her laugh; but I was the one chosen for the secret missions to Derham's bar, down Church Lane from the house, when she needed a Baby Power's whiskey on credit. She took inordinate pride in any accomplishments of mine at school, no matter how trivial. Among her many worries as I was growing up was my stubbornly fragile health. My undeniable love for her seems always clouded by agonized exasperation.

In the years following my father's death, alcoholism, mine and hers, made terrible inroads on our relationship. We quarrelled; others made our quarrel theirs. We didn't talk to each other for several years; at some point in this period I emigrated to America. After my first divorce, we made contact again by letter, and it was as if those years of silence

between us had never been. But she died before I could find a means of
returning to Ireland.

The first time I ever flew in a plane was on the trip to Beirut, in April
1963. I had never flown—nor had any of the family, so far as I know—
during my father's career as a pilot. I flew to London on Aer Lingus, the
Irish airline my father joined in 1938, after a ten-year stint as a fighter
pilot. He had joined the Royal Air Force a few months after his twenty-
first birthday, over my grandfather's opposition. He was Chief Pilot and
Chief Technical Advisor of Aer Lingus until 1951, when, as President of
the Airline Pilots Association, he led a series of one-day stoppages to win
a pension scheme for Aer Lingus aircrew, and he ran afoul of Manage-
ment.

He went back to England after severing the Aer Lingus connection,
and flew jockeys and film-stars from location to location for a charter
company. Then he was based in Hamburg while he flew the Berlin Airlift
for about a year. Thereafter he flew all kinds of propellor-driven craft in
Europe, British Guiana, Pakistan, even a stint training pilots on Lockheed
planes in Burbank, California, before joining a British freight line in
1959, which later seconded him to TMA, and he moved his domicile to
Beirut. He never took out a license to fly jets.

From London, I flew to Beirut via Geneva on a Middle East Airlines
DeHavilland Comet IV, the successor to the ill-fated first-generation
passenger jet, that comely, lethal Comet I, with the engines built into the
wings, five of which disappeared over the ocean before one crashed on
a Spanish mountain, and the cause of failure was discovered: metal
fatigue.

Over the Alps, after a couple of hours on the ground in Geneva, the
captain brought me into the cockpit. The crew was British; they had
known my father, who was regarded as something of a character in
Beirut, especially among the cooler jet-age pilots. They genuinely
mourned his passing.

The Comet cockpit was a perfectly mystical experience for me. I saw
and heard what my father had been doing for all his adult life. From
there, where our amazing speed was just the hiss of wind against the
fuselage, the spectacle of the Alps, and then the Dolomites, so close
under the wings, was a blur of blue-white glaciers and sharp crags of

smoky grey between rags of cumulus. They might as well have been merely a batch of picture-postcards, so engrossing were the rituals of the flight-deck.

Cryptic monosyllables crossed from captain to co-pilot, concerning trim and power and position. What was the little radar screen telling them? They were constantly checking the route-map unfolding in an endless roll between them under the throttles, occasionally directing my attention to some feature below. The engineer kept an amiable silence while he monitored the instruments for engine temperatures, fuel, hydraulics. Over Rome, we altered course and began the descent to Beirut. I learned more about my father than I'd ever learned in his lifetime during the hour I spent in the jump-seat behind the captain of that Comet, on the way to Beirut.

The Beirut authorities had sealed my father's apartment after his death. I was required to appear in court and prove, in French, my right to take possession of my father's belongings—and also pay off any debts he owed in Lebanon. I was given the keys in due course, and taken to the diplomatic quarter, overlooking the harbor.

After the policeman accompanying me removed the seals, I let myself into a spacious second-floor apartment, with a huge living-room, a verandah front and back, a cavernous cool bathroom, and a fully equipped modern kitchen. He was constantly referring to his frugal life-style, but only the bedroom fitted his description of the monastic conditions he'd lived in—a cell-like windowless place between bathroom and kitchen, with a bed and a built-in closet and an improvised bedside ledge to hold a radio and books and magazines.

A jacket hung on the back of a chair. A coffee cup sat crusted in the sink; something in the refrigerator had gone off. Piles of magazines spilled over onto each other in the utility room—including, to my embarrassment (and further education), several years of *Playboy*. His ulcer medicine was still in the bathroom cabinet—he'd forgotten to pack it with his shaving gear.

I found Nellie Conroy's letters among his personal papers in a drawer somewhere. I found the briefcase she'd given him, more like a great leather satchel, capable of carrying a quarter-century's worth of vital documents. I found the books of my poems I'd sent him. At times

I couldn't bear to stay in the place, and went off to one or other of his hang-outs which the Europeans frequented, near the big new hotel on the beach, the Phoenicia.

His friends came to my rescue, and helped me dispose of his battered old Jaguar Mark VII and the sparse furnishings from the apartment, and his cabin at a resort on the beach, which I didn't bother to visit. Soon the apartment echoed emptily. The only furniture remaining was the twin-size box-spring and mattress, which I left behind when I eventually vacated the apartment.

One of the more shameful things I've done in a far from blameless life was to sit on my father's bed in Beirut and read through Nellie Conroy's letters. They covered many more years than I'd expected, yet referred to few events in my father's life that I knew about. Even now, thirty years later, I feel dismayed by how separate their life together had been from his life with us, his children. And they too had spent so much time apart from each other. It was like a story from Chekhov, full of bleak, benign hopelessness, in which everyone concerned had been waiting for the change that would bring the happiness that they secretly knew would never come.

My profound shame was the intimacy I invaded by reading those letters—the intimacy of a passion so fiery, so durable—my first encounter with the power of erotic love. Not Anna Karenina, not Emma Bovary, not Edna O'Brien's country girl—no fictional mistress has taught me so much.

At our meeting in the Wicklow Hotel lounge in Dublin, when I returned the battered old briefcase and a few other mementos with her letters, she asked me if I had read them. No, I said, half indignantly, of course not. And indeed I hadn't read them all: my shame had overcome me at a certain point. I did read enough to know she had never been my mother's enemy as she had been portrayed by the propagandists for my mother. I'm sure my demeanor showed that much, at least; in any case, she knew I lied, but was not much put out. She had a quizzical squint to her expression when she heard my disclaimer. And then she did me the great favor of assuring me, when I intimated to her that I'd always thought the Old Man rather despised me for a lily-livered henpecked failure (I didn't express it quite in those terms), that he'd actually been quite proud of the family poet.

She won me over, did Nellie Conroy, and I resolved to keep in contact with her after that meeting. But of course I never revealed to her my confused feelings for her, and never did see her again, though I learned that she frequently visited my grandparents. If there were divorce in Ireland she would have been my stepmother. I'm told that when she died in her early seventies a few years ago in Dublin, she was still a handsome woman, and played golf fairly regularly.

She had a reputation for asperity, though my own impression, from those letters and from our only meeting, was of taciturnity, of a woman tragically wounded by her love for my father, yet bound by force of character to conceal her wound with a deceptive equanimity. No doubt, neither her reputation nor my impression of her is anywhere close to the truth.

*David Huddle*
# Thinking About My Father

I have to go back
past the way he was
at the end, panting
for breath, begging
for medicine, crazy
from medicine taken
for years. This is
hard because in his
dying, he was vivid,
excruciatingly slow,
and profoundly self-
absorbed, as if his
death required more
energy and devotion
than we could ever
bring to his bedside.

But then there he is
at home, at his desk
in the den, where he
was able to be most
truly himself, paying
bills—he was happy
doing that—reading
the paper, then best
of all, beautifully
solving its crossword
puzzle. My father was
the absolute master

of crossword puzzles
in the *Roanoke Times*.

I do not mean to say
that he shut himself
off from us. It was
just that we learned
to approach his desk
for quiet attention.
He breathed a light
whistle between his
teeth while he helped
me balance my paper
route money, coat my
model airplane's silk
wing with banana oil,
hinge a new Brazilian
stamp into my album.

My father did things
with a care that was
more important to him
than the thing itself.
For example, painting
by the numbers: no one
ever number-painted so
gravely and precisely.
His Saint Bernards hang
over his desk, his blue
jays over the toilet so
that every peeing male
must witness the craft
of his terrible picture.

His pleasures were fresh
things, mail just pulled
from his post office box,

unthumbed newspapers, new
model airplane kits, sets
of mint-condition stamps
in glassine envelopes.
With his hands he savored
a new harmonica so that I
still see as sacred those
little Hohner boxes with
pictures on them of old-
time German concert bands.

I don't have any fresh
insight into my father
or his life. Thinking
about him like this, I
miss him, and I forget
how horrible his death
was. Some mornings I
wake up feeling bad for
no reason I can think of,
and then all day he'll be
on my mind, dying again.

I have no memory of his
holding me as an infant,
but we have an old home
movie in which my twenty-
two year old mother walks
out onto the front porch
and hands a baby to this
thin young man. Some days
I wake up limp and happy
as that child, smiled at
and lifted up to the sun
by someone who wanted me
right here in this world.

*Frank O'Connor*

# My Oedipus Complex

Father was in the army all through the war—the first war, I mean—so, up to the age of five, I never saw much of him, and what I saw did not worry me. Sometimes I woke and there was a big figure in khaki peering down at me in the candlelight. Sometimes in the early morning I heard the slamming of the front door and the clatter of nailed boots down the cobbles of the lane. These were Father's entrances and exits. Like Santa Claus he came and went mysteriously.

In fact, I rather liked his visits, though it was an uncomfortable squeeze between Mother and him when I got into the big bed in the early morning. He smoked, which gave him a pleasant musty smell, and shaved, an operation of astounding interest. Each time he left a trail of souvenirs—model tanks and Gurkha knives with handles made of bullet cases, and German helmets and cap badges and button-sticks, and all sorts of military equipment—carefully stowed away in a long box on top of the wardrobe, in case they ever came in handy. There was a bit of the magpie about Father; he expected everything to come in handy. When his back was turned, Mother let me get a chair and rummage through his treasures. She didn't seem to think so highly of them as he did.

The war was the most peaceful period of my life. The windows of my attic faced southeast. My mother had curtained it, but that had small effect. I always woke with the first light and, with all the responsibilities of the previous day melted, feeling myself rather like the sun, ready to illumine and rejoice. Life never seemed so simple and clear and full of possibilities as then. I put my feet out from under the clothes—I called them Mrs. Left and Mrs. Right—and invented dramatic situations for them in which they discussed the problems of the day. At least Mrs. Right did; she was very demonstrative, but I hadn't the same control of Mrs. Left, so she mostly contented herself with nodding agreement.

They discussed what Mother and I should do during the day, what Santa Claus should give a fellow for Christmas, and what steps should be taken to brighten the home. There was that little matter of the baby, for instance. Mother and I could never agree about that. Ours was the only house in the terrace without a new baby, and Mother said we couldn't afford one till Father came back from the war because they cost seventeen and six. That showed how simple she was. The Geneys up the road had a baby, and everyone knew they couldn't afford seventeen and six. It was probably a cheap baby, and Mother wanted something really good, but I felt she was too exclusive. The Geneys' baby would have done us fine.

Having settled my plans for the day, I got up, put a chair under the attic window, and lifted the frame high enough to stick out my head. The window overlooked the front gardens of the terrace behind ours, and beyond these it looked over a deep valley to the tall, red-brick houses terraced up the opposite hillside, which were all still in shadow, while those at our side of the valley were all lit up, though with long strange shadows that made them seem unfamiliar; rigid and painted.

After that I went into Mother's room and climbed into the big bed. She woke and I began to tell her of my schemes. By this time, though I never seem to have noticed it, I was petrified in my nightshirt, and I thawed as I talked until, the last frost melted, I fell asleep beside her and woke again only when I heard her below in the kitchen, making the breakfast.

After breakfast we went into town; heard Mass at St. Augustine's and said a prayer for Father, and did the shopping. If the afternoon was fine we either went for a walk in the country or a visit to Mother's great friend in the convent, Mother St. Dominic. Mother had them all praying for Father, and every night, going to bed, I asked God to send him back safe from the war to us. Little, indeed, did I know what I was praying for!

One morning, I got into the big bed, and there, sure enough, was Father in his usual Santa Claus manner, but later, instead of uniform, he put on his best blue suit, and Mother was as pleased as anything. I saw nothing to be pleased about, because, out of uniform, Father was altogether less interesting, but she only beamed, and explained that our prayers had been answered, and off we went to Mass to thank God for having brought Father safely home.

The irony of it! That very day when he came in to dinner he took off his boots and put on his slippers, donned the dirty old cap he wore about the house to save him from colds, crossed his legs, and began to talk gravely to Mother, who looked anxious. Naturally, I disliked her looking anxious because it destroyed her good looks, so I interrupted him.

"Just a moment, Larry!" she said gently.

This was only what she said when we had boring visitors, so I attached no importance to it and went on talking.

"Do be quiet, Larry!" she said impatiently. "Don't you hear me talking to Daddy?"

This was the first time I had heard those ominous words, "talking to Daddy," and I couldn't help feeling that if this was how God answered prayers, he couldn't listen to them very attentively.

"Why are you talking to Daddy?" I asked with as great a show of indifference as I could muster.

"Because Daddy and I have business to discuss. Now, don't interrupt again!"

In the afternoon, at Mother's request, Father took me for a walk. This time we went into town instead of out in the country, and I thought at first, in my usual optimistic way, that it might be an improvement. It was nothing of the sort. Father and I had quite different notions of a walk in town. He had no proper interest in trams, ships, and horses, and the only thing that seemed to divert him was talking to fellows as old as himself. When I wanted to stop he simply went on, dragging me behind him by the hand; when he wanted to stop I had no alternative but to do the same. I noticed that it seemed to be a sign that he wanted to stop for a long time whenever he leaned against a wall. The second time I saw him do it I got wild. He seemed to be settling himself forever. I pulled him by the coat and trousers, but, unlike Mother who, if you were too persistent, got into a wax and said: "Larry, if you don't behave yourself, I'll give you a good slap," Father had an extraordinary capacity of amiable inattention. I sized him up and wondered would I cry, but he seemed to be too remote to be annoyed even by that. Really, it was like going for a walk with a mountain! He either ignored the wrenching and pummelling entirely, or else glanced down with a grin of amusement from his peak. I had never met anyone so absorbed in himself as he seemed.

At teatime, "talking to Daddy" began again, complicated this time by the fact that he had an evening paper, and every few minutes he put it down and told Mother something new out of it. I felt this was foul play. Man for man, I was prepared to compete with him any time for Mother's attention, but when he had it all made up for him by other people it left me no chance. Several times I tried to change the subject without success.

"You must be quiet while Daddy is reading, Larry," Mother said impatiently.

It was clear that she either genuinely liked talking to Father better than talking to me, or else that he had some terrible hold on her which made her afraid to admit the truth.

"Mummy," I said that night when she was tucking me up, "do you think if I prayed hard God would send Daddy back to the war?"

She seemed to think about that for a moment.

"No, dear," she said with a smile. "I don't think he would."

"Why wouldn't he, Mummy?"

"Because there isn't a war any longer, dear."

"But, Mummy, couldn't God make another war, if He liked?"

"He wouldn't like to, dear. It's not God who makes wars, but bad people."

"Oh!" I said.

I was disappointed about that. I began to think that God wasn't quite what he was cracked up to be.

Next morning I woke at my usual hour, feeling like a bottle of champagne. I put out my feet and invented a long conversation in which Mrs. Right talked of the trouble she had with her own father till she put him in the Home. I didn't quite know what the Home was but it sounded the right place for Father. Then I got my chair and stuck my head out of the attic window. Dawn was just breaking, with a guilty air that made me feel I had caught it in the act. My head bursting with stories and schemes, I stumbled in next door, and in the half-darkness scrambled into the big bed. There was no room at Mother's side so I had to get between her and Father. For the time being I had forgotten about him, and for several minutes I sat bolt upright, racking my brains to know what I could do with him. He was taking up more than his fair share of the bed, and I couldn't get comfortable, so I gave him several kicks that made him grunt and stretch. He made room all right, though. Mother waked and felt for me. I settled back comfortably in the warmth of the bed with my thumb in my mouth.

"Mummy!" I hummed, loudly and contentedly.

"Sssh! dear," she whispered. "Don't wake Daddy!"

This was a new development, which threatened to be even more serious than "talking to Daddy." Life without my early morning conferences was unthinkable.

"Why?" I asked severely.

"Because poor Daddy is tired."

This seemed to me a quite inadequate reason, and I was sickened by the sentimentality of her "poor Daddy." I never liked that sort of gush; it always struck me as insincere.

"Oh!" I said lightly. Then in my most winning tone, "Do you know where I want to go with you today, Mummy?"

"No, dear," she sighed.

"I want to go down the Glen and fish for thornybacks with my new net, and then I want to go out to the Fox and Hounds, and—"

"Don't-wake-Daddy!" she hissed angrily, clapping her hand across my mouth.

But it was too late. He was awake, or nearly so. He grunted and reached for the matches. Then he stared incredulously at his watch.

"Like a cup of tea, dear?" asked mother in a meek, hushed voice I had never heard her use before. It sounded almost as though she were afraid.

"Tea?" he exclaimed indignantly. "Do you know what time it is?"

"And after that I want to go up the Rathconney Road," I said loudly, afraid I'd forget something in all those interruptions.

"Go to sleep at once, Larry!" she said sharply.

I began to snivel. I couldn't concentrate, the way that pair went on, and smothering my early-morning schemes was like burying a family from the cradle.

Father said nothing, but lit his pipe and sucked it, looking out into the shadows without minding Mother or me. I knew he was mad. Every time I made a remark Mother hushed me irritably. I was mortified. I felt it wasn't fair; there was even something sinister in it. Every time I had pointed out to her the waste of making two beds when we could both sleep in one, she had told me it was healthier like that, and now there was this man, this stranger, sleeping with her without the least regard for her health!

He got up early and made tea, but though he brought Mother a cup he brought none for me.

"Mummy," I shouted, "I want a cup of tea, too."

"Yes, dear," she said patiently. "You can drink from Mummy's saucer."

That settled it. Either Father or I would have to leave the house. I didn't want to drink from Mother's saucer; I wanted to be treated as an equal in my own home, so, just to spite her, I drank it all and left none for her. She took that quietly, too.

But that night when she was putting me to bed she said gently: "Larry, I want you to promise me something."

"What is it?" I asked.

"Not to come in and disturb poor Daddy in the morning. Promise?"

"Poor Daddy" again! I was becoming suspicious of everything involving that quite impossible man.

"Why?" I asked.

"Because poor Daddy is worried and tired and he doesn't sleep well."

"Why doesn't he, Mummy?"

"Well, you know, don't you, that while he was at the war Mummy got the pennies from the Post Office?"

"From Miss MacCarthy?"

"That's right. But now, you see, Miss MacCarthy hasn't any more pennies, so Daddy must go out and find us some. You know what would happen if he couldn't?"

"No," I said, "tell us."

"Well, I think we might have to go out and beg for them like the poor old woman on Fridays. We wouldn't like that, would we?"

"No," I agreed. "We wouldn't."

"So you'll promise not to come in and wake him?"

"Promise."

Mind you, I meant that. I knew pennies were a serious matter, and I was all against having to go out and beg like the old woman on Fridays. Mother laid out all my toys in a complete ring around the bed so that, whatever way I got out, I was bound to fall over one of them.

When I woke I remembered my promise all right. I got up and sat on the floor and played—for hours, it seemed to me. Then I got my chair and looked out the attic window for more hours. I wished it was time for Father to wake; I wished someone would make me a cup of tea. I didn't feel in the least like the sun; instead, I was bored and so very, very cold! I simply longed for the warmth and depth of the big featherbed.

At last I could stand it no longer. I went into the next room. As there was still no room at Mother's side I climbed over her and she woke with a start.

"Larry," she whispered, gripping my arm very tightly, "what did you promise?"

"But I did, Mummy," I wailed, caught in the very act. "I was quiet for ever so long."

"Oh, dear, and you're perished!" she said sadly, feeling me all over. "Now, if I let you stay will you promise not to talk?"

"But I want to talk, Mummy," I wailed.

"That has nothing to do with it," she said with a firmness that was new to me. "Daddy wants to sleep. Now, do you understand that?"

I understood it only too well. I wanted to talk, he wanted to sleep—whose house was it, anyway?

"Mummy," I said with equal firmness, "I think it would be healthier for Daddy to sleep in his own bed."

That seemed to stagger her, because she said nothing for a while.

"Now, once for all," she went on, "you're to be perfectly quiet or go back to your own bed. Which is it to be?"

The injustice of it got me down. I had convicted her out of her own mouth of inconsistency and unreasonableness, and she hadn't even attempted to reply. Full of spite, I gave Father a kick, which she didn't notice but which made him grunt and open his eyes in alarm.

"What time is it?" he asked in a panic-stricken voice, not looking at Mother but at the door, as if he saw someone there.

"It's early yet," she replied soothingly. "It's only the child. Go to sleep again. . . . Now, Larry," she added, getting out of bed, "you've wakened Daddy and you must go back."

This time, for all her quiet air, I knew she meant it, and knew that my principal rights and privileges were as good as lost unless I asserted them at once. As she lifted me, I gave a screech, enough to wake the dead, not to mind Father. He groaned.

"That damn child! Doesn't he ever sleep?"

"It's only a habit, dear," she said quietly, though I could see she was vexed.

"Well, it's time he got out of it," shouted Father, beginning to heave in the bed. He suddenly gathered all the bedclothes about him, turned to the wall, and then looked back over his shoulder with nothing showing only two small, spiteful, dark eyes. The man looked very wicked.

To open the bedroom door, Mother had to let me down, and I broke free and dashed for the farthest corner, screeching. Father sat bolt upright in bed.

"Shut up, you little puppy!" he said in a choking voice.

I was so astonished that I stopped screeching. Never, never had anyone spoken to me in that tone before. I looked at him incredulously and saw his face convulsed with rage. It was only then that I fully realized how God had coddled me, listening to my prayers for the safe return of this monster.

"Shut up, you!" I bawled, beside myself.

"What's that you said?" shouted Father, making a wild leap out of the bed.

"Mick, Mick!" cried Mother. "Don't you see the child isn't used to you?"

"I see he's better fed than taught," snarled Father, waving his arms wildly. "He wants his bottom smacked."

All his previous shouting was as nothing to these obscene words referring to my person. They really made my blood boil.

"Smack your own!" I screamed hysterically. "Smack your own! Shut up! Shut up!"

At this he lost his patience and let fly at me. He did it with the lack of conviction you'd expect of a man under Mother's horrified eyes, and it ended up as a mere tap, but the sheer indignity of being struck at all by a stranger, a total stranger who had cajoled his way back from the war into our big bed as a result of my innocent intercession, made me completely dotty. I shrieked and shrieked, and danced in my bare feet, and Father, looking awkward and hairy in nothing but a short gray army shirt, glared down at me like a mountain out for murder. I think it must have been then that I realized he was jealous too. And there stood Mother in her nightdress, looking as if her heart was broken between us. I hoped she felt as she looked. It seemed to me that she deserved it all.

From that morning out my life was hell. Father and I were enemies, open and avowed. We conducted a series of skirmishes against one another, he trying to steal my time with Mother and I his. When she was sitting on my bed, telling me a story, he took to looking for some pair of old boots which he alleged he had left behind him at the beginning of the war. While he talked to Mother I played loudly with my toys to show my total lack of concern. He created a terrible scene one evening when he came in from work and found me at his box, playing with his regimental badges, Gurkha knives and button-sticks. Mother got up and took the box from me.

"You mustn't play with Daddy's toys unless he lets you, Larry," she said severely. "Daddy doesn't play with yours."

For some reason Father looked at her as if she had struck him and then turned away with a scowl.

"Those are not toys," he growled, taking down the box again to see had I lifted anything. "Some of those curios are very rare and valuable."

But as time went on I saw more and more how he managed to alienate Mother and me. What made it worse was that I couldn't grasp his method or see what attraction he had for Mother. In every possible way he was less winning than I. He had a common accent and made noises at his tea. I thought for a while that it might be the newspapers she was interested in, so I made up bits of news of my own to read to her. Then I thought it might be the smoking, which I personally thought attractive, and took his pipes and went round the house dribbling into them till he caught me. I even made noises at my tea, but Mother only told me I was disgusting. It all seemed to hinge round that unhealthy habit of sleeping together, so I made a point of dropping into their bedroom and nosing round, talking to myself, so that they wouldn't know I was watching them, but they were never up to anything that I could see. In the end it beat me. It seemed to depend on being grown-up and giving people rings, and I realized I'd have to wait.

But at the same time I wanted him to see that I was only waiting, not giving up the fight. One evening when he was being particularly obnoxious, chattering away well above my head, I let him have it.

"Mummy," I said, "do you know what I'm going to do when I grow up?"

"No, dear," she replied. "What?"

"I'm going to marry you," I said quietly.

Father gave a great guffaw out of him, but he didn't take me in. I knew it must be only pretence. And Mother, in spite of everything, was pleased. I felt she was probably relieved to know that one day Father's hold on her would be broken.

"Won't that be nice?" she said with a smile.

"It'll be very nice," I said confidently. "Because we're going to have lots and lots of babies."

"That's right, dear," she said placidly. "I think we'll have one soon, and then you'll have plenty of company."

I was no end pleased about that because it showed that in spite of the way she gave in to Father she still considered my wishes. Besides, it would put the Geneys in their place.

It didn't turn out like that, though. To begin with, she was very preoccupied—I supposed about where she would get the seventeen and six—and though Father took to staying out late in the evenings it did me no particular good. She stopped taking me for walks, became as touchy as blazes, and smacked me for nothing at all. Sometimes I wished I'd never mentioned the confounded baby—I seemed to have genius for bringing calamity on myself.

And calamity it was! Sonny arrived in the most appalling hullaba-loo—even that much he couldn't do without a fuss—and from the first moment I disliked him. He was a difficult child—so far as I was concerned he was always difficult—and demanded far too much attention. Mother was simply silly about him, and couldn't see when he was only showing off. As company he was worse than useless. He slept all day, and I had to go round the house on tiptoe to avoid waking him. It wasn't any longer a question of not waking Father. The slogan now was "Don't-wake-Sonny!" I couldn't understand why the child wouldn't sleep at the proper time, so whenever Mother's back was turned I woke him. Some-times to keep him awake I pinched him as well. Mother caught me at it one day and gave me a most unmerciful flaking.

One evening, when Father was coming in from work, I was playing trains in the front garden. I let on not to notice him; instead, I pretended to be talking to myself, and said in a loud voice; "If another bloody baby comes into this house, I'm going out."

Father stopped dead and looked at me over his shoulder.

"What's that you said?" he asked sternly.

"I was only talking to myself," I replied, trying to conceal my panic. "It's private."

He turned and went in without a word. Mind you, I intended it as a solemn warning, but its effect was quite different. Father started being quite nice to me. I could understand that, of course. Mother was quite sickening about Sonny. Even at mealtimes she'd get up and gawk at him in the cradle with an idiotic smile, and tell Father to do the same. He was always polite about it, but he looked so puzzled you could see he didn't know what she was talking about. He complained of the way Sonny cried at night, but she only got cross and said that Sonny never cried except when there was something up with him—which was a flaming lie, because Sonny never had anything up with him, and only cried for attention. It was really painful to see how simple-minded she was. Father wasn't attractive, but he had a fine intelligence. He saw through Sonny, and now he knew that I saw through him as well.

One night I awoke with a start. There was someone beside me in the bed. For one wild moment I felt sure it must be Mother, having come to her senses and left Father for good, but then I heard Sonny in convulsions in the next room, and Mother saying: "There! There! There!" and I knew it wasn't she. It was Father. He was lying beside me, wide awake, breathing hard and apparently as mad as hell.

After a while it came to me what he was mad about. It was his turn now. After turning me out of the big bed, he had been turned out himself. Mother had no consideration now for anyone but that poisonous pup, Sonny. I couldn't help feeling sorry for Father. I had been through it all myself, and even at that age I was magnanimous. I began to stroke him down and say: "There! There!" He wasn't exactly responsive.

"Aren't you asleep either?" he snarled.

"Ah, come on and put your arm around us, can't you?" I said, and he did, in a sort of way. Gingerly, I suppose, is how you'd describe it. He was very bony but better than nothing.

At Christmas he went out of his way to buy me a really nice model railway.

*Tom Whalen*
# The Missing Part

Today now at fifty he awoke with an image in his mind, a memory of an image of absence, the finger of his father or rather the missing finger, the hand, the right hand of his father that was missing its middle finger, only this, he knew not why this today at fifty would return to him, a memory of his father's hand that was missing its finger, the middle finger of his right hand, just that, this memory, the hand he recalled seeing as a child as a deformity, huge hand, strange hand, the knuckle knobbed, he would rub cream on it, he saw his father massage this area with cream for hours in his chair massaging with cream the knuckle that had no finger attached to it, sitting in his so-called easy chair, his feet up on the ottoman, massaging for hours his knuckle, staring off into space, only that, thinking he, the child, knew not what, possibly of the war in which his father lost his finger, the war he never told him anything about, only from his mother did he know the finger had been shot off by a sniper in the war and the rest, the night, the flares, the scream of the weaponry, the mud, the rain, the pain, all the rest he knew only by imagining at night before sleep in bed what it must have been like, but he was never sure, only imagined it, he was told only what his mother told him, his father never talked about the hand or the war in which he lost his finger, never talked about the war, had thrown, as his mother said, all his medals away, he had been a captain in the infantry, he avoided the VFW, he did not talk about the war yet oddly at the bottom of the ottoman, as if they were pornography, he hid novels with lurid covers of combat, men grimy and grimacing while grenades exploded behind the barbed wire in the background, but he never saw his father reading one, but the books were worn, the pages loose from the spine, but he never saw his father with one in his hand, did he read them at night when the boy was asleep, he never heard him up at night though sometimes they argued, his mother and father, argued and fought long into the night, argued and fought and his mother wore bruises on her arms, and once the hand without a finger, he remembered, now held in it a gun pointed at the two of them and he remembered not the circumstance but only the hand holding the gun on them, only that, the hand and the gun, how big they both looked to his eyes when he was a child, was he afraid, he must have been afraid of the hand to remember it now at fifty long after his father's death, why else this image in his mind of the hand without a finger, it did not dominate his home, his childhood, in fact had he not in time paid no attention to it at all, his father never talked about it, but was the finger still there, was there still as paraplegics so often say the feeling of the missing part still there and would this make the hand feel in time more normal or less, he wondered, did his father still feel the finger there even though it had been shot off a few years before, was the finger there as a spirit pulsing through the empty space, through time, a ghost, a phantom finger, was it there even though it was not, did it hurt, did it twitch, did it move, did he have control over it or not, none of this did he ask his father, he asked his father nothing about the war, later he understood and agreed with this, but as a child he was curious but he knew somehow not to ask about the war or how he lost the finger of his right hand, never to ask though it looked strange, the hand, gripping the steering wheel as they drove into the country, strange at the dinner table, strangest of all to his eyes then as a child under the eggblue sky of a summer afternoon as he watched his father pitch a softball game under the blue sky, the white ball gripped in the hand with its middle finger missing and released into the empty space between the hand and the batter into the air, the sky with its cavalcade of clouds, that strange hand holding the ball on the mound, a hand unlike any other, perhaps that was why now this morning with the night still in his head he remembered at fifty this image of the hand missing its middle finger shot off in the war by a sniper one night, or was it day, he did not know, now would never know anything more about the hand of his father, and why now even think about it at fifty this morning not even yet fully awake to the day, why remember it now, this image of absence, of presence where there was only absence like the cut-out of a bird in a sky-puzzle, the shape there but the thing missing, the finger absent, the three fingers of the hand holding in the morning a coffee cup, only that, only the hand, not the face bent over the cup, only the hand turning the pages of the paper, the fingers blackened, the whorls blackened from working all day

with carbon paper, tearing off strips of carbon paper, calculating receipts
all day, always with the right hand, the left clean, the left hand forgotten,
an accessory, always the right hand, for he was right-handed though the
son was not, or holding them in winter, the two hands, over the fire, the
light from the embers warming the finger, shining through the space
where the finger should have been, he wondered if it was cold, did the
fire warm the absence, strange thought, he thought, funny to think it
now, why he did not know, did not ask ever about the hand, not at the
table, not at the fire, not while his father sat in his so-called easy chair
rubbing cream on the dry skin-cracking knuckle, he did not ask while the
embers warmed their hands in the silence, he did not ask, only stared at
the hand, at the space where the finger should have been, until his father,
he now recalled, once turned his head and saw him staring, and in the
silence told him all he needed to know, and told him nothing.

*Stephen Shu-ning Liu*

# My Father's Martial Art

When he came home Mother said he looked
like a monk and stank of green fungus.
At the fireside he told us about life
at the monastery; his rock pillow,
his cold bath, his steel-bar lifting
and his wood-chopping. He didn't see
a woman for three winters, on Mountain O Mei.

"My Master was both light and heavy.
  He skipped over treetops like a squirrel.
  Once he stood on a chair, one foot tied
  to a rope. We four pulled; we couldn't
  move him a bit. His kicks would split
  a cedar's trunk."

I saw Father break into a pumpkin
with his fingers. I saw him drop a hawk
with bamboo arrows. He rose before dawn, filled
our backyard with a harsh sound hah, hah, hah:
there was his Black Dragon Sweep, his Crane Stand,
his Mantis Walk, his Tiger Leap, his Cobra Coil . . .
Infrequently he taught me tricks and made me
fight the best of all the village boys.

From a busy street I brood over high cliffs
on O Mei, where my father and Master sit:
shadows deepen across their faces as the smog
between us deepens into a funeral pyre.

But don't retreat into night, my father.
Come down from the cliffs. Come
with a single Black Dragon Sweep and hush
this oncoming traffic with your hah, hah, hah.

*e.e. cummings*

# 34

my father moved through dooms of love
through sames of am through haves of give,
singing each morning out of each night
my father moved through depths of height

this motionless forgetful where
turned at his glance to shining here;
that if(so timid air is firm)
under his eyes would stir and squirm

newly as from unburied which
floats the first who,his april touch
drove sleeping selves to swarm their fates
woke dreamers to their ghostly roots

and should some why completely weep
my father's fingers brought her sleep:
vainly no smallest voice might cry
for he could feel the mountains grow.

Lifting the valleys of the sea
my father moved through griefs of joy;
praising a forehead called the moon
singing desire into begin

joy was his song and joy so pure
a heart of star by him could steer
and pure so now and now so yes
the wrists of twilight would rejoice

keen as midsummer's keen beyond
conceiving mind of sun will stand,
so strictly(over utmost him
so hugely)stood my father's dream

his flesh was flesh his blood was blood:
no hungry man but wished him food;
no cripple wouldn't creep one mile
uphill to only see him smile.

Scorning the pomp of must and shall
my father moved through dooms of feel;
his anger was as right as rain
his pity was as green as grain

septembering arms of year extend
less humbly wealth to foe and friend
than he to foolish and to wise
offered immeasurable is

proudly and(by octobering flame
beckoned)as earth will downward climb,
so naked for immortal work
his shoulders marched against the dark

his sorrow was as true as bread:
no liar looked him in the head;
if every friend became his foe
he'd laugh and build a world with snow.

My father moved through theys of we,
singing each new leaf out of each tree
(and every child was sure that spring
danced when she heard my father sing)

then let men kill which cannot share,
let blood and flesh be mud and mire,
scheming imagine,passion willed,
freedom a drug that's bought and sold

giving to steal and cruel kind,
a heart to fear,to doubt a mind,
to differ a disease of same,
conform the pinnacle of am

though dull were all we taste as bright,
bitter all utterly things sweet,
maggoty minus and dumb death
all we inherit,all bequeath

and nothing quite so least as truth
—i say though hate were why men breathe—
because my father lived his soul
love is the whole and more than all

*Andrew Hudgins*
# My Father's Rage

As I kicked through the swinging door,
the turkey shifted on the platter.
I juggled, lost it, clipped the bird
with the platter's edge, and the hot meat
slid, skittered—greasy—on the floor,
and smacked the polished army boots
of Sergeant Turner, our Thanksgiving guest.
My Daddy grabbed me by the throat
and slammed me up against the wall,
which boomed. My mother gasped. I lost
my breath and couldn't get it back.
"You stupid idiot!" my father screamed.
Then Sergeant Turner touched Dad's arm.
"Lon," he said, "we've eaten worse—
when we were growing up." Dad sighed,
and then, reluctantly, he let me drop.
But now his crazy rage is gone
to whole days watching teevee, watching
golf, football, news. His rage gone to whole days
watching the fucking weather channel.
And I, goddamn his eyes, I want it back.

*Charles David Wright*
# Shaving

When his match, when his match kept missing
his pipe, I knew from my father's face,
sharp grey stubs in a cornfield reaped and dry,
he hadn't begun a beard out of an old man's right
or November whimsy, but that his hands were going.
Watching him there fumbling the light again,
I went back to another Sunday with him
when on small boy's legs I fell behind him
in the snow going to church. He came back for me
laughing and boosted me to his chest. My cheeks
touched then two smoothnesses at once:
the velvet collar of his Lord Chesterfield
and the warm plains of his best Sunday face.

I lit his pipe and said, "Smoke that while I shave you
for Sunday." He sat on the toilet seat like
a good boy taking medicine. My fingers
touched through the lather the cleft of his chin
and the blade made pink and blue swaths
in the snowy foam, and we were done.
Pretending to test, I bent down my cheek to his
a moment, and then we went to church.

*Samuel Hazo*
# Carol of a Father

He runs ahead to ford a flood of leaves—
he suddenly a forager and I
the lagging child content to stay behind
and watch the gold upheavals at the curb
submerge his surging ankles and subside.

A word could leash him back or make him turn
and ask me with his eyes if he should stop.
One word, and he would be a son again
and I a father sentenced to correct
a boy's caprice to shuffle in the drifts.

Ignoring fatherhood, I look away
and let him roam in his Octobering
to mind the memories of those few falls
when a boy can wade the quiet avenues
alone, and the sound of leaves solves everything.

# II
# Birth

---

*Another life before us glows*
*Casts on all faithful souls its gleam.*

Louis Honoré Fréchette

*What use to me the gold and silver hoard?*
*What use to me the gems most rich and rare?*
*Brighter by far—ay' bright beyond compare—*
*The joys my children to my heart afford!*

Yamagami no Okura

*Stephen Sandy*
# Expecting Fathers

"It's not the way it was supposed to be,"
The laboring mother muttered when the neuter
Light plumed on paper toweling, fluorescent medley
Of edges in the hall half laundry and half lab.

The play-offs make more sense. Dads eddy, cowed,
In the TV lounge. They want something they can handle.
No padded diapers, their boys wear shoulder pads.
Then what is this, a cameo appearance by a primate?

I put him down too fast on the bunting in the cradle
Near the stove he'll sleep beside. His arms startle,
Reach up, catching at air; the fingers clench,
The Moro reflex, reaching for a branch.

I hear the tiny yodel, a far blood-curdling yell
As if he called out to me, shouted in fear
A half a field, not half a yard, away.
I sit back, drawing great blanks on the years to come.

*Michael Dennis Browne*

# Breech

We called and called but he did not come. We stared
at each other. So we ran looking for him,
twisting, panting among the trees, losing sight
of each other, making contact again, even colliding
once, more than once, sweat-stung, salt-smarting,
asking: Did you see? Did you? Was there anything?
It was when we were standing panting in front of
the same thick oak where we began that we saw him,
or saw his feet first, descending out of the tree
where he had been hiding, saw him sliding wordless
backwards, striped with blood, his skin creased
and cheesy, slowly, slowly, as the tree bark
yielded him, his legs, his buttocks, his little
wrinkled back, and at last the matted, clotted hair
on the back of his head, until, with the tree's
last effort and the wordless closing over of its bark,
he slid onto the muddy ground and lay there, lips
slightly parted, panting, and we forgave him.

*Galway Kinnell*

# The Olive Wood Fire

When Fergus woke crying at night
I would carry him from his crib
to the rocking chair and sit holding him
before the fire of thousand-year-old olive wood,
which it took a quarter-hour of matches
and kindling to get burning right. Sometimes
—for reasons I never knew and he has forgotten—
even after his bottle the big tears
would keep on rolling down his big cheeks
—the left cheek always more brilliant than the right—
and we would sit, some nights for hours,
rocking in the almost lightless light
eking itself out of the ancient wood,
and hold each other against the darkness,
his close behind and far away in the future,
mine I imagined all around.
One such time, fallen half-asleep myself,
I thought I heard a scream
—a flier crying out in horror
as he dropped fire on he didn't know what or whom,
or else a child thus set aflame—
and sat up alert. The olive wood fire
had burned low. In my arms lay Fergus,
fast asleep, left cheek glowing, God.

*Michael Dennis Browne*

# To My Brother Peter,
# on the Birth of His First Child

You who love to climb
the mountains you live among,
now you are roped to someone;
and when one day you fall
as you will,
why, you've a son to swing from.

# III
# A Father's Love

---

*No sweeter, holier sound to heaven can float*
*Than childhood's laughter, or the free bird's note.*
                              Guy de Maupassant

*John Updike*
# Son

He is often upstairs, when he has to be home. He prefers to be elsewhere. He is almost sixteen, though beardless still, a man's mind indignantly captive in the frame of a child. I love touching him, but don't often dare. The other day, he had the flu, and a fever, and I gave him a back rub, marvelling at the symmetrical knit of muscle, the organic tension. He is high-strung. Yet his sleep is so solid he sweats like a stone in the wall of a well. He wishes for perfection. He would like to destroy us, for we are, variously, too fat, too jocular, too sloppy, too affectionate, too grotesque and heedless in our ways. His mother smokes too much. His younger brother chews with his mouth open. His older sister leaves unbuttoned the top button of her blouses. His younger sister tussles with the dogs, getting them overexcited, avoiding doing her homework. Everyone in the house talks nonsense. He would be a better father than his father. But time has tricked him, has made him a son. After a quarrel, if he cannot go outside and kick a ball, he retreats to a corner of the house and reclines on the beanbag chair in an attitude of strange—infantile or leonine—torpor. We exhaust him, without meaning to. He takes an interest in the newspaper now, the front page as well as the sports, in this tiring year of 1973.

He is upstairs, writing a musical comedy. It is a Sunday in 1949. He has volunteered to prepare a high-school assembly program; people will sing. Songs of the time go through his head, as he scribbles new words. *Up in de mornin', down at de school, work like a debil for my grades.* Below him, irksome voices grind on, like machines working their way through tunnels. His parents each want something from the other. "Marion, you don't understand that man like I do; he has a heart of gold." His father's charade is very complex; the world, which he fears, is used as a flail on his wife. But from his cringing attitude he would seem to an outsider the one being flailed. With burning red face, the woman accepts the role of aggressor as penance for the fact, the incessant shameful fact, that *he* has to wrestle with the world she hides here, in solitude, at him. This is normal, but does not seem to them to be so. Only by convolution have they arrived at the dominant/submissive relationship society has assigned them. For the man is maternally kind and with a smile hugs to himself his jewel, his certainty of being victimized; it is the mother whose tongue is sharp, who sometimes strikes. "Well, he gets you out of the house, and I guess that's gold to you." His answer is "Duty calls," pronounced mincingly. "This social contract is a balance of compromises." This will infuriate her, the son knows; as his heart thickens, the downstairs overflows with her hot voice. "*Don't* wear that smile at me! And *take* your hands off your hips; you look like a fairy!" Their son tries not to listen. When he does, visual details of the downstairs flood his mind: the two antagonists, circling with their coffee cups; the shabby mismatched furniture; the hopeful books; the docile framed photographs of the dead, docile and still like cowed students. The matrix of pain that bore him—he feels he is floating above it, sprawled on the bed as on a cloud, stealing songs as they come into his head. (*Across the hallway from the guidance room/Lives a French instructor called Mrs. Blum*), contemplating the view from the upstairs window (last summer's burdock stalks like the beginnings of an alphabet, an apple tree holding three rotten apples as if pondering why they failed to fall), yearning for Monday, for the ride to school with his father, for the bell that calls him to homeroom, for the excitements of class, for Broadway, for fame, for the cloud that will carry him away, out of this, out.

He returns from his paper-delivery route and finds a few Christmas presents for him on the kitchen table. I must guess at the year. 1913? Without opening them, he knocks them to the floor, puts his head on the table, and falls asleep. He must have been consciously dramatizing his plight: his father was sick, money was scarce, he had to work, to win food for the family when he was still a child. In his dismissal of Christmas, he touched a nerve: his love of anarchy, his distrust of the social contract. He treasured this moment of revolt; else why remember it, hoard a memory so bitter, and confide it to his son many Christmases later? He had a teaching instinct, though he claimed that life miscast him as a schoolteacher. I suffered in his classes, feeling the confusion as a persecution of him, but now wonder if his rebellious heart did not court confusion, not as Communists do, to intrude their own order, but, more radical still, as an end pleasurable in itself, as truth's very body. Yet his handwriting (an old pink permission slip recently fluttered from a book where it had been marking a page for nearly twenty years) was always considered legible, and he was sitting up doing arithmetic the morning of the day he died.

And letters survive from that yet prior son, written in brown ink, in a tidy tame hand, home to his mother from the Missouri seminary where he was preparing for his vocation. The dates are 1887, 1888, 1889. Nothing much happened: he missed New Jersey, and was teased at a school social for escorting a widow. He wanted to do the right thing, but the little sheets of faded penscript exhale a dispirited calm, as if his heart already knew he would not make a successful minister, or live to be old. His son, my father, when old, drove hundreds of miles out of his way to visit the Missouri town from which those letters had been sent. Strangely, the town had not changed; it looked just as he had imagined, from his father's descriptions: tall wooden houses, rain-soaked, stacked on a bluff. The town was a sepia postcard preserved in an attic. My father cursed: his father's old sorrow bore him down into depression, into hatred of life. My mother claims his decline in health began at that moment.

He is wonderful to watch, playing soccer. Smaller than the others, my son leaps, heads, dribbles, feints, passes. When a big boy knocks him down, he tumbles on the mud, in his green-and-black school uniform, in an ectasy of falling. I am envious. Never for me the jaunty pride of the school uniform, the solemn ritual of the coach's pep talk, the camaraderie of shook hands and slapped backsides, the shadow-striped hush of late afternoon and last quarter, the solemn vaulted universe of official combat, with its cheering mothers and referees exotic as zebras and the bespectacled timekeeper alert with his claxon. When the boy scores a goal, he runs into the arms of his teammates with upraised arms and his face alight as if blinded by triumph. They lift him from the earth in a union of muddy hugs. What spirit! What valor! What skill! His father, watching from the sidelines, inwardly registers only one complaint: he feels the boy, with his talent, should be more aggressive.

• •

They drove across the Commonwealth of Pennsylvania to hear his son read in Pittsburgh. But when their presence was announced to the audience, they did not stand; the applause groped for them and died. My mother said afterwards she was afraid she might fall into the next row if she tried to stand in the dark. Next morning was sunny, and the three of us searched for the house where once they had lived. They had been happy there; I imagined, indeed, that I had been conceived there, just before the slope of the Depression steepened and fear gripped my family. We found the library where she used to read Turgenev, and the little park where the bums slept close as paving stones in the summer night; but their street kept eluding us, though we circled in the car. On foot my mother found the tree. She claimed she recognized it, the sooty linden tree she would gaze into from their apartment windows. The branches, though thicker, had held their pattern. But the house itself, and the entire block, was gone. Stray bricks and rods of iron in the grass suggested that the demolition had been recent. We stood on the empty spot and laughed. They knew it was right, because the railroad tracks were the right distance away. In confirmation, a long freight train pulled itself east around the curve, its great weight gliding as if on a river current; then a silver passenger train came gliding as effortlessly in the other direction. The curve of the tracks tipped the cars slightly toward us. The 'Golden Triangle, gray and hazed, was off to our left, beyond a forest of bridges. We stood on the grassy rubble that morning, where something once had been, beside the tree still there, and were intensely happy. Why? We knew.

" 'No,' Dad said to me, 'the Christian ministry isn't a job you choose, it's a vocation for which you got to receive a call.' I could tell he wanted me to ask him. We never talked much, but we understood each other, we were both scared devils, not like you and the kid. I asked him. Had he ever received the call? He said No. He said No, he never had. Received the call. That was a terrible thing, for him to admit. And I was the one he told. As far as I knew he never admitted it to anybody, but he admitted it to me. He felt like hell about it, I could tell. That was all we ever said about it. That was enough."

• •

He had made his younger brother cry, and justice must be done. A father enforces justice. I corner the rat in our bedroom; he is holding a cardboard mailing tube like a sword. The challenge flares white-hot; I roll my weight toward him like a rock down a mountain, and knock the weapon from his hand. He smiles. Smiles! Because my facial expression is silly? Because he is glad that he can still be overpowered, and hence is still protected? Why? I do not hit him. We stand a second, father and son, and then as nimbly as on the soccer field he steps around me and out the door. He slams the door. He shouts obscenities in the hall, slams all the doors he can find on the way to his room. Our moment of smilingly shared silence was the moment of compression: now the explosion. The whole house rocks with it. Downstairs, his siblings and mother come to me and offer advice and psychological analysis. I was too aggressive. He is spoiled. What they can never know, my grief alone to treasure, was that lucid many-sided second of his smiling and my relenting, before the world's wrathful pantomime of power resumed.

As we huddle whispering about him, my son takes his revenge. In his room, he plays his guitar. He had greatly improved this winter; his hands getting bigger is the least of it. He has found in the guitar an escape. He plays the Romanza wherein repeated notes, with a sliding like the heart's valves, let themselves fall along the scale.

The notes fall, so gently he bombs us, drops feathery notes down upon us, our visitor, our prisoner.

*Robert Hayden*

# Those Winter Sundays

Sundays too my father got up early
and put his clothes on in the blueblack cold,
then with cracked hands that ached
from labor in the weekday weather made
banked fires blaze. No one ever thanked him.

I'd wake and hear the cold splintering, breaking.
When the rooms were warm, he'd call,
and slowly I would rise and dress,
fearing the chronic angers of that house,

Speaking indifferently to him,
who had driven out the cold
and polished my good shoes as well.
What did I know, what did I know
of love's austere and lonely offices?

*Coventry Patmore*
# The Toys

My little Son, who looked from thoughtful eyes
And moved and spoke in quiet grown-up wise,
Having my law the seventh time disobeyed,
I struck him, and dismissed
With hard words and unkissed,
—His Mother, who was patient, being dead.
Then, fearing lest his grief should hinder sleep,
I visited his bed,
But found him slumbering deep,
With darkened eyelids, and their lashes yet
From his late sobbing wet.
And I, with moan,
Kissing away his tears, left others of my own;
For, on a table drawn beside his head,
He had put, within his reach,
A box of counters and a red-veined stone,
A piece of glass abraded by the beach,
And six or seven shells,
A bottle with bluebells,
And two French copper coins, ranged there with careful art,
To comfort his sad heart.
So when that night I prayed
To God, I wept, and said:
Ah! when at last we lie with tranced breath,
Not vexing Thee in death,
And Thou rememberest of what toys
We made our joys,
How weakly understood
Thy great commanded good,

Then, fatherly not less
Than I whom Thou hast moulded from the clay,
Thou'lt leave Thy wrath, and say,
'I will be sorry for their childishness.'

*Richard Blessing*

# The Poet's Dream the Night After His Son Scores 36 in a Little Dribbler's Game

When I shoot, the glass board bends triple like a tailor's mirror,
and the ball splits like a bullish stock, vanishes
down a tunnel of refractions.
                                        Someone keeps doubling up
on me. He is short when I dribble, tall when I jump.
He shadows me in corners like quick death.

                                        I am home,
but my shirt says "Visitors." It is July in Bradford, Pennsylvania.

I know everything before it happens.

Soon an old man will come through a grove of slack-leaved trees.
He will move down the dusty path that leads to this park
as if he would die if both feet did not always touch the ground.
He will sit on the low stone wall beside the asphalt court.

It is all as I say.

                    Under the shade of his old man's hat
his eyes are cheering my name as a boy. They are screaming
I must win this one time for him. Everything depends on it.

I am confused. I call time-out, but the clock still runs.

The shadow who guards me has stolen the old man's hat.
*I'm quick as a sneeze,* he whispers, *tough as week-old cake.*
*I'm faster than you will be again in your life.*

I throw an elbow and he starts to cry. I stoop to comfort him,
but he is gone with the ball. His sweet base-line jumper
swells the net, swells my heart.

                                        Time's running out.
We've lost for good, I tell the old man. Together we sit
on the low stone wall, loving him, hating him, rooting him home.

*Irv Broughton*

# Shagging

*For Sayer*


The haul of pigskin rises   comes side-
     long   between my eyes   and the sun
               a sleep mask   to lose   my sense of time.


          Propped like a head   in some ancient ceremony,
     the ball   waits   as if driven in the ground   there
               my son's mark.


     I step. He delivers   something of legs grown   stronger.
          I have to reach       for his precise message.


          The ball          turns around          in air.
                    In the hoop of sleep or dreams
          you roll toward me          bound into
                    my hands like a pup. Other
times the ball rises, sputters,
rises high       on a bolt-like       last step which has
          sprung with intention. High in the breeze the balls
     travel.       I am now an animal       following
          something       in the grass
                              But it lies   there
instead an old shoe   in the size-mixed closet.
               I am comfortable   like the shoe   prancing
          the fields and onto the
     road          pride-driven among the flights
of my child's foot.   Points gather   in threes.
The vanished air   rubs the skin
          Now shoe-bare son's dirt-scaled sock
     is a shark moving                    edging
               toward the ball   attacking as it bobs

like a buoy      then veering
          from the dark boot of ball      slamming
its side      sending it   skyward   soccer-style
          like the Hanson boys          through.
    The metal goalpost   clangs   a dinner bell.


          I am tiring   across fifty yards   fifty years.
      I imagine a goalpost   struck down   a folded cross.
Florida State's Buddy Reynolds   galloping off   on one knee
          To Hollywood: What will be, is. A hit.
          Three in a row   tumble toward me.      I gather them in


              like leaves.   As balls fly   I fill
                    with guilt      for the lost host
                         and the mistletoe   now hanging   with only
          the crosslimbs              of stars              and still
                    I am fielding         this season              next
                where the dandelion seed-heads sit up
                         like baseballs         dancing   all over
          the spring practice field.


              We stop to look more   and punt.   Here another leg
of my son      powers forward,   another ball suppressing
the air.          "Oh, to keep my child's      feet on the green field
      radiating spheres!"   The pigskin now      grown thinner


          for you;   you unmoor it   from your hands
                    furiously,   dealing sky.   The rubber bladder
      bulges                    through the pigskin   my shirt rides
              high      proud shirt, drooped with sweat,
          my back      pains sharply.

Forty-two years ago   with my father,
this was life. I never was   done.   Father is seizing
the balls, returning them   like gifts. They spin   like tops
in the gold heavens.

One must   at least   be a star-crossed
lover      a child waking
a blind-squinting hunter   adjusting to outside
silence        a father        a gatherer
to pick up            everything            everything one sees
as I walk      slowly the beaches        the rail-
yards       the rescinding hills      woods
cast green      by all future      fields, shagging.

*Lucien Stryk*
# Rites of Passage

Indian river swollen brown and swift:
the pebble from my hand sounds above
           the southfield—

soybeans, corn, cicadas. Stone rings
touch the bank, ripple up my arm.
           In the grass

a worm twists in webbed air (how things
absorb each other)—on a branch
           a sparrow

tenses, gray. As grass stirs it bursts
from leaves, devouring. I close my book.
           With so much

doing everywhere, words swimming green,
why read? I see and taste silence.
           Starlings flit,

blue/black feathers raising spume
of dandelions, young fluttering
           in the twigs.

I think of my grown son who runs
and heaves me to my feet—our
           promised walk

through woods. As he pulls back a branch
hair on his forearm glistens
       like the leaves

we brush by. I follow down the path
we've loved for years. We try to
       lose ourselves,

yet there's the river, churning south.
I muse on what I've given,
       all I can't.

My son moves toward the bank, then turns.
I stop myself from grasping
       at his hand.

# IV
# Lessons

*"My son," said he, "we're surely fools*
*To wait for other people's tools . . ."*
                    Jean de la Fontaine

Ernest Hemingway
# Fathers and Sons

There had been a sign to detour in the center of the main street of this town, but cars had obviously gone through, so, believing it was some repair which had been completed, Nicholas Adams drove on through the town along the empty, brick-paved street, stopped by traffic lights that flashed on and off on this trafficless Sunday, and would be gone next year when the payments on the system were not met; on under the heavy trees of the small town that are a part of your heart if it is your town and you have walked under them, but that are only too heavy, that shut out the sun and that dampen the houses for a stranger; out past the last house and onto the highway that rose and fell straight away ahead with banks of red dirt sliced cleanly away and the second-growth timber on both sides. It was not his country but it was the middle of fall and all of this country was good to drive through and to see. The cotton was picked and in the clearings there were patches of corn, some cut with streaks of red sorghum, and, driving easily, his son asleep on the seat by his side, the day's run made, knowing the town he would reach for the night, Nick noticed which corn fields had soy beans or peas in them, how the thickets and the cut-over land lay, where the cabins and houses were in relation to the fields and the thickets; hunting the country in his mind as he went by; sizing up each clearing as to feed and cover and figuring where you would find a covey and which way they would fly.

In shooting quail you must not get between them and their habitual cover, once the dogs have found them, or when they flush they will come pouring at you, some rising steep, some skimming by your ears, whirring into a size you have never seen them in the air as they pass, the only way being to turn and take them over your shoulder as they go, before they set their wings and angle down into the thicket. Hunting this country for quail as his father had taught him, Nicholas Adams started thinking about his father. When he first thought about him it was always the eyes. The big frame, the quick movements, the wide shoulders, the hooked, hawk nose, the beard that covered the weak chin, you never thought about—it was always the eyes. They were protected in his head by the formation of the brows; set deep as though a special protection had been devised for some very valuable instrument. They saw much farther and much quicker than the human eye sees and they were the great gift his father had. His father saw as a big-horn ram or as an eagle sees, literally.

He would be standing with his father on one shore of the lake, his own eyes were very good then, and his father would say, "They've run up the flag." Nick could not see the flag or the flag pole. "There," his father would say, "it's your sister Dorothy. She's got the flag up and she's walking out onto the dock."

Nick would look across the lake and he could see the long wooded shore-line, the higher timber behind, the point that guarded the bay, the clear hills of the farm and the white of their cottage in the trees but he could not see any flag pole, or any dock, only the white of the beach and the curve of the shore.

"Can you see the sheep on the hillside toward the point?"

"Yes."

They were a whitish patch on the gray-green of the hill.

"I can count them," his father said.

Like all men with a faculty that surpasses human requirements, his father was very nervous. Then, too, he was sentimental, and, like most sentimental people, he was both cruel and abused. Also, he had much bad luck, and it was not all of it his own. He had died in a trap that he had helped only a little to set, and they had all betrayed him in their various ways before he died. All sentimental people are betrayed so many times. Nick could not write about him yet, although he would, later, but the quail country made him remember him as he was when Nick was a boy and he was very grateful to him for two things: fishing and shooting. His father was as sound on those two things as he was unsound on sex, for instance, and Nick was glad that it had been that way; for some one has to give you your first gun or the opportunity to get it and use it, and you have to live where there is game or fish if you are to learn about them, and now, at thirty-eight, he loved to fish and to shoot exactly as much as when he first had gone with his father. It was a passion that had never slackened and he was very grateful to his father for bringing him to know it.

While for the other, that his father was not sound about, all the equipment you will ever have is provided and each man learns all there is for him to know about it without advice; and it makes no difference where you live. He remembered very clearly the only two pieces of information his father had given him about that. Once when they were out shooting together Nick shot a red squirrel out of a hemlock tree. The squirrel fell, wounded, and when Nick picked him up bit the boy clean through the ball of the thumb.

"The dirty little bugger," Nick said and smacked the squirrel's head against the tree. "Look how he bit me."

His father looked and said, "Suck it out clean and put some iodine on when you get home."

"The little bugger," Nick said.

"Do you know what a bugger is?" his father asked him.

"We call anything a bugger," Nick said.

"A bugger is a man who has intercourse with animals."

"Why?" Nick said.

"I don't know," his father said. "But it is a heinous crime."

Nick's imagination was both stirred and horrified by this and he thought of various animals but none seemed attractive or practical and that was the sum total of direct sexual knowledge bequeathed him by his father except on one other subject. One morning he read in the paper that Enrico Caruso had been arrested for mashing.

"What is mashing?"

"It is one of the most heinous crimes," his father answered. Nick's imagination pictured the great tenor doing something strange, bizarre, and heinous with a potato masher to a beautiful lady who looked like the pictures of Anna Held on the inside of cigar boxes. He resolved, with considerable horror, that when he was old enough he would try mashing at least once.

His father had summed up the whole matter by stating that masturbation produced blindness, insanity, and death, while a man who went with prostitutes would contract hideous venereal diseases and that the thing to do was to keep your hands off of people. On the other hand his father had the finest pair of eyes he had ever seen and Nick had loved him very much and for a long time. Now, knowing how it had all been, even remembering the earliest times before things had gone badly was not good remembering. If he wrote it he could get rid of it. He had gotten rid of many things by writing them. But it was still too early for that. There were still too many people. So he decided to think of something else. There was nothing to do about his father and he had thought it all through many times. The handsome job the undertaker had done on his father's face had not blurred in his mind and all the rest of it was quite clear, including the responsibilities. He had complimented the under- taker. The undertaker had been both proud and smugly pleased. But it was not the undertaker that had given him that last face. The undertaker had only made certain dashingly executed repairs of doubtful artistic merit. The face had been making itself and being made for a long time. It had modelled fast in the last three years. It was a good story but there were still too many people alive for him to write it.

Nick's own education in those earlier matters had been acquired in the hemlock woods behind the Indian camp. This was reached by a trail which ran from the cottage through the woods to the farm and then by a road which wound through the slashings to the camp. Now if he could still feel all of that trail with bare feet. First there was the pine-needle loam through the hemlock woods behind the cottage where the fallen logs crumbled into wood dust and long splintered pieces of wood hung like javelins in the tree that had been struck by lightning. You crossed the creek on a log and if you stepped off there was the black muck of the swamp. You climbed a fence out of the woods and the trail was hard in the sun across the field with cropped grass and sheep sorrel and mullen growing and to the left the quaky bog of the creek bottom where the killdeer plover fed. The spring house was in that creek. Below the barn there was fresh warm manure and the other older manure that was caked dry on top. Then there was another fence and the hard, hot trail from the barn to the house and the hot sandy road that ran down to the woods, crossing the creek, on a bridge this time, where the cat-tails grew that you soaked in kerosene to make jack-lights with for spearing fish at night.

Then the main road went off to the left, skirting the woods and climbing the hill, while you went into the woods on the wide clay and shale road, cool under the trees, and broadened for them to skid out the hemlock bark the Indians cut. The hemlock bark was piled in long rows of stacks, roofed over with more bark, like houses, and the peeled logs lay huge and yellow where the trees had been felled. They left the logs in the woods to rot, they did not even clear away or burn the tops. It was only the bark they wanted for the tannery at Boyne City; hauling it across the lake on the ice in winter, and each year there was less forest and more open, hot, shadeless, weed-grown slashing.

But there was still much forest then, virgin forest where the trees grew high before there were any branches and you walked on the brown, clean, springy-needled ground with no undergrowth and it was cool on the hottest days and they three lay against the trunk of a hemlock wider than two beds are long, with the breeze high in the tops and the cool light that came in patches, and Billy said:

"You want Trudy again?"

"You want to?"

"Un Huh."

"Come on."

"No, here."

"But Billy——"

"I no mind Billy. He my brother."

Then afterwards they sat, the three of them, listening for a black squirrel that was in the top branches where they could not see him. They were waiting for him to bark again because when he barked he would jerk his tail and Nick would shoot where he saw any movement. His father gave him only three cartridges a day to hunt with and he had a single-barrel twenty-gauge shotgun with a very long barrel.

"Son of a bitch never move," Billy said.

"You shoot, Nickie. Scare him. We see him jump. Shoot him again," Trudy said. It was a long speech for her.

"I've only got two shells," Nick said.

"Son of a bitch," said Billy.

They sat against the tree and were quiet. Nick was feeling hollow and happy.

"Eddie says he going to come some night sleep in bed with you sister Dorothy."

"What?"

"He said."

Trudy nodded.

"That's all he want do," she said. Eddie was their older half-brother. He was seventeen.

"If Eddie Gilby ever comes at night and even speaks to Dorothy you know what I'd do to him? I'd kill him like this." Nick cocked the gun and hardly taking aim pulled the trigger, blowing a hole as big as your hand in the head or belly of that half-breed bastard Eddie Gilby. "Like that. I'd kill him like that."

"He better not come then," Trudy said. She put her hand in Nick's pocket.

"He better watch out plenty," said Billy.

"He's big bluff," Trudy was exploring with hand in Nick's pocket, "but don't you kill him. You get plenty trouble."

"I'd kill him like that," Nick said. Eddie Gilby lay on the ground with all his cheek shot away. Nick put his foot on him proudly.

"I'd scalp him," he said happily.

"No," said Trudy. "That's dirty."

"I'd scalp him and send it to his mother."

"His mother dead," Trudy said. "Don't you kill him, Nickie. Don't you kill him for me."

"After I scalped him I'd throw him to the dogs."

Billy was very depressed. "He better watch out," he said gloomily.

"They'd tear him to pieces," Nick said, pleased with the picture. Then, having scalped that half-breed renegade and standing, watching the dogs tear him, his face unchanging, he fell backward against the tree, held tight around the neck, Trudy holding, choking him, and crying, "No kill him! No kill him! No kill him! No. No. No. Nickie. Nickie. Nickie!"

"What's the matter with you?"

"No kill him."

"I got to kill him."

"He just a big bluff."

"All right," Nickie said. "I won't kill him unless he comes around the house. Let go of me."

"That's good," Trudy said. "You want to do anything now? I feel good now."

"If Billy goes away." Nick had killed Eddie Gilby, then pardoned him his life, and he was a man now.

"You go, Billy. You hang around all the time. Go on."

"Son a bitch," Billy said. "I get tired this. What we come? Hunt or what?"

"You can take the gun. There's one shell."

"All right. I get a big black one all right."

"I'll holler," Nick said.

Then, later, it was a long time after and Billy was still away.

"You think we made a baby?" Trudy folded her brown legs together happily and rubbed against him. Something inside Nick had gone a long way away.

"I don't think so," he said.

"Make plenty baby what the hell."

They heard Billy shoot.

"I wonder if he got one."

"Don't care," said Trudy.

Billy came through the trees. He had the gun over his shoulder and he held a black squirrel by the front paws.

"Look," he said. "Bigger than a cat. You all through?"

"Where'd you get him?"

"Over there. Saw him jump first."

"Got to go home," Nick said.

"No," said Trudy.

"I got to get there for supper."

"All right."

"Want to hunt tomorrow?"

"All right."

"You can have the squirrel."

"All right."

"Come out after supper?"

"No."

"How you feel?"

"Good."

"All right."

"Give me kiss on the face," said Trudy.

Now, as he rode along the highway in the car and it was getting dark, Nick was all through thinking about his father. The end of the day never made him think of him. The end of the day had always belonged to Nick alone and he never felt right unless he was alone at it. His father came back to him the fall of the year, or in the early spring when there had been jacksnipe on the prairie, or when he saw shocks of corn, or when he saw a lake, or if he ever saw a horse and buggy, or when he saw, or heard, wild geese, or in a duck blind; remembering the time an eagle dropped through the whirling snow to strike a canvas-covered decoy, rising, his wings beating, the talons caught in the canvas. His father was with him, suddenly, in deserted orchards and in new-plowed fields, in thickets, on small hills, or when going through dead grass, whenever splitting wood or hauling water, by grist mills, cider mills and dams and always with open fires. The towns he lived in were not towns his father knew. After he was fifteen he had shared nothing with him.

His father had frost in his beard in cold weather and in hot weather he sweated very much. He like to work in the sun on the farm because he did not have to and he loved manual work, which Nick did not. Nick loved his father but hated the smell of him and once when he had to wear a suit of his father's underwear that had gotten too small for his father it made him feel sick and he took it off and put it under two stones in the creek and said that he had lost it. He had told his father how it was when his father had made him put it on but his father had said it was freshly washed. It had been, too. When Nick had asked him to smell of it his father sniffed at it indignantly and said that it was clean and fresh. When Nick came home from fishing without it and said he lost it he was whipped for lying.

Afterwards he had sat inside the woodshed with the door open, his shotgun loaded and cocked, looking across at his father sitting on the screen porch reading the paper, and thought, "I can blow him to hell. I can kill him." Finally he felt his anger go out of him and he felt a little sick about it being the gun that his father had given him. Then he had gone to the Indian camp, walking there in the dark, to get rid of the smell. There was only one person in his family he liked the smell of; one sister. All the others he avoided all contact with. That sense blunted when he started to smoke. It was a good thing. It was good for a bird dog but it did not help a man.

"What was it like, Papa, when you were a little boy and used to hunt with the Indians?"

"I don't know," Nick was startled. He had not even noticed the boy was awake. He looked at him sitting beside him on the seat. He had felt quite alone but this boy had been with him. He wondered for how long. "We used to go all day to hunt black squirrels," he said. "My father only gave me three shells a day because he said that would teach me to hunt and it wasn't good for a boy to go banging around. I went with a boy named Billy Gilby and his sister Trudy. We used to go out nearly every day all one summer."

"Those are funny names for Indians."

"Yes, aren't they," Nick said.

"But tell me what they were like."

"They were Ojibways," Nick said. "And they were very nice."

"But what were they like to be with?"

"It's hard to say," Nick Adams said. Could you say she did first what no one has ever done better and mention plump brown legs, flat belly, hard little breasts, well holding arms, quick searching tongue, the flat eyes, the good taste of mouth, then uncomfortably, tightly, sweetly, moistly, lovely, tightly, achingly, fully, finally, unendingly, never-endingly, never-to-endingly, suddenly ended, the great bird flown like an owl in the twilight, only it daylight in the woods and hemlock needles stuck against your belly. So that when you go in a place where Indians have lived you smell them gone and all the empty pain killer bottles and the flies that buzz do not kill the sweet grass smell, the smoke smell and that other like a fresh cased marten skin. Nor any jokes about them nor old squaws take that away. Nor the sick sweet smell they get to have. Not what they did finally. It wasn't how they ended. They all ended the same. Long time ago good.

And about the other. When you have shot one bird flying you have shot all birds flying. They are all different and they fly in different ways but the sensation is the same and the last one is as good as the first. He could thank his father for that.

"You might not like them," Nick said to the boy. "But I think you would."

"And my grandfather lived with them too when he was a boy, didn't he?"

"Yes. When I asked him what they were like he said that he had many friends among them."

"Will I ever live with them?"

"I don't know," Nick said. "That's up to you."

"How old will I be when I get a shotgun and can hunt by myself?"

"Twelve years old if I see you are careful."

"I wish I was twelve now."

"You will be, soon enough."

"What was my grandfather like? I can't remember him except that he gave me an air rifle and an American flag when I came over from France that time. What was he like?"

"He's hard to describe. He was a great hunter and fisherman and he had wonderful eyes."

"Was he greater than you?"

"He was a much better shot and his father was a great wing shot too."

"I'll bet he wasn't better than you."

"Oh, yes he was. He shot very quickly and beautifully. I'd rather see him shoot than any man I ever knew. He was always very disappointed in the way I shot."

"Why do we never go to pray at the tomb of my grandfather?"

"We live in a different part of the country. It's a long way from here."

"In France that wouldn't make any difference. In France we'd go. I think I ought to go to pray at the tomb of my grandfather."

"Sometime we'll go."

"I hope we won't live somewhere so that I can never go to pray at your tomb when you are dead."

"We'll have to arrange it."

"Don't you think we might all be buried at a convenient place? We could all be buried in France. That would be fine."

"I don't want to be buried in France," Nick said.

"Well, then, we'll have to get some convenient place in America. Couldn't we all be buried out at the ranch?"

"That's an idea."

"Then I could stop and pray at the tomb of my grandfather on the way to the ranch."

"You're awfully practical."

"Well, I don't feel good never to have even visited the tomb of my grandfather."

"We'll have to go," Nick said. "I can see we'll have to go."

William Stafford
# Listening

My father could hear a little animal step,
or a moth in the dark against the screen,
and every far sound called the listening out
into places where the rest of us had never been.

More spoke to him from the soft wild night
than came to our porch for us on the wind;
we would watch him look up and his face go keen
till the walls of the world flared, widened.

My father heard so much that we still stand
inviting the quiet by turning the face,
waiting for a time when something in the night
will touch us too from that other place.

*Michael Dennis Browne*
# Peter and Thunder

Your face when you heard it. How you looked up.
How, crouched over toy parts,
suddenly you stiffened. How then you turned,
how you stared up in the direction
of the thunder. **They are at the gates.**
How then you looked at me, as if
I might send them away, as if with a few
low-toned, well-chosen words I could
send the thunder-gangs scuttling back
through all the holes in the sky.
As if there were no thunder deep
down in my own bones, no thunder
in yours, little son.

*Henry Taylor*

# Green Springs the Tree

My young son lurches halfway down the stair
or shrieks and totters midway through a climb
from the wobbling bookcase to the rocking chair.
I freeze and hold my breath. Most of the time
I am too far away to break the fall
that seldom comes. Instead, I stoop and bend
with him, as if threads of remote control
could reel out and connect him to my hand
that strains against his fall, against my leap
to rescue him. My twisting body prays
for skill in this, the high wire he will keep
both of us on as we rehearse the ways
to braid these strands of our inheritance
and teach poor body english how to dance.

*Robert Bagg*

# My Father Plays the 17th

Before I had discovered my own boyhood,
Dad, you filled me with yours in Gloversville—
those trout so sluggish in the cold March brooks
your hands once culled two still rainbows, and laid
both shivering awake on the frost-white bank.
You skinned muskrats trapped in that same stream
for selling to the glovers—out of their factory
Naphtha would sometimes spill into the rapids,
set on swirling fire once by a tossed match.
Downstream, deer hunting with a yew bow,
you flew a whistling shot into a mule's flank,
an error it took painful weeks to heal.
Your father had been so flawless a rifle shot
the town forever banned him from the turkey shoot.
Soft and powerful, your dog Kibo pulled you
everywhere in his wagon, then one day vanished.
Your cousin and best friend, Ben Grager, fell
from your climbing tree and slowly died.
I took your stories much to heart: if I couldn't
find them in Millburn, my poems would find them—
setting pigeons on fire, exploring storm sewers,
constructing soap-box racers that free fell
through my stomach at night, wheels feeling
for Mountain Street, sparks arcing as the brakes froze.

As soon as I could hold a cut-down shaft,
your fingers from behind pressed mine to the leather,
to help me hit a golf ball—at first, light
soft cotton ones that carried the backyard shrubs,
but magnified a slice boomerang wild. You sent me

out, but nine years, with Stu McCornack, and six
new Truflites on an eighteen hole safari
that lasted two hundred and eighteen
adventurous and persistent strokes.
But your own swing, so sure and nonchalant,
had as much of the twenties in it as Gatsby,
the club-head flowing out like a scarf past your head,
then sweeping through the turf to fly the ball
almost uncoerced to its destination;
a secret never learned by me, who struck
in savage fifties' style, taking turf
and cracking harsh complaining arcs.
But when we played as partners in tournaments,
hitting alternate shots in a scotch foursome,
we played a game in which our boyhoods almost touched.
My drive that found a cuppy lie behind a birch
you calmly extricated with a seven iron
to the edge of the green and we were down in two.
And playing with you now on Dennis Pines
we're even coming to the seventeenth,
a long par three across a rock-studded gorge;
my iron is wide; you used your blessed driver
and hit it with your fullest strength,
skimming the club-head so close to the earth
I hardly hear your shot, but see it fly
over everything toward the green,
in whose uncut heaviness of drenched grass
the ball dies in a luxurious lingering
to sit up, white and huge, seven feet from the flag.

*David Bottoms*
# Sign for My Father Who Stressed the Bunt

On the rough diamond,
the hand-cut field below the dog lot and barn,
we rehearsed the strict technique
of bunting. I watched from the infield,
the mound, the backstop
as your left hand climbed the bat, your legs
and shoulders squared toward the pitcher.
You could drop it like a seed
down either base line. I admired your style,
but not enough to take my eyes off the bank
that served as our center-field fence.

Years passed, three leagues of organized ball,
no few lives. I could homer
into the garden beyond the bank,
into the left-field lot of Carmichael Motors,
and still you stressed the same technique,
the crouch and spring, the lead arm absorbing
just enough impact. The whole tiresome pitch
about basics never changing,
and I never learned what you were laying down.

Like a hand brushed across the bill of a cap,
let this be the sign
I'm getting a grip on the sacrifice.

*William Humphrey*

*from* Home from the Hill

H e was Mrs. Hannah's only child, but he was his father's son. From this distance in time it is possible to say that perhaps there was nothing so very self-sacrificing about it, but rather more self-satisfaction: but whatever her motive, true to her word, Mrs. Hannah said nothing to the boy against his father. If on the other hand she did not say quite as much for him as she liked to think, and as she had told her mother she did, why, this must have struck Theron as the only fitting praise for a man to whom no words could have done justice.

Growing up meant just one thing: he thought always of the time when he would sit beside his father in that ring of men, hunters—the two words were synonymous for him—on the corner of the town square on Saturday afternoons, or above a smouldering fire deep in the woods listening to the hounds run foxes, of the time when he would have a gun of his own, when he would shoot over the fine bird dogs, read the animal signs, know the weather, find his way in the big woods.

He lived out of doors, in all weathers, from the time he could dress himself; when in the house, making his model airplanes or mounting his stamps or just dreaming, he was in his father's den. It was too rough a room and his father too plain a man to call it a den; that was his mother's word. It was a big room, forty feet long, and had no ceiling. From the exposed beams hung all manner of hunting gear. In the center of the room hung a two-man boat, a double-pointed duck punt, and scattered throughout the room hung trotlines and steel traps, boat oars and a fish seine like a giant spider's web spun between two beam struts, and in clusters of a dozen or so strung together by the necks hung over a hundred wooden duck decoys: greenhead mallards, redheads, pintails, canvasbacks—hens and drakes.

In the gun cabinet were five guns, two shotguns, two rifles, and a pistol. The bird gun was English, a Purdey, a famous make, a double barrel 12 gauge, and had been custom built for his father at a cost of over

a thousand dollars. But it was the other shotgun that was really fabulous.
It too was a Purdey. It too had been custom built. It had cost nearer two
thousand dollars. It was a magnum 10 gauge double with barrels thirty-
three inches long and weighed just under fourteen pounds. No man but
the Captain, it was said, could take the punishment it dealt the shoulder
in a day in a duck blind, and on the still damp foggy air of a good duck
day in the marshes it could be heard for miles, like the boom of a
cannonade. The rifles were a Model 94 Winchester .30-30 carbine with
the blue worn completely off, and a Remington hammerless pump .22
squirrel rifle. The pistol was a .22 revolver, a Colt Single Action Army,
that had killed untold rattlers and cottonmouth moccasins, and with
which Theron had seen his father hit a bottletop spun high into the air.

Over the floor of the room were scattered deer hide rugs, and in front
of the gun cabinet was a black bearskin rug with the head attached. There
were foxhides, gray and red, and polecat, bobcat, and coon skins
stretched and tacked on the walls. Beside the fireplace hung his father's
shapeless, blood-stiffened old hunting coat. Beside the coat stood an old
chiffonier with the drawers hanging permanently open, containing relics
which as a boy his father had dug from the Indian burial mounds, and
on top of which stood the skull of an Indian with a hole in his right
temple. Until he was ten years old Theron had the idea that his father had
shot that Indian.

But it was glory enough that he had shot the wild boar whose head
was mounted over the mantel, looking as if he had charged through the
wall, covered with black, white, and gray bristles like porcupine quills,
the long blunt black snout drawn back in wrinkles baring the long yellow
tusks. And to have shot the deer whose antlers were mounted over each
of the room's ten windows—all prizes, one of eighteen points.

It was a disorderly but clean room, man-kept, with things left lying
about to be seen and handled and enjoyed rather than put away in closets
and drawers. It was rich in smells, the banana odor of nitro gunpowder
solvent, the manly smells of leather and steel and gun oil and boot grease,
the smells his father brought in, of the woods, damp and mouldering, the
strong, hot, rutty reek of game, and the odor of dogs, for there were
always three or four dogs there, brought in from the pens outside to
recover from scratchings got in a coon fight, or retired there full of scars
and honors, too old to run the foxes or point the birds anymore.

• •

One day his father, who had become a little more respectful of the game laws now that Theron was with him, said, "Squirrel season opens a week from today. On opening day we'll go."

He told his mother about it while he skinned the squirrels.

Above the hind feet he made a cut all around, then he slipped the blade under the skin and down the legs drew slits that met in the crotch. He sliced through the tail bones, then with one foot holding down the tail, peeled out the silvery-red body. With a quick shallow jab he then slit down the belly, ripped out the entrails and flung them over the fence against which two hounds strained, eager but quiet. Turning, he caught his mother's glance and he smiled with embarrassed pride.

He placed the raw carcass on the newspaper in the row where the others lay already darkening in the sun and wind, and he wiped the gore from his hands on the fur of the one remaining. He picked out the largest squirrel and plied its stiffened joints. "This one is mine," he said. "My first. Or rather, the first that I did as I should have. I could tell Papa knew it was a big one from the noise it made in the cane. He didn't say, and yet I knew he meant for me to take this one. That's how it is in the woods. You understand each other without speaking. I shot well on this one, see?"

At first they had done none of the sly stalking he had imagined they would. His father scorned to use a dog for hunting squirrels. He believed in the method known as still-hunting. "You don't go after them," he said. "Not as long as you can help it. You make them come to you." And so they had sat leaning against a sweetgum tree on the edge of a canebrake, both chewing wads of the sticky, resinous-tasting sweetgum.

"I didn't want to hurt his feelings by not seeming to like it," said Theron. "Besides, he didn't want me to know he'd given it to me to keep me from falling asleep. As if I could!"

For it was just past four in the morning. It was that expectant time in the woods when the night sounds have just died away and the day sounds not quite started up, and when the trees, as they darken and solidify with the coming of the light, seem to grow up around you. He had known he must not talk and had felt proud of resisting such a strong urge to talk as he felt. In the advancing light he had watched the rifle grow

distinct upon his lap, feeling now for the first time that it really belonged
to him.

He had seen his first squirrel at daybreak. It seemed to have been
there just waiting for him. Day had come as a rain blows up; there was
a distant rustle high in the treetops and the wind came down in whiffs,
warm then cool. Then the sun was up. You knew it not by seeing, for the
thick-leaved redoaks, small leaves but thick already in May there in
Sulphur bottom, the tall scalybark hickories, and the tall, long-needled
pines would admit the sun for only a few hours in the middle of the day.
You knew it by the commencement of sounds. From afar off came three
rapid crow calls, like the sound of an old person clearing his throat on
getting out of bed, and the woods close around were jerked awake by the
testy yammering of a peckerwood.

His father had whispered, "Hear that?" and he nodded, though he
had no idea which of the many sounds he heard was the meaningful one.

It was then he saw his squirrel. No telling how long it had been there,
watching him with no sign of fright, but merely with a mild interest,
fanning his tail as he hung head down, head stuck out at a right angle
to his body, on the trunk of a hickory forty feet away.

"I was watching Papa, not the squirrel," he said. "And I was afraid
I'd spoil my shot because I was almost laughing aloud at how clever I
was."

Then the squirrel turned and started up the tree and he forgot all his
training, forgot to let out his breath, pulled violently on the trigger and
sighted not only not with both eyes open, but—"Like a baby! I told
myself in the very instant of doing it,"—with both shut.

Despite all this, he had hit it. With disbelief he watched the squirrel
stop, quiver, then slip downwards, clawing at the bark, then catch itself
by one paw and hang quivering, then drop to the ground. By this time
he was on his feet, running.

Bending over the still-quivering squirrel, watching the blood trickle
through its fur, he sensed the commotion overhead. He looked up. The
tree had become like a cherry tree full of birds. Squirrels were everywhere, dashing distractedly up and down branches, running down the
trunk and almost on top of him before wheeling with a frantic scratching
of claws and swirling up again to the big leafy nest high in a fork of the
limbs. One big old boar squirrel was hopping up and down in place on

a limb and screeching with a noise like a buzz saw cutting through a knot. He turned to go for his rifle, knew it was useless, and realized that his father had known all along that the first squirrel was there and had not fired but waited because he knew all these others were there too. So he stood and listened to them leaping into the nearby trees with a noise like rocks thrown through the leaves, until all was still. He knew then how still the big woods could be, how much life there had been in what before he had thought was stillness.

He had two humiliations yet to come. His father had left the rifle as he had tossed it: pointed straight at him and with the safety off. That the gun was a single-shot made this harmless but hardly excusable. He had violated the first, most important rule of the woods.

"I thought then of what you had told me," he said to his mother. "That accidents happen to the best. And I remembered how I had answered—that I wasn't going to get hurt. I was sick. It never occurred to me you could have been thinking I might hurt somebody."

He had reloaded then and sat reproaching himself, glad that his father at least said nothing, at least gave him the credit of realizing what he had done. He knew now that shooting the squirrel, jumping the gun, bad as it was, had not been his worst blunder. After shooting it he should have kept still, just have left it where it fell. He should have shot well enough, and known it, especially having only a single-shot rifle, to be sure the squirrel was going to stay where it fell. After no more disturbance than the shot the others would have come out soon to feed and play. But he had broken stand and, like an untrained bird dog pup, had flushed a covey to get a single. He supposed they were sitting yet, instead of moving on and taking up another stand, so he could do just what he was doing—reproach himself with what a mess he had made of things.

And then—perhaps it was another of those things you understood, without being told, in the woods—he realized that his father had known every thought in his head, every move, every mistake he would make, knew the impulse to be his own man that would overcome him when he saw his first squirrel, and had allowed him to go ahead. But instead of feeling that his father had let him misbehave in order to mortify him, he felt suddenly filled with love at the understanding of him it showed. He saw his father for a moment as a boy, really as himself, and it gave him a feeling of the deep affinity between them.

Then the second humiliation: after five minutes of sitting, after giving him five minutes to think of it himself, his father turned and silently took the rifle from him and with a twig reamed out the muzzle and shook into his palm enough dirt to have blown the barrel off in his face the next time he pulled the trigger.

They sat through five minutes more of silence. Suddenly his father broke forth with the most outlandish and inimitable sound he had ever heard come from a person's mouth. It was, to the life, the chatter of that treeful of squirrels, only with the difference, noticeable even to his green ear, that now it was an all-clear signal instead of an alarm. And in no time at all the canebrake began to twitch with life. Soon the stalks were clacking and swishing together as though a wind was in them.

A big fox squirrel darted out, making for a hickory tree, saw them, wheeled, and sped up too fast for a shot. His father gave a sharp, shrill whistle. The squirrel stopped in his tracks and lifted his head. He was left where he lay. In this way they killed ten in an hour, five of them Theron's.

Later in the day when their feeding time was over and you had to stir yourself and go after the squirrels, he marveled at the way his father, who weighed almost as much again as he, could step on that dry and littered ground so completely without sound that you could not say at what moment his weight came to rest on his foot, or if it ever did; cheating the earth of the sound it exacted of his, Theron's, foot. He marveled at his ear. He not only heard every sound the forest made, but knew what had made it and why and exactly where it came from, and how to imitate it or its natural enemy or friend. But most of all he marveled at his eye. Within the range of a rifle he could spot a squirrel among the leaves, and it seemed that just as he could call them up by imitating their chatter, he could conjure squirrels into a spot just by looking at it.

They took a roundabout way in leaving, so Theron could see something of the Bottom, though as his father said, this was only the margin. His father showed him the tracks of a deer, said he believed they were a doe's and had been made that day. They followed the trail until his father stopped. In the next fifteen minutes he took just ten steps. Then he motioned Theron to come up. He did, conscious of sounding like a herd of mules, and looking through the leaves that his father held parted for him, saw, standing so delicately upon the edge of a little pool that it seemed her feet rested upon the surface of the water, his first deer. She scented something and looked up. He saw her delicate nostrils and soft eyes, and thought she was as pretty as a girl.

On their way out Theron followed behind and watched his father lead them through the trees until at a certain one, indistinguishable from all the rest to anyone but him, he would turn as purposefully and as casually as at the corner of his block in town. They were not hunting now, both having got their legal limits (which his father, it being too warm to wear the big hunting coat, carried in a game belt around his waist, twenty-four squirrels, fox and cat, with their heads looped into dangling thongs, so that it looked as if he was wearing a squirrel kilt)—they were merely strolling, so that there was no call for stealth; yet his father could walk in the woods in no other way except as noiselessly as ever, seeming to glide across the clearings like the shadow of a bird overhead and to melt into the shadow of the trees.

He finished telling her and fell silent for a moment, thinking of it all again, reliving it, wondering with a mixture of pride and despair how he would ever be worthy of such a father, when his mother said, "Well now, it'll be no time at all before you're every bit as good as he is yourself."

*Lewis Nordan*
# Field and Stream

My gift under the Christmas tree the year I turned twelve was a single-shot .410 gauge shotgun. It was a fine looking little gun, with a dark-wood stock and forepiece. It breeched with a sharp metallic crack, so that a shell might be dropped into the chamber.

The shells were another gift, a bright box of number six shot. And also a canvas hunting jacket with a game bag built into the lining, and a canvas cap as well, with earflaps that could be pulled down in case of cold weather. Next to these was a stiff bright pair of lace-up leather boots with rawhide laces, and a pair of wool boot socks, gray with a red stripe around the tops.

Not only were these things under the tree, which would have made my life complete in any case, but there was also a small sturdy metal box with two suitcase-like latches. I flipped open the latches and saw what was almost too good to be true, a sectional ramrod, a bottle of cleaning solvent, patches of cotton swabbing and a length of soft cotton rope. Also a can of gun oil, and a bottle of something called "blueing." There was a thin pamphlet titled "Care and Cleaning of Firearms."

It was just daylight Christmas morning. My father was puking in the bathroom from drinking too much the night before. The fat red Christmas tree lights were shining and there was an angel on top of the tree. My grandfather—my blind bitter well-dressed grandfather, who lived with us—was in his room smoking a cigar, though it was only six o'clock on a misty Mississippi morning and the house stunk weirdly of tobacco and oranges.

I was holding the shotgun across my lap where I sat on the floor.

My mother said, "Do you like it?"

I said, "It's okay. Yeah, it's fine."

She said, "I wasn't sure it would be what you wanted. I was guessing. I hope I guessed right. Is a .410 all right? Is a .410 what you wanted?"

I said, "You can't hunt deer with it. It's too small for deer hunting."

My mother said, "Well, but maybe you wouldn't want to start with, you know, big game. Maybe you'll want to hunt, maybe, squirrels at first, until you're more experienced, maybe. Maybe rabbits."

I turned the gun on its side. I had to force myself not to caress it, pet it, like a living thing. I read the trademark and the other writing stamped into the barrel. *Winchester .410 gauge Full Choke*

I said, "Full choke."

My mother said, "Was full choke the wrong thing to get? Mr. Gibson at the Western Auto Store didn't mention anything about 'choke.' Or if he did, well, I mean, I guess I didn't hear, wasn't listening carefully. I don't even know what 'choke' means. Is full choke all right?"

We could hear my father finishing up in the bathroom. The big finish, this morning, with the final gags of dry heaving and the soft scuffing sounds of his crawling on the floor, where he had been lying with his head in the toilet. Now the spitting and the cursing. Next the gargling.

There was so much noise even my mother had to notice. She said, "Dad's driving the porcelain bus this morning."

I said, " 'Modified' or 'Open' choke would be better for quail."

She said, "But how about squirrels, or maybe rabbits. Just to start, you know, to get some experience at first. Would full choke be all right for either of them?"

I waited a long time before I answered. My mother was sitting on the floor beneath the Christmas tree with her hands in her lap. The fat red bulbs burned among the tinsel behind her. I cocked the hammer, and then eased the hammer back to the 'Safe' position. I sighted along the barrel, out the window at a pecan tree, black with rain from the night before.

I knew nothing at all about guns. This was the first gun I had ever held in my hands. I lowered it from my shoulder and did not look up.

I said, "Full choke is perfect for squirrels."

In my room, behind the closed door I held the gun, I breeched it, and cocked the hammer. I even loaded it once, dropped a dangerous little cylinder of a bright plastic-coated shell into the chamber and snapped the gun shut and cocked the hammer and aimed from the hip at my closed door and knew that I could shoot right through it.

I took it apart, barrel and stock, and laid each piece on my bed separately, neatly apart. I looked at each part, and then I put the parts back together.

I read *Field and Stream* magazine. I read articles on rifled slugs. I read articles on removing musk glands from animals. I read articles describing recipes for wild duck. I read about the construction of a dove blind in a harvested corn field. I read advertisements for insulated boots, for "pocket warmers," for battery operated socks, for long underwear and waterproof shell bags. I looked at the faces of the men in the ads, and in the articles. Men in flannel and leather and canvas and rubber. Smiling healthy men with pipes in their mouths and color and health in their faces.

And sometimes I even took the gun to bed with me, beneath the covers. I dumped the shells out of their box and scrambled them with my hand over the sheet, just to listen to the click. I picked them up and let them run through my fingers like gold.

Though I did these things, I did not go hunting. With the exception of one aborted attempt soon after Christmas my father resisted steadfastly all my mother's suggestions that he take me. Whenever the subject came up, he lapsed into sentimental memory. He remembered and told repeatedly of a man who hunted with "a little beagle dog, sweetest baby voice you ever heard on a dog, like banjoes far off in the woods somewhere," and when that poor man accidentally shot and killed that sweetest of animals one day, why, my father said, "He set down on the bumper of his truck and believe it or not because he was a big man, six foot ten or eleven, he set down on the front chrome bumper of his truck and he cried. I mean *cried like a baby.*" He would tell this story several times in rapid succession, only varying the height of the crybaby on the bumper of the truck.

And yet, at night beneath the covers with the gun and the shotgun shells and my flashlight and with page worn copies of *Field and Stream* I fed a romance of the great pornography of nature and all its rhythms of forest and field.

By February the .410 had only once been outside my room. For weeks my mother had worked her small manipulations upon my father's guilt. "You know, there's nothing quite so beautiful to me as a father and a son together," she might say to him at the dinner table. She might actually stand between us where we sat and place her right hand on my father's shoulder and her left hand on my shoulder and make a physical connection between us. Her words were the blessing and benediction that should have made the magic work.

Nothing did work, of course, hinting least of all. And not direct pleading. "Please take him, Gilbert. Take the boy hunting. Get to know him, you hardly know the child." She said this as well, and it had as little effect as her subtler attempts.

But then one frozen Saturday morning in February, when for all I knew both my parents had forgotten that a single-shot shotgun had been my gift under the Christmas tree, I woke up with both of them standing above my bed and my father saying, "Get up, Sugar, I'm taking you hunting."

My mother was actually wringing her hands. The wedding ring on her left hand, a simple thin gold band that fitted loosely beneath the knuckle, was for a moment the only thing of her that I could see, and it struck me to the heart with loneliness.

"Get up," my father was saying, harshly. "We're going hunting."

I rubbed my eyes and sat up against my pillows.

My mother said, "But will you be careful? You will be careful, won't you? Sugar, please be careful, listen to your father. Gilbert, teach him about safety. I'd just, I mean, if anything happened to him, I'd just, just . . ."

My mother and father had had a fight. It could have been about anything. This was his punishment of her.

My father took the canvas coat and canvas hunting cap from my closet and tossed them onto the bed beside me. He said, "Dress up like a hunter. Let's have a look at Mama's little hunter."

My mother wrung her hands and then picked at the frayed sleeve of her robe. She said, "Teach him safety, Gilbert. Please? Teach him all about safety."

He said, "You're the one wants him to go hunting."

To me he said, "Bring along that fine gun cleaning kit too. You might need to clean your gun, you don't know. You never can tell when you might need a gun cleaning kit along with you."

•  •

My father was wearing no hunting clothes, and he had no gun. He was wearing a pair of slick polyester pants, shiny as a lizard, and he had on a heavy corduroy coat and a pair of yellow plastic shoes, loafers of an unbelievable strangeness, that somebody had told him were the latest thing, and for which he had paid five dollars. It was difficult, in the presence of those plastic shoes, to keep on believing that I was a person who would ever resemble the men in *Field and Stream* who stirred fragrant pots of wild stew over campfires in the wilderness.

We left the house with my mother still wringing her hands and saying, in as cheerful a voice as she could invent from her despair, "Now you boys be careful, be just real extra careful, and, uh, and have yourselves a, uh, you know, good time." As we pulled away in the car, she called out, "Teach him firearm safety, Gilbert!"

As I've said, this was not the first time my father had set out with me to go hunting. The other time was a few days after Christmas, before the first of the year. Then he had said, "Hole up just a minute, Sugar, I'm thinking I might stop off at the Delta Cafe for a minute."

He was stopping to drink, of course. "You stay out in the car," he said. "I'm not going to be but one minute."

I stayed in the car for an hour. And then I took off my canvas jacket and hat and walked to the big plate glass window and looked through the sign painted on it—I peered through the big hole in the D of Delta—and saw my father sitting on a stool at the counter with many other men. One of the men had a wicker basket full of newly born puppies. He must have been trying to give them away, to find homes for them.

Then I saw my father take one of the pups from the wicker basket and rub its little head with his forefinger. He held the pup up to his face and seemed to be talking to it, sweetly I thought, and then he talked to the man with the basket in his lap. My father drank a shot of whiskey and made his face, like oh yes! and then took a sip of beer behind the whiskey. Then he did the most remarkable thing I had ever seen anyone do.

He turned the puppy around and took the dog's tail in his mouth, between his teeth, and bit the dog's tail off, clean off, and spit it onto the linoleum floor, under a table where a couple was eating catfish. I could hear no sound, but the puppy was obviously squealing with surprise and pain.

There was blood all over the front of my father's shirt and on his chin. He was grinning proudly, as if he had done something fine. When the dog's owner had recovered himself—it took only a second or two— he took the pup from my father and looked at the other astonished faces sitting behind beers at the counter and said not a word. The expression of complete disgust for my father was sufficient. No words were necessary. He wrapped the puppy's tail in a napkin and picked up the rest of the pups, in the basket, and turned to leave the cafe. I wanted to run, but I stayed there and watched the man come out the door.

As the door opened I could hear my father's voice. He said, "Put a little salt on that nubbin to help it heal!"

So it is miraculous that for even one second I had been deceived by the romance of this possibility of a hunting trip.

Mr. Shanker was the pharmacist. This time my father and I were not stopping at the Delta Cafe for shots and beers. We were stopping at the drug store for opium. Mr. Shanker and my father often drank paregoric together. My father said it was good for a hangover if you didn't mind the constipation. And to be helpful my father sometimes gave Mr. Shanker an injection of morphine to help him sleep. My father liked Mr. Shanker, because he was the only man in town to whom my father seemed sober in comparison.

Immediately now I received a clear picture of how the two of us looked, my father and I. We were clowns. He was wearing yellow plastic shoes and pants the unreal colors of a lizard, and I was wearing stiff new canvas clothing several sizes too large for me, and the new leather of my unoiled boots was almost as yellow as my father's. My feet hurt like torture.

I was paralyzed by shame for the two of us. I was my father's son, there was no doubt in my mind, and it was impossible for me to tell which of us was more worthy of loathing and disdain. In addition to my preposterous outfit, I was carrying a shotgun and a metal box with the words Gun Cleaning Kit stenciled on the front. "Don't forget your hunting equipment," my father insisted in his ironic way when I tried to leave the gun and kit behind in the car.

I followed my father through the front door of the drug store and breathed in the strange chemical fragrance that hung forever in its unholy air.

There was no one in the drug store.

My father called out, "Shank!"

There was no answer. Mr. Shanker was rarely conscious.

Again, he said, "Shank, where are you, boy?" He said this in his ironic voice, and then looked at me and gave me a sharp wink.

I felt loaded down with clothing and the shotgun and the gun cleaning kit. There was a long soda fountain with a marble top, and a long mirror behind the counter.

In the reflection I could see clearly the shelves of things behind me, the tonics and patent medicines and mustard plasters and bunion pads and suppositories and boxes of Kotex, all the bright primary colors of their bottles and boxes and packaging. I could see a glass counter where Mr. Shanker had placed costume jewelry for sale, large gold-looking earrings and necklaces, impressive large bottles of perfume with French words in the name and glass stoppers as big as the bottles themselves, bud vases and ceramic masks and even chocolates in gold foil, stale for a decade.

But I could not see myself. The reason was that I could not bear to look. I could not permit the reality of who I was and what I looked like so utterly to swamp the invention of myself that I had brought with me from *Field and Stream* magazine. I looked in the mirror and saw the drug store, but I could not, would not see myself.

Mr. Shanker was in the back room, my father told me.

Still carrying the .410 and the gun cleaning kit and with a loose box of shells click-clacking in my jacket pocket, I followed my father through the large silent old barn of a pharmacy, with its perpetual chemistry and perpetual twilight and antique soda bar.

Mr. Shanker was in the back room all right. He was not dead yet, but he soon would be. He was filthy and soaked in his own urine and lying on an army cot beneath a wool army blanket. He was shivering so hard I thought he would fall right off the cot onto the floor. There was no twilight here. The room was narrow and high-ceilinged and cramped and black dark, and everything I needed to know of it I could smell or hear, the piss and the rattling of the cot against the floor, the rattling of something else, something inside Mr. Shanker, some clatter in his chest.

My father groped around above his head in the darkness and finally laid a hand on a string hanging from the ceiling. He gave the string a yank and an enormous light bulb flashed on and filled the cave-like room with harsh light.

Mr. Shanker's eyes looked like a busted-out windshield. His face was an incredible orange color in the glare of the electric bulb. He was literally bouncing on the cot, his shivering was so extreme. The smell of his urine was strong.

Even so, Mr. Shanker made the last joke of his life. He said, "Gilbert, they won't no need for the boy to shoot me. Those yaller shoes of yours'll do the trick by theyself." When he finished saying this, he opened his mouth and his enormous blue tongue rolled out like a snake. There was no sound, but I understood this to be laughter.

My father said, "Look like you bout to need a pick-me-up."

Mr. Shanker finished with his weird tongue-laughter and motioned with his eyes to the syringe and morphine in a small black leather case on a low table nearby. The tongue sucked back into Mr. Shanker's mouth like a blue runner into a hole.

I said, "Daddy, he's dying."

My father said, "Lemme see that kit." He meant the gun cleaning kit I was holding in my arms like a baby.

Mr. Shanker had swallowed his tongue and was choking to death.

I was rigid with fear.

My father said, "Gimme that goddamn kit, Sugar, you want to kill Mr. Shanker or what!"

I shoved the metal box toward my father and he took it in his hands. He set it on the low table and snapped open the latches. He said, "Now ain't that just the way the Lord his mighty works doth perform?" He was saying what a fortunate thing that we had this gun cleaning kit along with us, just at a time when Mr. Shanker was swallowing his tongue. My father was in a spiritual mood.

My father stripped the shortest section of the ramrod loose from the velvet lined box and jammed it between the choking man's teeth and pried open Mr. Shanker's mouth. He said, "Hand me that box of swipes." He meant the package of cleaning swabs that normally fit at the end of the ramrod to clean gunpowder residue from a barrel.

Now he had Mr. Shanker's mouth open with one section of the ramrod cracking the enamel off Mr. Shanker's teeth and his fingers down

Mr. Shanker's gullet groping around for his tongue. The cleaning swab between my father's fingers gave him a good grip on the slick tongue, and so it was not long before he had grabbed hold of it pulled it up to the surface like a fish. Mr. Shanker was actually breathing again.

My father was competent and calm and in control of the situation. For a moment I felt almost good about my life, I felt less lonely and more hopeful than I had for a long time. Mr. Shanker's tongue was as big as a bullfrog, and while it was no longer hopping, it did seem to have life, a life of its own, it seemed to breathe in a more or less healthy and regular rhythm, though Mr. Shanker's own real breathing was less healthy and regular than the tongue's.

My father said, "Hole on to this thang for minute, Sugar."

He meant the tongue. He meant Mr. Shanker's unbelievable reptilian tongue.

I said, "I cain't do it, Daddy."

He said, "Shore now. Jess put down your mighty weapon there and grab holt of it."

Mr. Shanker's eyes were popped out and throbbing with blood and jaundice.

I leaned the .410 against the wretched army cot and moved into position behind my father. He set the gun cleaning kit carefully on the cot beside the shotgun.

He said, "Use that-air swipe. You can get a better grip."

I said, "I don't think I can do it, Daddy." I took a cleaning swab between my fingers and reached around for Mr. Shanker's tongue.

My father said, "Have you got it?"

I was holding the tongue on one side and my father still had a grip on the end of it.

He said, "Okay, I'm letting go."

I said, "You're letting it go? You're letting it go right now?"

He said, "Have you got a-holt of it? Are you ready?"

I said, "I got it. I think I've got it."

He said, "All right then, I'm doing it, I'm letting go."

My father let go, and I held on like a bulldog. I had Mr. Shanker's tongue by the balls. This tongue was going nowhere. We had passed the baton.

My father said, "Good, good. Good work, Sugar-man."

I stood there holding the tongue while my father prepared the shot of morphine. Mr. Shanker's tongue was as passive as a fed and sleepy cat.

It was almost like hunting. It was almost like *Field and Stream*. The great strange electrical bulb swinging from a cord above us was the blazing Mississippi sun, it was the bright yellow of cornfields and sorghum and sugarcane, it was a campfire and shadows in the woodlands, it was a lantern to skin squirrels by, it was the harvest moon to sleep beneath in a down-filled sleeping bag, it was the Milky Way and all the stars above, it was the warmth of love and the warmth of electrical socks and the warm bowl of a briar pipe and chocolatey tobacco, it was father and son together in a place so primitive that age and old hatred and old habitual love and all of history made no difference, it was bright water and dark wood.

My father filled the syringe and found an uncollapsed vein in Mr. Shanker's skeletal black-and-blue arm, and swabbed the vein with cleaning solvent from a bottle in the kit, and tied a tourniquet from the small coil of soft cotton rope.

He said, "Keep a holt on that tongue," and I tightened my grip so hard that I pinched a blood blister into it with the fingers of my right hand.

There is not much way to tell the next part except just to go on and tell it.

My father inserted the needle in the vein of Mr. Shanker's bruised and filthy arm, and pumped the little handle of the syringe, and filled Mr. Shanker's blood with morphine, and killed him dead.

There was a brief seizure and a few seconds of jerkiness, and maybe even a little vomit, but not much. It was a sudden death, if you look at it the right way. Mr. Shanker was dead of an overdose of morphine that my father had administered thirty seconds after saving his life from suffocation by tongue.

My father said, "Some days I swear to God it don't pay to get out of the damn bed."

What happened next is a strange and marvelous thing.

There was nothing to be done for Mr. Shanker. He was dead. I don't know what I expected my father to do, or say. I had never seen a dead person before, though I suppose my father had.

My father sat down slowly on the edge of the cot beside Mr. Shanker. The electric light bulb overhead still cast its odd harsh light over everything, the filthy cot, the army blanket, the table, the drugs and crumpled clothing on the floor.

My father said, "I'll have to call Big Boy." He meant Mr. Chisholm, the town marshall.

I said, "Are we in trouble?"

He said, "No, Sugar. We're not in any trouble. Shank wouldn't want me to say I killed him."

I said, "We just found Mr. Shanker here like this?"

He said, "I'll work this all out with Big Boy. Don't you worry, Sugar-man."

My father kept on sitting there. He patted Mr. Shanker once on the knee, and then sat a little longer.

At first I didn't move, and then I started to pick up the bits and pieces of my gun cleaning kit and put them away, the tip section of the ramrod, with Mr. Shanker's spit and tooth enamel still on it, the solvent that my father had used to sterilize Mr. Shanker's arm before administering the morphine, the used swabs, the soft cotton rope that had been the tourniquet. All of it I fitted carefully back into the velvet lined box, and then I snapped shut the latches.

For a little while neither of us spoke.

My father said, "I look like a fucking fool in these shoes."

It is hard to say why, but I am certain that this was the closest moment my father and I had ever shared. I was very much in love with my father, though I might have known even in this moment that something inside me had frozen solid and would be a long time in thawing.

I said, "Is the hunting trip, you know, is it off again?"

My father rubbed his unshaven face with both his hands.

He said, "Do you still want to go hunting?"

I said, "Well, I wouldn't mind. Sure. Okay."

He said, "You're not just saying this? You really want to?"

I said, "Well, you know—if you want to."

He shook his head. He said, "Tell you the truth, if I was a fine boy like you I wouldn't much want to go hunting with a man like me."

He put his hands in his lap and studied the backs of them.

I said, "You mean a murderer?"

He looked up. He said, "Oh, well yeah, that too. I was more thinking about, you know, these damn shoes. Going hunting with somebody wearing yellow plastic shoes."

I sat down on the cot beside my father and the late Mr. Shanker. I could feel the warmth of my father's arm against my arm, and the warmth of Mr. Shanker's dead body against my butt and lower back. I leaned comfortably into the corpse.

My father said, "Do you really think I'm a murderer?"

I said, "I don't know." I said, "But you could throw the shoes away. That's something you could do"

My father said, "You're right there. I could do that. I could get rid of these damn shoes."

My father slipped off one shoe, very slow, and held it a moment and then dropped it into Mr. Shanker's paraphernalia-cluttered wastebasket. Then with the other shoe he did the same. He crossed his legs and rubbed his foot with his hands.

He said, "They won't even comfortable."

Mr. Shanker was very warm. I wondered how long it took for a body to grow cold.

I said, "You could cry like a baby."

My father said, "I couldn't do that, Sugar-man. Oh-no, I don't think I could do that."

I said, "I guess not."

I thought of my father's father, the blind bitter old man back at the house. What did he have to do with this strange moment in my family's history? I could smell cigars and oranges.

I said, "I've never fired a gun."

My father said, "Well, you're right. You're right about that. And that's another thing we can do something about."

He stood up and took the gun and the gun cleaning kit out of my hands.

He said, "Here you go, let me carry these for a while."

I handed everything over to him.

He said, "I think we'd better find me some decent shoes and call Big Boy Chisholm and figure out some way for me and you to burn some gunpowder before this day turns out to be a total loss."

*Peter Meinke*
# Scars

When I was young, I longed for scars
like my father's. They were the best
scars on the block, startling, varied,
pink as a tongue against his whiskey skin.

The longest bolted from his elbow,
finger-thick where the barbed wire plunged in,
a satin rip thinning toward the wrist.
I read the riddle of my father's body

like a legend punctuated by pale hyphens,
neat commas, surgical asterisks, and exclamation
points from scalp to ankle. His tragic knuckles
spoke violence in demotic Greek.

My silent father said little—too little, it seems—
but after the divorce he told me, tracing
the curved path on his skull where hair never grew,
"It's the ones you can't see that kill you,"

and it's true our doctor said his liver,
which did him in, was scarred like an old war horse.
Still, the wound I knew best I gave him myself, hitting
a pop fly straight up and swinging the child's bat again

with all my might as the ball descended
over the plate. He had run in to catch it
and the bat cracked him under his chin, dropping
my father like a murdered king, peeling a wound

no butterfly bandage could cover. I was too stunned
to move, but the look my mother gave me proved,
no matter what happened later, this man bleeding
like Laius on the ground was the one she loved.

*Herbert Gold*
*from* Fathers

Skinny and prideful, I moved underfoot in the steam room like a drenched rat, learning the ways of men. Just as a few years later a uniform would reduce me—or raise me—to being a man exactly like all other men, except courageous or cowardly, evasive or direct, foolish in life or getting through, so the uniform of nakedness removed all these men from the pride, disgrace, and works of their days. In my child's eyes they were very much alike—swollen sex, hanging gourds, purplish veins, creased bellies—and to them I was different: a child. "Sam's kid! Lookit the kid, little Sam, he's learning the steam room! Sam Gold's boy! You making out, kid, with all you got is that pinkie of yours?"

I hid myself in shame and giggled. I was only a child, agreed for the sake of peace, but I was the only child whose father trusted him here. And Dad said I was no bother to him, not too much anyway, as briskly, grunting, enjoying, he rubbed salt into his velvety pelt until the skin beneath flamed pink, glowed. And therefore I was a gladiator. I sloshed through the drain that lay at dead center of the tiled steam room, and then climbed the hot and hotter wooden shelves along the wall. Dad pushed me out when he thought I might get dizzy, and once when I felt abruptly soft and faint, he carried me into the locker room and made me drink salt water. Hot and sulky, I tasted blood on my tongue. I thought I looked like a man and smiled at my father.

*Simon J. Ortiz*

# My Father's Song

Wanting to say things,
I miss my father tonight.
His voice, the slight catch,
The depth from his thin chest,
The tremble of emotion
in something he has just said
to his son, his song.

> We planted corn one Spring at Acu—
> we planted several times
> but this one particular time
> I remember the soft damp sand
> in my hand.

> My father had stopped at one point
> to show me an overturned furrow;
> the plowshare had unearthed
> the burrow nest of a mouse
> in the soft moist sand.

> Very gently, he scooped tiny pink animals
> into the palm of his hand
> and told me to touch them.
> We took them to the edge
> of the field and put them in the shade
> of a sand moist clod.

> I remember the very softness
> of cool and warm sand and tiny alive mice
> and my father saying things.

*Thomas Lynch*
# Like My Father
# Waking Early

Even for an undertaker, it was odd.
My father always listened through the dark,
half-dreaming hours to a radio
that only played police and fire tunes.
Mornings, he was all the news of break-ins, hold-ups,
now and then a house gone up in flames
or a class of disorder he'd call, frowning,
a *Domestic*. They were dying in our sleep.
My father would sit with his coffee and disasters,
smoking his Luckies, reading the obits.
"I've buried boys who played with matches
or swam alone or chased balls into streets
or ate the candy that a stranger gave them . . ."
or so he told us as a form of caution.
When I grew older, the boys he buried toyed
with guns or drugs or drink or drove too fast
or ran with the wrong crowd headlong into peril.
One poor client hung himself from a basement rafter—
heartsick, as my father told it, for a girl.
By sixteen, I assisted with the bodies,
preparing them for burial in ways
that kept my dread of what happened to them busy
with arteries and veins and chemistries—
a safe and scientific cousin, once removed
from the horror of movements they never made.
Nowadays I bury children on my own.
Last week two six-year-olds were through the ice
and bobbed up downstream where the river bends
through gravel and shallows too fast to freeze.
We have crib deaths and cancers, suicides,

deaths in fires, deaths in cars run into trees,
and now I understand my father better.
I've seen the size of graves the sexton digs
to bury futures in, to bury children.
Upstairs, my children thrive inside their sleep.
Downstairs, I'm tuning in the radio.
I do this like my father, waking early,
I have my coffee, cigarettes and worry.

# V
# Grandfather

---

*Old Man: You get old and you can't do anybody*
  *any good any more.*
*Boy: You do me some good, Grandpa. You tell me things.*

Robert Penn Warren

*Ted Kooser*

# Grandfather

Driving the team, he came up over
the hill and looked down. In the white bowl
of the snow-covered valley, his house
was aflame like a wick, drawing up
into itself all that he'd worked for.

Once, forty years later, we passed.
It was October. The cellar
was filled by a flame of young trees.
I got out, but he sat in the back
and stared straight ahead, this old, old man,
still tight on the reins of his years.

*George Garrett*
# The Gift: A Recapitulation

Y ou know how he died. Died not badly. If, by that, by badly you
mean dying after a long, slow, painful and probably inordinately
expensive illness. Was more than ninety years old, still able if
somewhat fragile, able to move about and to look after himself, still alert
and thoughtful and blessed and cursed by a clear memory; though he
sometimes complained, saying that he remembered or dreamed things
he would rather not have. Died quietly, dreaming or dreamless in deep
sleep in his own bed and his own house after only a few days of not
feeling so very well. Feeling a little poorly, thank you.

Died not badly or poorly, though he did sure enough die poor. Not
as poor as you can be and still be alive, that's true. God knows, and so
do we, that we bear witness to enough of that in fact and flesh and in the
flickering images on our TV screens. He had his social security and a few
dollars above and beyond that thanks to some of his working children
and grandchildren. Lived those last years, after busy years spent elsewhere, in a raw and simple frame house, a sturdy, one-story shack, really,
set up on stilts because it was built on a little spit of land close by tidal
water. Certain winds and tides would sometimes get together and let the
rising water come to leap against the front steps. He said at times it was
like being on a boat again.

Lived not all alone, but with always a couple of hound dogs (who,
like the animals out of the old stories and myths, crawled up under the
house and cried and howled for three days after he died). Always dogs
and cats and some chickens and once upon a time a pet turkey gobbler
and, oh yes, a country woman, lean and pale and younger by many years,
a cracker woman if the truth is known and said out loud. (Which was and
is seldom if ever.) A lean, pale, more than a little careless and slovenly
cracker woman who could cook the plain southern food that suited him
and also kept his house for him, more or less, as clean as she knew how
to. A companion, then. Some kind of a distant cousin and blood kin to

him and to all the rest of us. Though that truth was seldom, if ever alluded
to, either. And when it unavoidably was mentioned, it was all vague
enough, the women, keepers of family and tribal flame and memories,
being uniformly unspecific as to how close and what kind of kin to us
that woman might be. When he died in his sleep and the dogs crept
underneath and took to howling, she, too, slipped away (with no tears
anybody heard or saw) and with most of the family flat silver and
whatever modest valuables were handy and portable. Though who could
blame her for taking anything she could carry with her? And, anyway,
she didn't take it all, not even very much of it, did she? There were things
left over, some of them precious only by memory and association, true,
for everyone in the family to have and to share, after all.

You, yourself, have his best gold pocket watch and watch chain,
don't you? Must remember to take it to a jeweler and have it cleaned and
set one of these days.

But this is not a story about that. Not exactly. Maybe not at all. We'll
see. This story goes back years and years before that. Before you were
born and able to see and feel and think for yourself. You were a witness
only to the last part, that part you have already told. And you probably
told it first, started there to try to identify and perhaps prove yourself at
the outset as a kind of credible witness. Someone at least entitled to
imagine and to believe in the time before your time.

This story begins by going back to the time when, for a time, he was
a rich man of good repute. A man with an earned reputation as a man
of honor and industry and dignity and integrity and courage and style
and so forth and so on. All of those things which facts of wealth and good
fortune, in and of themselves, could not and cannot confer outright upon
anyone. But nevertheless there are, as we well know, qualities which
wealth and good fortune can greatly enhance and help to maintain and
preserve. Whereas the chief qualities of character and repute which can
conceivably arise out of conditions of poverty and bad luck are apt to be
more inward and spiritual than outward and visible. Way of the world.

Old father Job has some words of wisdom on that subject. But this
is not a story as bleakly sad as his. Nor does ours come, as you already
know, to a happy ending.

Our man made two great fortunes in his lifetime and he spent three.
Which is how they always politely described it. He made his money

honestly and honorably enough, according to the lights and mores of those times. (Which, may I say, were in many ways and means more strict than our own hypocritical guidelines.) Made it not by stealing anything from anyone. Not by any kind of clever gouging or any sharp practices. Not by cruelty and arrogant indifference to the needs of others. Not by tricks of the trade.

Hard to believe or imagine such things nowadays, isn't it? In part you choose to credit it to the circumstances of the times. A time when good name seemed to matter so very much, maybe most of all. Therefore a time when shame was still possible. Call it all a kind of hypocrisy, if you choose to, but bear in mind how many of our own hypocrisies are the forces which lead us, ready and willing or not, to try to act virtuously.

In some ways the whole story is so aptly familiar to its times, so shaped like a work of fiction, that it may challenge credulity. Consider the orphan child raised by poor kinfolk and coming to manhood and maturity in the long shadowy days of the Reconstruction South. Growing up, in fact as it happened, only a few hundred yards away and in the same village as the place he returned to and died in. From early childhood having learned to be perfectly at home in deep woods and on the open water. His first work for a living, while still no more than a large child, involved both sea and forest. Cutting timber and bringing it out with mules. Then with an old man in charge, sailing boatloads of timber down the coast and into Charleston harbor. Where once, when he was still very young, not yet twelve years old, the old man was knocked unconscious by the boom and the boy had to bring in the large clumsy schooner, through wind and rough water, all by himself. As soon as he was old enough he was licensed as a pilot. Then earned and saved and with those earnings and savings studied and learned the Law. Then practiced Law, soon with success and later on with honor and high offices. Married a beautiful and gifted woman and with her had and raised his family of five sons and three daughters.

And you have seen them for yourself in old and slowly fading photographs, all standing solemnly, straightfaced together. Except, sometimes, for a white-haired great-grandmother sitting on an incongruous chair in the midst of them. Live oaks set the scene like columns. Leafy, mossy canopies all around them, casting a wealth of light and shadow. And themselves standing together a little stiffly, darkly handsome and somehow enigmatic as they squint to stare out of that dappled shade and across time as if from some other, far shore, all attention fixed on an unseen and now unknown photographer.

It is another side of that life and times, his, that has always interested you most. You were a child, then a young man, and loved to hear anything and everything about his passion rooted in the cold indifference of the archetypal gambler. Gambling meant not merely with money and possessions, which he surely did, but, in his daily courtroom trade, for instance, with life and death. Betting it all on life and love and light as you, yourself, wrote about it in a poem a long time ago.

Lucky and at the very peak of his good luck and worldy wisdom, he had a whole and enviable stable of horses—trotters and pacers and jumpers and fine carriage horses and riding horses and ponies for the children. And automobiles, too, when they began to arrive and to be part of the scene. Because his sons, your uncles, rose early to take the cars before he could or was ready to, he had six automobiles, finally, scattered all around the yard. They were living in those days in Ortega across the wide St. John's River from Jacksonville. And, so the story goes, one morning he took his car, last of the six remaining, when he finished breakfast, and drove it to town to work. Stalled on the narrow drawbridge at its high center. Couldn't start that car if his life depended on it. Struggled with the obstinate machine while all behind him a restless line, a mob of other cars and horse-drawn carriages, and probably the crowded streetcar, too, honked and hooted and tooted, jeered and hollered. Then he, weary of all that, climbing out of his car, stepping lightly off the high runningboard and walking to the edge of the bridge and dropping the car keys over the rail, seeing them glint and glitter in the light and flash, white and brief as a gull's wing, as they hit and splashed and sank to the deep bottom. Looked down and saw the keys vanishing forever, then walked away to his office, to work, never looking back and (as they all said ever after) never once asking about and never once caring what became of that stalled automobile.

What a time he had!

Hunted big game in far places—Africa and India and the Arctic. And when the family enjoyed an inland vacation, in the mountains of western North Carolina or maybe in the villages and old farms of Vermont, why it took a whole railroad car to carry them and their companions and servants there and back. By sea he had the use of his own steam yacht, the *Cosette,* lean and fast at ninety feet and drawing so little water that he could nose her into many a small harbor, shallow river or creek. In the open sea, the Atlantic, he, himself, handled her in good weather and foul. For the fun of it sometimes challenged other yachts to race. None ever came close to beating the *Cosette.*

All of that and almost everything else except for odds and ends, flotsam and jetsam of his life, was long gone before you were born. Gone, too, now that you suddenly think about it, gone by the time he was your age.

Anyway all of this interests you, fascinates with an odd kind of feeling, as you grow old with your few and perfectly commonplace possessions, owning nothing at all you would fear to shed, nothing you cheerfully couldn't do without. Nothing you have is worth more than a shrug, really. Except for memories. Which, of course, have to include his life and the lives of others.

Remembering now, at least for here and now, one moment among them all.

He would have been middleage then. Getting on, as they used to say. All of his children grown up and gone away except for the two youngest—Jack and Chester. Jack who would soon become a fine professional golfer and later a drunkard. Chester, the dancer, soon to dance in great cities all over the world. And then soon after that to fight in the Second World War and live to see it end at Linz, meeting the Russians on the bridge over the Danube there. There where, by the mysterious and wonderful synchronicity of things, you were to find yourself on duty, sometimes on guard duty at a checkpoint on the selfsame bridge.

But then, on that day, in those days, they were boys still. The last of his boys. And it was, happened to be the birthday of one or the other of them. I forget which. And does it matter? Not worth mentioning or worrying about now, really, except insofar as it gives an apt occasion and an edge of anticipation to the playing out of the story. At least from their point of view. For, in a sense, it's their story more than his, even though it is about him.

As they would learn gradually and later it was on this very same day, and all day long, that he gambled grandly and lost his last fortune. Last of it. All of it. Everything he owned in the world. Except for the house in Ortega which he would soon enough have to sell just to make ends meet. In one bad day he had managed to lose everything except the cash he had in his wallet. Two hundred dollars. Which was no small sum by any standard or measure in those days. Ten or twenty times what it would be equal to today.

They had come over to town in one of the cars to pick him up at the office and to bring him home for the birthday dinner. He came out of the front door of the office building at a minute or two past five, neat as a pin in his threepiece suit, his tailored shirt and tie. From high white separate collar to the fold of his cuffs as neat and crisp, unwilted and unwrinkled as he had looked in the morning when he left for work. That was his style and was not even noticed by them until much later when they tried together to reconstruct that day when he had lived through, spent, even as all his little house of cards collapsed and fell apart and was shuffled and then he was dealt out a sequence of impossible and implausible hands to play and to lose with. He came out of the entrance to the building, most likely nodding a good evening to the doorman, crossed the sidewalk, smiling a greeting to them where they sat in the car, parked with the motor running, at the curb.

"It's a lovely day," he said looking up and around at blue skies, thin clouds, light breeze. "And I've been cooped up in my office all day long. Let's leave the car and walk home."

A walk of several miles. But it was a fine day. And why not? He gave the doorman the keys to the car and a coin or two. They set off walking in the direction of the St. John's River.

Closer to the water, they came across a hand-lettered sign, pointing down a narrow lane to a dock. Advertising a boat for sale. They paused a moment, went to take a look.

It was a fat little wooden sailboat, single mast, cockpit, high-railed. A native version, squat and sturdy, of a New England catboat. Only a little bit larger. Looked in pretty good shape, all in all, though no doubt she could use some paint on her bottom. The man who owned her and was selling her came out of an unpainted shed nearby. Fellow with rubber boots and a beard flecked with pieces of gray and a grin with raggedy teeth.

And then their father, your grandfather, took off his coat, loosened his necktie and hunkered down with the old fellow to bargain for the boat. A duet of mumbling and of pauses. More muttering and silence. Oldtimer stood up and hawked and spit a gob over the edge of the dock into the lapping water.

Your grandfather stands up, too, and shakes his legs lightly to let his trousers fall neatly into place.

"Done, then," he says.

Offers his hand and shakes on it. Then pulls out his wallet and counts off a hundred dollars to pay the old man.

"It's yours," he says to the boys, or to whichever one whose birthday it was then and nobody can remember now. "Let's sail home. Plenty of time left before the light starts to fade and . . ." (here looking out at wrinkles of wind sprinting across the river, at the wind and the glitter of small waves) ". . . it's a nice breeze."

They sit down side by side on the dock and untie and remove their street shoes and socks. Barefoot they step on board and stow their shoes. Carefully stow his folded coat. Unfurl and check the sail. Fix the center-board, rudder and tiller in place. The old man returns and adds a paddle to the deal. They untie the ropes fore and aft, paddle a moment or two to clear the end of the dock. And then your grandfather settles into place and taxes up the tiller and the sheet. She luffs briefly, catches wind, and in a moment is pointed and skimming, heeling slightly, on a starboard tack.

It's going to take them an hour or so, not a lot more, taking turns at the tiller, to bring her home to their own dock and float at their house. When they do get there, the wind will be up and shifting direction and the tide will be turning. And it will be a little tricky to come in and dock her gracefully. The boys will ask him to do it himself, half hoping, it may well be, that he has lost his touch and will bang and shake them all when he rams the float. Unspoken, it's a kind of a bet or a dare. And, of course, he takes the dare. A kind of a last bet (as he has always bet on life and love and light) with half of all his remaining wealth in the world. Betting nothing at all and yet, for a moment, that one, everything that matters. He takes hold of the tiller and sheet, swings around and runs with the wind as if to crash into the float. Boys are holding tight now and gritting their teeth when he suddenly yanks the tiller toward him and jibes her. She swings around and he lets the sheet loose and the sail crackles and luffs as, urged on by her own slight wake, she lightly touches the float.

They leap out and snub and tie her fast. Remove the mast and furl the sail. Pull up the rudder and raise the centerboard and then sit side by side to put on their shoes. Sun going down, wind touched with a chill and the salty sense of the open sea.

"Nice little boat," he tells them. "A little clumsy, but she'll get you there."

They tote all the things including the paddle. While he walks in the middle between them, his arms over their shoulders as they go along up the twisty path from the riverbank towards the shape of the house among the trees, house where, window by window, evening lights are coming on.

"You know," one of those brothers, your uncles, will tell you so many years later, "I don't think I ever saw Papa as happy as that. Sailing that boat home with not a worry in the world."

That's how he sees it and remembers it. How he takes it to be.

Well, why not? This is not the story of Job. Nothing like that. Only another story of winning and losing. Lightened by a gesture, the last real gift. Anyway, the children of fortune seldom arrive at happy endings.

Of course, it's not the same for you at second hand. You can't and won't come to believe that the inevitable shabby end of things would not lie heavy upon even the stoutest of hearts. But, still, consider that he seems to have known a blithe and simple way to lift his flagging spirits. First by an impulse and an act of unthinking generosity. And next by giving himself over to it—to water and air, to the fire of fading sunlight on the river and to the solid earth of a smooth landing and a safe return. And thereby all the rest of it, beginning and end, bitter or sweet, is nothing at all. Good luck and bad luck, all the rest of it, none of it means or matters anything at all.

*Philip Levine*
# Zaydee

Why does the sea burn? Why do the hills cry?
my grandfather opens a fresh box
of English Ovals, lights up, and lets the smoke
drift like clouds from his lips.

Where did my father go in my fifth autumn?
In the blind night of Detroit
on the front porch, Grandfather points up
at a constellation shaped like a cock and balls.

A tiny man, at 13 I outgrew his shirts.
I then beheld a closet of stolen suits,
a hive of elevator shoes, crisp hankies,
new bills in the cupboard, old in the wash.

I held the spotted hands that passed over
the breasts of airlines stewardesses,
that moved in the fields like a wind
stirring the long hairs of grain.

Where is the ocean? the flying fish?
the God who speaks from a cloud?
He carries a card table out under the moon
and plays gin rummy and cheats.

He took me up in his arms
when I couldn't walk and carried me
into the grove where the bees sang
and the stream paused forever.

He laughs in the movies, cries in the streets,
the judges in their gowns are monkeys,
the lawyers mice, a cop is a fat hand.
He holds up a strawberry and bites it.

He sings a song of freestone peaches
all in a box,
in the street he sings out Idaho potatoes
California, California oranges.

He sings the months in prison,
sings salt pouring down the sunlight,
shovelling all night in the stove factory
he sings the oven breathing fire.

Where did he go when his autumn came?
He sat before the steering wheel
of the black Packard, he turned the key,
pressed the starter, and he went.

The maples blazed golden and red
a moment and then were still,
the long streets were still and the snow
swirled where I lay down to rest.

*Claude Koch*

# Grandfather

The major event of Andrew's ninth birthday was his introduction to semaphore and the Morse code. "You have to know both," his Grandfather said; "there's no point in doing anything halfway."

"Now semaphore," his Grandfather said, "is 'a system of visual signaling by two flags held one in each hand.' That definition is precise." He reared up from his chair in the garden, using his cane like a vaulter's pole: "It happens I have only one flag at the moment, but we'll make it do." He held out a two-by-four inch American flag that had been on Andrew's birthday cake that afternoon. "You go down to the end of the garden."

There were obstacles to getting to the end of the garden. Grandfather's Spring enthusiasm had somewhat waned, and the zucchini he had planted where he meant to have lettuce had done very well—so that the mid-portion of the yard that was the garden was largely impassable. "Now, Andrew, watch were you walk. A garden is an extraordinary thing—and the seedlings are our charge." The zucchini seedlings were a foot high and four feet across.

"Shall I walk around the block?" Andrew asked.

"It might be wise," Grandfather said.

So Andrew left by the iron gate of Grandfather's house, its forbidding points softened by late honeysuckle and blue morning glory, where his Mother as a child had swung creaking into the path of progress (as, indeed, his father said she still could do, on occasion) and entered upon the road of her childhood, crossing ragged plots of chicory and snow-on-the-mountain to the back lane and the back gate and the lower yard and the mulch pile, that grew mountainous year after year because Grandfather never got around to using it. The tomato vines cut Grandfather off at the waist, but he was tall and dignified—like a scarecrow or Don Quixote—and he waited with arms outstretched and a pigeon circling his head.

One of Grandfather's projects was to tell Andrew about Don Quixote, and he would have related more except that he had not yet gotten in his own reading beyond chapter one of Book One. But he had pointed out at St. Philomena's Church how the elongated statue of St. Francis (feeding the birds) bore some resemblance to the noble Spaniard, and Andrew could see how they all came together in that gaunt figure whose interest in nature and peanuts had brought squirrels to his feet and pigeons to other parts of his anatomy at the top of the autumn garden beyond the tomato vines.

"Andrew!" Grandfather had a voice for amphitheatres and large rooms that had lately been reduced by a numbing cough. "The message is: 'You may fire when you are ready, Girdley!' " That was when Andrew became aware that Father had been watching the entire performance from the second-floor back window.

When Father spoke of Grandfather he had always a rasp in his throat, as though he were suppressing a roar. He had said to Mother more than once in Andrew's hearing: "It's good for 'Grand' to live where he does. If he lived with us it would curtail his independence." Hence, because of Grandfather's advanced age, Andrew's birthdays were always held at Grandfather's house, a good five miles and one wide river from Andrew's home, and yet, Andrew's father sometimes said, hardly far enough. (Then Mother would explain that it was Father's work that made him impatient. He was a medical proofreader, and he worried about his memory. "Not like Grand, of course," he would say, in a tone that Andrew did not quite understand.)

Now Father was half out the back window. "It's *Gridley,* damnit. And remember that child's *polyarthritis rheumatica."* Then he slammed the window, and squirrels and pigeons took flight.

"Watch me," Grandfather raised his right hand, from which the American flag peeped forth, at approximately ten o'clock; his left hand clutching unshelled peanuts, held firm at three. "This is Y, Andrew. Commit it to memory. You never know when it may come in handy."

"Got it, Grand." And Andrew heard the salvoes of the guns.

"Where are you, boy? Come out from under those vines. You're supposed to be on the flag deck."

In the crotch of the pear tree there was room for a signalman. There, while the bees (that father called *multitudinous* with the emphasis he reserved for certain words) tumbled up from the fallen pears, Andrew held on, and his eyes filled with pride as Grand snapped to an O. "That's an O, boy, an O. Never forget it." He didn't. He tried the signal, and there was a breathless minute when he almost pitched from the tree, while through his legs he saw Grandfather, his hands outstretched and angled up, like St. Peter crucified upside-down at St. Philomena's. "U," Grandfather shouted; "U, never forget it." Then Mother came to the door, and it was supper time, when there were always plenty of cucumbers because the vines had gotten away from Grandfather this year and roamed wantonly over the front porch railing.

After supper, while Mother and Father did the dishes, they were to catch a cricket in the cage that Grand had gotten for Andrew's birthday, but Grandfather thought it best to put that off to another day. "I want to show you, 'And,' the uniform I wore with Dewey at Manila."

There was a familiar noise that could best be described as a growl from Father's throat, and Mother said: "Now, now Drew." Grandfather looked archly around at them all and crooked a finger at Andrew. "Go ahead, dear," Mother said; "go up with Grand, and we'll have some of the cake that's left when you come down."

The back stairs wound to the second floor, and Grand and Andrew were halfway up when Father said *"cockamanie."*

"Go on, Grand. I'll just be a minute." Andrew came back and sat on the fourth step, just beyond the corkscew turn in the stairs.

"What'll it do to the child when he discovers it's all *cockamanie,"* his Father was saying. Andrew puffed his lips to get them around the word. Father was doing crossword puzzles again.

When Father did crosswords his family was in for a hard time. "Damnit," Father would say, "how could that escape me?" It affected his digestion. And then, after he'd discovered the word, and used it religiously for a week or so, perhaps he'd forget its definition. So that if Andrew asked him, he'd groan and clutch his stomach. But sometimes the words were magnificent, and Andrew would try them at school. *Dizzard* had gotten him a reprimand. He still did not know what it meant; his nun's reaction to the epithet inhibited his question, and he dared not ask Father, who had long since gone on to *gowk* and *jabbernowl.* Ordinarily, Mother would simply say: "I can't imagine, dear."

"I don't want the child knocked into a cokamanie."

"I'm sure you mean 'a cocked hat,' Drew." Mother's voice was compounded of the pile of soft blankets on an autumn evening and the cupped palm of Indian summer sun on his face. Then his father growled again, and Andrew knew the discussion was at an end.

Just at the second floor landing, outside the door to Grandfather's room, Grand was tapping on the railing: *tap tap* pause *tap tap,* then a long pause while Andrew sat on the steps and listened. *Tap tap tap,* and again a pause. "Listen carefully," Grandfather said; "it's important." *Tap tap bang.* "There it is. If you're going to know semaphore, you might as well know Morse. That was Y-O-U. The first word of that memorable message: 'You may fire when you are ready, Girdley.' We'll learn the rest later—but keep that in mind." There was an old wood smell to the stairs, as though the sunlight had never reached them and time was pausing there. The presences of Grandfather's house were all about him. And Andrew could hear the inexorable statement of the railway clock in Grandfather's room, that never rang, but added second to second without emphasis, and sometimes frightened him because it seemed the beating of his heart, and he'd think of his heart swaying back and forth on a frail string and then it would thunder a warning in his ears.

"Come on up, child," Grandfather said. And Andrew came up under his arm. "That Morse, now; I could do it with the shade. Up and down, with a long pause for the dash. Not right now, though. That shade needs adjustment. I've been kind of busy—haven't gotten around to it. Just now, it doesn't come down."

There were books in all corners of the room. Over a rolltop desk (that didn't exactly work because Grandfather had misplaced the key) were the two volumes of the Oxford English Dictionary that Grandfather had gotten for five dollars at the Salvation Army, and that Father used when he came to Grandfather's. In fact, that was probably why he was in Grandfather's room when the matter of Gridley arose. Grandfather couldn't use the dictionary because it was fourteen volumes reduced to two, and a magnifying glass was necessary to read the print and Grandfather hadn't gotten around to getting one. Father's eyes were sharp.

"Grand," Andrew said, "tell me about all of them again, . . ." He leaned his chin on the mahogany table where daguerreotypes and yellowing photographs were displayed. "Well, yes, I will," Grandfather said, "but there's something more important. I have a surprise. Did I say I'm going to show you the uniform I wore with Dewey at Manila? On the very bridge where the signal was given: 'You may fire when you are ready'? Yes, I had the real signal flags in my hands then—the Real McCoy."

"Gosh," Andrew said.

Sometimes his friends made fun of him. There were those words Grandfather had taught him, not quite like Father's words: gosh, the Real McCoy, even magic lantern—and Grandfather had one of those in his closet. It didn't work (the lens had gotten misplaced): Grandfather said it was mice, but no one at St. Philomena's Grammar School had heard of it anyway. And no one had heard of Manila either, but Andrew had seen pictures in the huge blue dog-eared two-volume history of the Spanish American War on Grandfather's table, and he had thought from certain hints that Grand had charged up San Juan Hill with Teddy Roosevelt. So it came as a surprise, but not an unpleasant one, that—all those years ago—his own Grandfather had served in the Great White Fleet, flag-draped and smoke-crowned, and ghostly as the dreams that awaited him on the edge of sleep. These were things he could not tell his friends, if only because of Grand's C.I.A. Connections.

"The Real McCoy," Andrew came over under his Grandfather's arm; "gosh."

"I've been saving this," Grandfather said. "I've been saving it until you could appreciate it." There was a cedar chest across from the foot of his four-poster, brass bound and brass locked, and the last secret place in the house that Andrew had not seen. It was a promise unfulfilled.

"Nine," Grandfather said; "that's a good time, a right time," and he sat on the bed to catch his breath.

"Does it hurt, Grand?"

"Sometimes." Grandfather's hand trembled as he pulled it from under his sweater and over the place where the Jezail bullet had entered his shoulder when he served with his friend Dr. Watson in the Second Afghan War. "But it's nothing that time won't cure."

Andrew understood. Sometimes he could feel it too, when his chest grew tight and there didn't seem to be enough air for everyone; and sometimes when his head grew hot and he had to rest, and there were dangers of fearful dreams if he let himself sleep, he knew what it must have been like in the Black Hole of Calcutta and on those dark ships to Van Dieman's Land.

"First," Grandfather used his arms again to thrust himself erect, "we want to go through it all again: semaphore and Morse—a Navy man must know them both." He sat down heavily: "You go across the room. Let's see it again. Y . . . O . . . U . . ." And Grandfather corrected him from his seat on the bed. "Good. This is just the beginning, you remember. Now Morse—tap it out with that slipper on the turret," and he pointed to the wooden castle that he'd started three years ago for Andrew, but that had gotten bogged down when he needed a certain type of sandpaper. Tap tap . . . tap tap . . . tap tap tap . . . tap bang. "Fine, fine. You've got a memory like a steel trap. You'll be on the bridge of a cruiser in no time. Perhaps we'd better skip ahead a bit. You've got to know S.O.S. Now tap this out: dot dot dot . . . dash dash dash . . . dot dot dot . . . We'll work on the semaphore." And then to his feet: "The piece d'resistance, now . . ." But a fit of coughing sent him back on the bed again.

"Shall I get Mother, Grand?"

"Of course not. It's just a touch of that malaria I got in the Solomons, coastwatching. Open that Maiori box on the bureau."

"Maiori?"

"Native New Zealanders—it's a gift from the Chief."

Andrew pulled Grandfather's stool over to the bureau and delicately opened the box. He had seen something resembling it in the Five and Ten in Wallingford, but an imitation just wasn't the real thing. He felt the rough edge of jungle and the prick of spears. Inside was a pair of cufflinks, a shoehorn, a tiepin, two liberty-head nickels, a frayed Mass card, and a large brass key.

"The key," Grandfather said "bring it here."

It was as large as his hand, and Andrew could believe in its secrets.

"Now what I'm going to show you is going to be yours someday." Grandfather paused and coughed a bit and was silent. Then: "This is to be kept just between us. Thieves, you know—and envious people."

"Gosh."

Grandfather lifted his hand and his long, bent forefinger toward the bay window. "That's it." The cedar chest was wedged in the bay between the three-legged table with the empty goldfish bowl (Grandfather had had other things on his mind while the water evaporated last winter), and the radiator that always in Andrew's imagination hissed and bubbled on the verge of leaping, barely restrained, like one of the hooting, brass-stacked engines on the B & O that Grand had driven in his youth.

"Can I turn the key?" Andrew held it up to the light like a monocle. "Can I?" The sun nicked its edges.

"I was about to suggest it." Grandfather settled back in a fit of coughing. "Open it carefully and wait for me."

The lid squeaked up on a brass hinge, and Andrew felt the presences about him again. There was an odd, clean, woodsy, weathered smell— heavy with the scent of Grandmother and her voluminous clothes; and he looked up, startled, into Grandfather's eyes that saw what he saw too. The room was filled with her presence, and she was no longer out there across the river where the early autumn sigh of wind rumbled leaves over the stones, and where sometimes Mother took him and stood as though there was something she had forgotten that a long look inward would reveal.

Grandfather said, very quietly: "Help me up, Andrew." He had never seemed so old to Andrew as when he knelt by the cedar chest. It was labor for him to lift out the layers of clothes.

"These were Mother's, Andrew," he said. "Handle them with care."

There was a white dress, intricately trimmed in lace.

"Did Grandma wear this?"

"This was your Grandmother's wedding dress." Grandfather spoke as though he had swallowed his voice. Then a strange, shiny black suit with velvet lapels; a very small, white First Communion gown; a pair of ballet shoes; a May crown of lace with withered flowers; a private sol- dier's fatigue cap from World War I; a veil spotted with tiny lavender knots...

"Ah," said Grandfather.

It was magnificent. First, on top of the dark blue uniform and the red velvet sash, was the sword, and the silver scabbard, and on top of the sword the long hat, pointed fore and aft, and crowned with a sweeping white plume.

"A sword!" Andrew wondered if he could continue to breathe. On the pommel of the sword, and on the left breast of the scarlet-lined cape, in gold and red and blue and white, were the letters of K of C, and Andrew knew that these were part of the Navy code that Admiral Dewey had used to conquer the Spanish Fleet at Manila. He drew his finger around K of C on the pommel of the sword and spelled out S. Phil. Chapter. "Is this part of the code, Grand?" His voice cracked with awe.

"Right," Grand said, "right. It's our secret. Now you know where to come and what is yours."

"The sword and all?"

"Yes, And. Sword and all." Grandfather slowly lowered the lid: "But we're surrounded by assassins, and we must be careful." Then, as though he had prepared for Andrew yet a fresh surprise, he gasped and fell to the floor.

Andrew slid down the last four steps, and Mother and Father were gentler than they had ever been with him as Grandfather was lifted by the strange men and taken away.

The next day they came back ("to get Grand's things," Father said). Mother had been the night before, and Father had been upset because Mother was upset. They passed the hospital on the way, across the river and only two blocks from their home. Andrew strained to see Grandfather at the window there, but Mother said that he was likely to be in bed. "Maybe the shade doesn't work," Andrew said. Back home Father had said something about *"hematoma"* but Andrew knew that he was at crosswords again.

"We'll see him every day, And," Mother said.

"I'll take him the semaphore flag. Grand is teaching me semaphore and Morse."

"Yes," Father said. "Fine." He cleared his throat: "But you must not expect to see him for a while. Just now only adults can be admitted. He can't stand any excitement."

"I'm not excitement," Andrew said.

"Yes. Well, that's the way it is," and Father raced the motor and pulled out belligerently into traffic.

At Grand's, Father discovered that he had forgotten the key. So they went from window to window, trying them all. Finally, Father had to break a cellar pane, and then they got in. But the house was awfully quiet, and there was no heat in the kitchen where Grandfather depended on the stove because the President had asked him to save energy, or in the parlor where he burned mostly wood brought from India long ago in the clippers, or in his room that had one of the very first electric heaters devised by Thomas A. Edison himself.

While Mother and Father packed odds and ends into a Pan-Am flight bag, Andrew stood at the window from which Grandfather had watched a runaway slave sneak up the back street in the old days. A squirrel sat in the crown of the dogwood that tapped the window, and ate berries redder than the lining of Grandfather's cape in the cedar chest. Andrew guarded the Maiori box and the chest out of the corner of his eye. There were some things even his parents couldn't know about, but they didn't seem interested and instead worried because they couldn't find a Medicare card. Then they would have forgotten Grandfather's slippers with the toe out, but Andrew brought them to Father who said: "There's no . . ." and then stopped and said, "Thank you, Andrew; Grandfather will need these." That was the first time Andrew had heard Father call 'Grand' Grandfather.

The days without Grand were strange. There had not been a week since Grandmother's death when they had not, two or three times, crossed the river to the old house, and when Father had not groaned and done his crosswords. But two weeks passed without And seeing the old house, and then his mother said: "Grandfather is sitting up in bed."

"I have to hand it to him," Father said; "he's perdurable."

"Can I see Grand today?" Andrew had trouble with the words; there was a place so large he seemed to wander in, so empty—though he never moved except between St. Philomena's Grammar School and the tidy split-level where his parents lived—that he felt as he had once when he was spun away, alone, on one of the whirling amusements at Fairaway. "Can I see Grand, Mother?"

"We'll walk to the hospital, and you can wait across the street in the playground. I'm sorry, son, but he can only see your Mother now." Father pulled his head against his chest and was kind. But there were so many things to be done; the fire to be built in Grandfather's yard for Tedyuscum of the Lenapes, should he return, the almost cake to be placed on Grandfather's mantel for Saint Nicholas, the candle for the spirits at All Souls. How could he do all this himself? Andrew sat in his room and hunched his shoulders and wondered where he could turn.

Then they went to the hospital, Andrew for the first time.

"Wait for us here," Mother said. "You can play on the slides, and it's fun to push that merry-go-round. There'll be other children here. We'll tell Grandfather where you are and that you're thinking of him. We'll be right back; Mother is only allowed to stay a moment." Then she stopped beside Andrew: "Look, that room just above the entrance is his."

The hospital windows were glinting at the edges like Grandfather's great key, and Andrew felt the lowering sun warm on his back as he peered to see Grand at that window above all others. Because it was Daylight Saving (and Grandfather's letter to the Governor had helped save Daylight for once and all) the lights did not begin to show until Andrew saw Mother and Father crossing the street, coming back toward the playground. They were almost up to him when the light went on in Grandfather's room . . . and off and on again and off . . . His father bridled, and said something about "cantankerous." But Andrew strained forward like a runner, though it was his heart that was reaching at the end of its frail string: "Look, look!" And he formed the letters silently on his lips: S . . . O . . . S, S . . . O . . . S, S . . . O . . . S . . .

"For heaven's sake, now what? Well, Grand's their problem." His Father's voice was really not unkind, and he and Mother almost smiled as they walked away.

Then Father turned: "Mother! Will you kindly tell me what's animating that child?"

Andrew's right arm was at approximately ten o'clock; his arm held firm at three. And while his father pointed and sighed, the arms moved, desperately: Y . . . O . . . U, Y . . . O . . . U, Y . . . O . . . U . . .

*Clive Wilmer*

# The Sparking of the Forge

Stiffened and shrunk by age, my grandfather
Leans forward now, confined within his chair,
Straining to raise a finger to point back
Over his shoulder, scarcely able to look
Over his shoulder through the darkening window
At the road behind him and before me where

The mailcoach ran just seventy years ago
He suddenly tells me, reaching to capture one
Glimpse of the road where memory finds its form
And in whose lamps so many memories burn:
The armed guard in the rear, behind bars;
Changing the horses at the road's end inn;

And where we buy his tobacco every day
Was once the blacksmith's forge. I watch him stare
Into the crumbling coal and feel the blaze
surge in the ancient forge and his childhood-eyes,
And whether the shoes were hammered on red-hot
Uncertain now, he recollects their glare.

His words uncertain now, I watch him see
Bright in his mind the sparking of the forge
The monstrous anvil and the sizzling steel,
The raising of the hammer high to feel
What once he had of muscle in his arm,
The hammer's beat sounding his deepest urge.

Each time recalled another fragment lost,
Still his past seeps back—with broken breath—
Continuous in a stream of memories.
I pick up only broken images:
Confined by time, as he is by his age,
My own time's loss I find in his lost youth.

An old man's death becomes a young man's rage;
I seize the coal-tongs; now the blacksmith's clamp
Shadows my tiny room with smouldering giants,
An arm is raised to fall which, falling, hurls
Hammer-blows forward rung with resonance;
And, shod with steel now, hear the hard hoof stamp.

*Donald Hall*

# Maple Syrup

August, goldenrod blowing. We walk
into the graveyard, to find
my grandfather's grave. Ten years ago
I came here last, bringing
marigolds from the round garden
outside the kitchen.
I didn't know you then.
                              We walk
among carved names that go with photographs
on top of the piano at the farm:
Keneston, Wells, Fowler, Batchelder, Buck.
We pause at the new grave
of Grace Fenton, my grandfather's
sister. Last summer
we called on her at the nursing home,
eighty-seven, and nodding
in a blue housedress. We cannot find
my grandfather's grave.
                              Back at the house
where no one lives, we potter
and explore the back chamber
where everything comes to rest: spinning wheels,
pretty boxes, quilts,
bottles, books, albums of postcards.
Then with a flashlight we descend
firm steps to the root cellar—black,
cobwebby, huge,
with dirt floors and fieldstone walls,
and above the walls, holding the hewn
sills of the house, enormous

granite foundation stones.
Past the empty bins
for squash, apples, carrots, and potatoes,
we discover the shelves for canning, a few
pale pints
of tomato left, and—what
is this?—syrup, maple syrup
in a quart jar, syrup
my grandfather made twenty-five
years ago
for the last time.
                    I remember
coming to the farm in March
in sugaring time, as a small boy.
He carried the pails of sap, sixteen-quart
buckets, dangling from each end
of a wooden yoke
that lay across his shoulders, and emptied them
into a vat in the saphouse
where fire burned day and night
for a week.
                    Now the saphouse
tilts, nearly to the ground,
like someone exhausted
to the point of death, and next winter
when snow piles three feet thick
on the roofs of the cold farm,
the saphouse will shudder and slide
with the snow to the ground.
                              Today
we take my grandfather's last
quart of syrup
upstairs, holding it gingerly,
and we wash off twenty-five years
of dirt, and we pull
and pry the lid up, cutting the stiff,
dried rubber gasket, and dip our fingers

in, you and I both, and taste
the sweetness, you for the first time,
the sweetness preserved, of a dead man
in the kitchen he left
when his body slid
like anyone's into the ground.

*Robert P. Tristram Coffin*

# A Father Is a Strange Thing

A father is a strange thing, he will leap
Across a generation and will peep
Out of a grandson's eyes when unexpected
With all the secrets of him resurrected.

A man is taken by complete surprise
To see his father looking from the eyes
Of a little boy he thought his own
And thought he had the breeding of alone.

His father looks direct through eyes new blue,
His father moves on stout thighs quick and new,
He takes hold of things as once he did
And none of his old handsomeness is hid.

The grace the father thought well hid away
Shines like the sun upon a boy at play,
The love he kept so close for none to see
Looks up naked at the father's knee.

All the proud, high ways his father had
Are lowered to his knee. A man is sad
To see them so, but then he catches breath
To see how one so loved has cheated death.

# VI
# Beautiful Dreams, Vicious Realities

*Sail fast, sail fast*
*Ark of my hopes. Ark of my dreams.*

Sidney Lanier

*The fathers have eaten sour grapes,*
*and the children's teeth are set on edge.*

Ezekiel

Steven Schwartz

# Madagascar

This is a story I know so well.

My father, who is twenty-one, is on his way home from finding food for his family. He has traded a gold brooch for a bottle of milk, some vegetables and a little meat. With his blue eyes and blond hair, my father is the only one in the family who has any chance to pass for gentile on the streets. He makes sure to sit on a public bench, to pick out a paper from the trash and look comfortable, then go on. Among the many edicts against Jews—no traveling in motor cars, no leaning out windows, no using balconies open to the street, no going outside after dark—is one that forbids them to sit on park benches.

On the way home he takes another chance, meeting his fiancée in South Amsterdam. Before the deportations started they were to be married; now they must wait until the war ends, each of them hidden in different areas of the city.

After dark when he returns to the apartment cellar where his father, mother, and sister hide, he sees the Gestapo drive up. It is May 26, 1943. Tomorrow he will learn that the Great Raid has taken away all the remaining Jews, those in rest homes, in mental institutions, in orphanages, those too sick to walk, those who have cooperated with the Germans thinking it would spare them. Even the entire Jewish Council will be shipped to the labor camps. Now he knows nothing, only that he must avoid the house, that if he is caught out after curfew he will be imprisoned or shot. He steps into a bakery where the baker—a gentile though trusted friend of the family—offers to hide my father. If someone has informed on the family and the Gestapo do not find all the members, the baker knows they will search the whole block; they have been through here before. They will check the back room, the bins of flour, the attic above. They will tap the floor and walls for any hollow spaces. But, ironically, they will not check the ovens.

The baker tells my father to climb into an oven no longer in use. At first my father resists. He is afraid. Afraid he will die in there. But there is no other way. The Gestapo will not think to look in such an obvious yet unlikely place.

My father crawls in. The sirens stop. His family is taken away to Majdanek, never to return. He lives in the oven until the end of the war, coming out every two hours when business has slowed sufficiently so that he may stretch. Some days the baker stays so busy that my father must be inside for three, four, and once even six hours. Without room to turn over or extend his legs, he remains curled up in a ball. On one occasion, much to his humiliation, he must go to the bathroom in his pants. The baker and his wife kindly provide him with a long apron while his trousers are washed in back. In the oven, he makes up waltzes in his head and has long, complex discussions with himself, marshaling arguments for each side, as to which of the two Strausses, father or son, is the true Waltz King, despite the son being known by the title. He re-creates each note of their compositions and discusses the works with a panel of experts, but always delays the final vote another day so he may weigh the evidence more carefully and reconsider the merits of "Joy and Greetings," "Lorelei-Rheinklange," "Shooting Stars," and a hundred others.

After the war my father will listen to music in a high-backed chair. The record player during my childhood, a hi-fi, will be near a whisper in volume, perhaps the loudness at which he originally heard the melodies in his head. When I come into the room, he does not mind being disturbed, but asks me to sit and listen with him. I am ten. "Ah, now," he says raising his hand when the French horns begin to play. "Our favorite part." I do not know if "our" includes me or someone else or if he just speaks of himself in the plural. Soon he closes his eyes, smiles and extends his hand for mine. Although we are sitting down, me at his feet, our arms sway together, my father waltzing with me from this position. Softly he releases my hand, tells me I have good timing and to remember practice practice practice. Mastering the clarinet is no easy task—even for a bright ten-year-old. He rises from his chair, pulls down the sides of his coat—on Sunday afternoons he wears a jacket and tie at home—returns the record to its sleeve, closes the lid of the hi-fi, and stands with his hands behind his back for a few seconds as though making a silent prayer. Then he says, "Ephram, would you like to accompany me on a walk in the park?" I have my coat on within five seconds.

In ninth grade, I am caught shoplifting. I steal a silver pen from a drugstore. I am taken to the police station in Haverford, the small town where we live outside of Philadelphia and where my father teaches European history at Haverford College. My mother is in New York visiting her sisters, so I must call my father. The department secretary informs me that he should return from class within the hour.

"Are you at home, Ephram?"

"I'm at the police station," I say, shocked by my own admission. Perhaps I want to confess right away and get it over with, not hide the shame I feel, or perhaps I want to boast.

Without comment, she makes a note of my situation and promises she will get the message to my father immediately.

While I wait for my father in front of the sergeant's desk, on a plastic chair a faded aqua color, I think how I've wanted to succeed at something, most recently sports. The basketball game I made sure my father attended, positive I would be put in since we were playing a much weaker team, we wound up only narrowly winning, coming from behind. I sat on the bench the whole time. "Very stirring match," my father said afterward, walking me to the car, his arm around me. He knew I felt bad, of course, but there was nothing he could do, nothing I could do.

I lack the speed and agility to be first string; and by this season I've lost interest in sports, don't even try out for the team, and instead have fallen in with a group of kids who hang out at the edge of the parking lot, wear pointed shoes with four-inch Cuban heels, pitch quarters during lunch, comb their hair in duck tails (a style that requires me to sleep with my hair parted the opposite way so that the curls will straighten out by morning), and who generally get in trouble for everything from smoking cigarettes to belching "The Star-Spangled Banner" in back of Spanish class. It is 1964. School has become intolerable.

My father soon comes to the police station. I am released into his custody and we leave the old armory building of massive, buff sandstone, me in a blue corduroy coat that says Haverford Panthers, my father with his walking stick and tweed overcoat, a cream-colored scarf tucked under his chin. He puts his hand lightly behind me and I involuntarily sink back against his open palm, no easy feat going down a flight of steps. I keep expecting him to ask me what happened. Though I know he won't raise his voice, he never does, let alone physically punish me, I anticipate a lecture, as is his custom when I've misbehaved, which to be honest has not happened all that often. An only child, I have learned how to fill my parents' wishes better than my own. They have little reason to find fault with me, so trained am I in the most subtle of ways—a raised eyebrow from my father, a frown from my mother—to find fault with myself first.

"Why don't we walk a little bit, Ephram." We stop at the post office. My father buys a roll of stamps and some airmail envelopes for letters to Holland. We have no relatives over there anymore but he keeps a regular correspondence with friends and some members of the Amsterdam Symphony. Before the war he, too, had studied the clarinet and planned to become a professional musician, a source of conflict with his father who wanted my father to have a career in business like himself. When I was younger I always eagerly awaited the letters from Holland so I could steam off the stamps for my collection.

We sit down on a bench in front of the post office. It is December but the sun is bright enough for us to rest a moment outdoors.

I am prepared to apologize, no longer able to stand my father's silence. At the same time I want to explain that school offers me nothing but hypocrisy, lies, false values, and mush-headed teachers who haven't read a book themselves in years, and that I know this frustration has something to do with what I've done. But before I have the chance, he says he wants to tell me something about the war, one subject in which I am intensely interested because I always hope he will speak, as he rarely does, of his own experience.

"You may not know," he says, "that Hitler had several plans for the Jews. The camps came much later, after he had ruled out other possibilities, such as selling Jews to different countries. He also considered sending the Jews to the island of Madagascar. He wanted to permanently exile them there. Not destroy them, just isolate them on a remote island. This was to be his answer to the Jewish question. I have imagined many times what this situation may have been. I see the beaches, I see the shops, I see the clothes my mother and father wear there—light fabrics, colorful, soft cotton, a little lace on holidays. The sea is blue, the houses white. My mother does not like the heat, but my father welcomes it every morning by doing calisthenics on the balcony. They have settled here, done well, as Jews will do most anywhere, even in Nazi Madagascar. But you see how childish this is of me, don't you? That I want there to be a refuge in the midst of such undeniable evil. Perhaps it is why I decided to study history after the war. I have the liberty to make sense of the many possible pasts historians can always imagine—but the duty to choose only one. Sometimes I fail to honor my task because it is too unbearable. I do not think you are in a very happy period of your life now, Ephram. We are perhaps letting you down, your mother and I. I hope, though, that you will see I am far from perfect and struggle to make meaning of things as much as you do. It is my wish only that you will not harm others in the process, nor assault your own dignity. Leave yourself a small measure of respect in reserve. Always. You see, even in my worst memories—and I know nothing that can be worse for a man than to remember his mother and father and sister while he walks free in the world—even here I have left myself an escape to Madagascar. So allow yourself the same opportunity and do not think so poorly of your own promise that you must succumb to the disgrace of crime. You are bright, imaginative, resourceful. Surely there is a way out of whatever hell it is you too experience. I do not doubt that you can do better than this."

Chastened, I sit in silence with my father while we drive home. After his intercession, charges will be dropped by the drugstore. My mother learns nothing of the incident, and I soon separate from the group of misfits I've joined earlier. I also give up the clarinet when I discover—as my teacher agrees—that I feel nothing for the instrument.

My college roommate freshman year is named Marshall X. Tiernan. I have chosen to go to a small liberal arts college in Ohio that is not too far from Haverford but far enough so I feel I'm leaving home. Every Tuesday afternoon he asks if I can vacate the room for three hours and fifteen minutes (exactly) so he can listen to music.

"I don't mind if you listen while I'm here," I tell him.

He shakes his head. He must have privacy. Marshall X. Tiernan, reedy and tall as elephant grass but not nearly so uncultivated, has an enormous collection of classical records that takes up one quarter of our room. He is studying to be an engineer. Unlike the rest of the men in my dorm, who in the fall of 1968 have grown their hair long and wear patched jeans and army surplus coats, Marshall dresses in Arrow shirts with button-down collars and keeps a well-inked pen protector in his pocket. He has an unfortunate stutter and does not socialize beyond a fellow engineering student he knows from home. We have a respectful relationship, but I can't say that Marshall is a friend.

I agree to leave him alone on Tuesday afternoons, but one time I come back early. I have forgotten some notes that I need to take with me to the library. Expecting to hear music outside the door, I hear nothing and decide to go in. On the bed, with large padded earphones, is Marshall, his thin body rigid as slate. He sees me but does not acknowledge that I am here. His clothes, the sheets, everything is drenched with sweat. His legs tremble, a kind of seizure starts. When the record ends, a composition by Satie, Marshall sits up, quickly strips the bed, throws the sheets in the closet (Tuesday the maids bring new linen), changes his clothes and returns to his desk to study.

We do not discuss the incident.

Shortly afterward he drops out of school and moves home. I have the privacy of my own room, a lucky situation that enables me to spend time alone with Jessica, whom I've met at an antiwar meeting. One night while I am telling her, with some amusement I am sorry to say, about Marshall X. Tiernan, I suddenly stop. Jessica says later the look on my face is as if I've seen a ghost, for that is what happens. I suddenly see—no, *feel*—a twenty-one-year-old man curled painfully in a baker's oven, his body kept alive by music.

Thanksgiving vacation my sophomore year I bring Jessica home with me. Several years older than I and a senior in anthropology, she helps my mother with Thanksgiving dinner, talks at length with my father who retains a lifelong interest in Margaret Mead, and makes such a positive impression on them both that my mother whispers to me as we are about to leave for the airport, *"She's a jewel."*

But at school I sink into a profound depression. My grades plummet and although Jessica tries to stand by me, I manage to chase even her away. She finds her own apartment yet continues to call every day to check up on me. I become more withdrawn, however, and after a while I ask her to stop phoning. I watch television and eat chocolate donuts, drink milk from the carton and stare at the dark smudge marks my lips leave on the spout.

My father appears one afternoon, a surprise visit, he says. I know by the look on his face, though, that he has come because of Jessica. I burst into tears when I see him.

"What has happened, Ephram?" he says.

But I don't know what has happened, only that I can no longer study, I don't care about school and have no chance of passing finals; I don't care if I flunk out.

"Your mother is very worried. She wanted to come with me but I thought it best if I came alone. Is there anything I can do to help you? Is there something wrong in school, you don't like your courses, the pressure perhaps of too many hours . . ."

"I haven't been to class in weeks," I say. "I can't go. Even a trip to the store is overwhelming." I start to cry again. "I want to go home. I want to go back with you."

"But what will you do back there?" my father says. "There is nothing at home for you now. You have your studies here, your friends."

I look at my father. As always, he is dressed neatly, and warmly, a blue blazer and gray slacks, a wool vest under his coat. Meanwhile, my apartment remains a mess, dishes in the sink, clothes everywhere, my hair unwashed.

"I'll find a job, I'll work and make money."

"And live at home?"

"Yes, what's wrong with that?"

My father pauses. "I don't know. I would think that you'd enjoy the freedom of living on your own."

"I have freedom and privacy at home. You've never told me what to do or when to come in. I'm not happy here."

"But Ephram, changing the place you live will not solve your problems. You need to get to the bottom of this."

"I don't care, I just want to go home! Can't you understand that?" I am almost screaming. "I have to go back. I can't make it here!"

For the rest of the winter, I work in a bubble gum factory near Philadelphia. It is miserable, but the more miserable the better because I feel as if I deserve the punishment of tedious, demeaning work for failing in school. I am paid minimum wage, $1.85 an hour. So much sugar hangs in the air—we throw bags of it into a mixing contraption resembling the gigantic maw of a steam shovel—that the people who have worked for years at the factory have lost many of their teeth. The gum itself comes out on long (and unsanitary) splintered boards that I carry to racks, which are taken to another station where these long tubular strips of bubble gum—more like waxy pink sausages than gum at this stage—are cut into bite-size pieces with a tool akin to a large pizza wheel.

One day at the beginning of spring I receive a letter from the draft board. According to their records, my student deferment has expired; I am now eligible to be considered for military service.

My father comes home early from his office hour at school. He himself hates the war, the senseless bombing and killing. He has marched with his college's students and protested the presence on campus of recruiters from a chemical company that makes napalm. He has, in fact, been more active than I, who have withdrawn into the routine and oblivion of factory labor, for which there are no deferments.

"What are your plans?" my father asks.

"I don't know. Canada, I suppose, if all else fails."

"And what is 'all else'?"

"A medical deferment."

"On what basis?"

"My mental condition."

"But you have never been to a psychiatrist. You have no history."

"I don't know then." I shrug. I feel numb, resigned. Why not basic training and then the jungles of Southeast Asia? Could it be much worse than the bubble gum factory?

"You will not go. That is all there is to it. We will make sure of that."

"And how will you do that?"

"We'll hide you, if necessary."

I look at my father and almost laugh. But I can see he is serious, alarmed.

"What are you talking about—hide me? Where?"

He picks up his newspaper and folds it back, once, twice, three times until he has a long strip of news in front of him. It is the idiosyncratic way he likes to read the paper—folding it up like a map until he is down to a small, tight square of information the size of a wallet or obituary. I think that it must make him feel some control over the world's chaotic events to read about them in such miniature, compressed spaces.

My mother brings in a stuck jar for one of us to loosen, and my father puts down his newspaper, which pops open on his lap like an accordion. I am still thinking about his wanting to hide me, aware that the draft has touched off buried fears for him, a flashback to the war, some instinctive response to the personal terror of his family being taken away from him. "I'll get out of it, Dad," I say. "Don't worry. I won't go."

"Don't worry, don't worry, is that what you think is the problem here? You have put yourself in this position, though I begged you not to. What is there to do now but worry!" He stands up. "I am *sick* with worry, if you must know. This is my fault. I should have demanded you stay in school, not let you come here!"

I have never heard him raise his voice like this. His body begins to tremble, and from the kitchen my mother hurries in with her hand over her heart. "What is going on here?" she says. "What are you arguing about?"

"Nothing," my father answers. "The argument is finished," and he goes into his study and closes the door—a sight I am used to from childhood. I hear him weep but rather than sadness I feel a great relief; finally, something I've done has touched him.

I do not get drafted but receive a high number in the first lottery. The long and tiresome depression, the deadness I have felt, is replaced with the exhilaration of a survivor, a life reclaimed. I make plans to visit Europe, use the money I've saved from the bubble gum factory to travel for three months. Guidebooks about England, France, Spain, and Italy cover my bed. I pore over them and come up with a tentative itinerary. But when I actually get to Europe, I find I make a detour from England to Holland. I locate the Jewish quarter where my father hid during the war, find his school—the Vossius Gymnasium—and then what I've come for: the bakery. It is still there, although the original owners who saved my father have long ago died. I explain to the current owners who I am; they tell me in broken English that yes, they have heard what happened here during the war, they know about my father and the Koops who saved him; the story is legend. "Does the oven still exist by any chance?" I ask.

They take me to the back, outside to a shed. It is here, covered with a tablecloth. I ask them if I can be by myself for a few moments and they say certainly, no one will disturb me.

A squat and solid object, the oven stands only chest high. I pull open the door and look inside. The opening is deeper than it is wide, the height a little less than two feet. I hoist myself up to sit on the edge. Then I swing my legs around and push my body in feet first. My neck is back against the left edge. I cannot go any farther. My shoulder sticks out too much even when I bend my knees into my chest. I do not understand how he did this, but I am determined to fit inside, so I slide out again and try to enter without my shoes and without my jacket. I tuck my legs under and pull my head inside, my back curved tight as an archer's bow. I hook my finger through the match hole and close the door. The stove smells of mildew and carbon; the scaled roughness of the iron ceiling grates against my cheek. It is pitch black except for the match hole through which I can see. I put my eye up to it and watch. Soon I hear footsteps and I feel frightened, but the footsteps recede into the distance and the bakery becomes silent.

Many years later my parents come out to celebrate the occasion of our son's fifth birthday. My father helps Philip build the space station they have brought him. I watch them play together, my father with no awareness of the world around him other than this mission to be his grandson's assistant.

While my mother and Judith, my wife, put Philip to bed, my father and I have coffee on the porch. It is a cool summer night and we are in Boulder, Colorado, where the shimmering night sky looks, to my parents, like a planetarium. Judith works in the university's office of communications, while I teach literature. Like my father, I have become a professor.

"What are you going to do now?" I ask him. He is on transitional retirement, half-time teaching, and is scheduled to leave the college next year. "Will you finally go to Europe?"

"Perhaps," he says, "but your mother's back may not permit it."

I nod. The trip out here has cost her a great deal of pain that she has accepted stoically. If she walks for more than half an hour or sits for that long, the result is the same, inflammation.

"Have you thought of going yourself?" I ask.

"I could not leave your mother for that long. She would not be well enough."

My father sits with the hiking boots he has bought for this trip out west laced tight on his feet. They are spanking new and he has already cleaned them of mud from our climb this afternoon. I take pleasure in seeing him so fond of the mountains, so open to the world out here. "You and I could go," I say. "Together. A nurse could help mother if we went next summer."

"I will give it some thought," my father says, but I can see that the veil has already dropped—the complex configuration of blank terror that can still scare me with its suddenness, the yearning on his face vanished. He has gone to Madagascar.

He empties the coffee he has spilled in the saucer back into his cup. "I have made a mess here," he says, replacing the dry saucer underneath. He stands up. Pulls down the sides of his jacket. Despite the hiking boots, he has dressed for dinner. "Would you like to go for a walk with me, Ephram?"

Yes, I say, and get my coat, eager as always.

Last summer Judith and I took Philip to Europe because I wanted to show him where his grandfather grew up. Though the bakery was no longer there—an insurance office now—I described everything about the original building, and the oven. I held him in my arms while he listened with intelligence and care, and I kissed his long lashes and felt his soft cheek against mine. I wondered what he knew that I would never know about him, what pleased him that could not be spoken. When would he grow past me, leave his fatherland, hack and chop and hew whole forests until he could find one piece of hallowed ground to plant the seed of his own self?

One night in our hotel I could not sleep and began to write: "Every son's story about his father is, in a sense, written to save himself from his father. It is told so that he may go free and in the telling the son wants to speak so well that he can give his father the power to save himself from his own father." I wrote this on a note card, put it in an airmail envelope, and planned to send it with its Amsterdam postmark to my father.

The following morning a call from my mother let us know that my

father had suffered a stroke. We flew home immediately, and I rushed to
see him in the hospital while Judith waited with Philip at the house. My
mother was there by his bed. An I.V. bottle was connected to his wrist.
His other arm I saw had purplish bruises from all the injections and from
the blood samples taken. The effects of the stroke made him confuse the
simplest of objects, or draw on archaic uses—a pen became a plume. A
part of his brain had lost the necessary signals for referencing things and
faces with words, and now dealt in wild compensatory searches to
communicate. When he spoke of Judith he referered to her as my
husband, called me "ram" trying to pronounce Ephram, and, saddest of
all, could not understand why I had so much trouble understanding him.
He had once spoken three languages fluently, and to see him in this state
was more of a shock than I could bear. When he fell asleep, I left his room
to speak with the doctor, a neurologist who explained to me that a
ruptured blood vessel was causing the illogical and distorted speech.
Bleeding in the brain. The image for me was vivid, his brain leaking, his
skull swelling from the fluid's pressure inside and all one could do was
wait.

One day while I sat and read by his bed, he said my name clearly and
asked if I could help him get dressed. He had a white shirt and tie in the
closet. He spoke with difficulty from the stroke, although his condition
had improved and we all believed he would be released soon. I dressed
him and because he was cold I put my sweater over his shoulders and
tied the arms in front so he looked like a college man again. While he
sat up in bed I held onto his hand to steady him, reminded of how we
used to waltz together when I was ten. I said something to him that I had
carried around with me for a long while, something that had no basis in
fact, only in the private burden of a son traversing the globe for a father's
loss. "I'm sorry if I've disappointed you," I told him and he answered me
in speech slowed by his stroke, "I forget everything, Ephram." I nodded,
but then cried later at his funeral because I thought and hoped he had
meant to say forgive.

*Sherman Alexie*
# Father Coming Home

THEN          Father coming home from work. Me waiting on the front steps, watching him walk slowly and carefully, like half of a real Indian. The other half stumbling, carrying the black metal lunch box with maybe half a sandwich, maybe the last drink of good coffee out of the thermos, maybe the last bite of a dream.

SPOKANE          Father coming home from work five days a week. Me, waiting every day until the day he doesn't come walking home, because he cut his knee in half with a chainsaw. Me, visiting with my father laying in bed in the hospital in Spokane. Both of us, watching the color television until my mother comes from shopping at Goodwill or Salvation Army or until the nurses come in telling us we have to go.

CEREMONIES          Father coming home from the hospital in a wheelchair. Me, waiting for him to stand up and teach me how to shoot free throws. Me, running up to him one day and jumping hard into his lap, forgetting about his knee. Father holding me tight against his chest, dark and muddy, squeezing his pain into my thin ribs, his eyes staying clear.

AFTER          Father coming home from the mailbox, exercising his knee again and again. Me, looking up from the floor as he's shaking his head because there is no check, no tiny miracles coming in the mail. Father bouncing the basketball, shooting lay-in after lay-in, working the knee until it bleeds along the scars. Father crying from the pain late at night, watching television. Me, pretending to be asleep. All of us listening to canned laughter.

INSOMNIA          Father coming home from another job interview,
                  limping only a little but more than enough to keep
                  hearing no, no, no. Me, eating potatoes again in
the kitchen, my mother's face growing darker and darker by halves. One
half still mostly beautiful, still mostly Indian, the other half something
all-crazy and all-hungry. Me, waking her up in the middle of the night,
telling her my stomach was empty. Her throwing me outside in my
underwear and locking the door. Me, trying anything to get back in.

HOMECOMING        Father coming home from drinking, after being
                  gone for weeks. Me, following him around all the
                  time. Him, never leaving my sight, going into the
bathroom. Me, sitting outside the door, waiting, knocking on the wood
every few seconds, asking him *Are you there? Are you there?*

NOW               Father coming home finally from a part-time job.
                  Driving a water truck for the BIA. Me, waiting on
                  the front steps, watching him come home early
every day. Him, telling my mother when they think I can't hear, he
doesn't know if he's strong enough. Father telling mother he was driving
the truck down Little Falls Hill, trying to downshift but his knee not
strong enough to keep holding the clutch in. Me, holding my breath.
Him, driving around the corner on two wheels, tons and tons of water,
half-insane. Me, closing my eyes. Him, balancing, always ready to fall.
Me, holding onto father with all my strength.

*Sherman Alexie*
# Crisis on Toast

We've been driving for hours
my father and I
through reservation farmland
talking the old stories:
Stubby Ford; Lana Turner
at the National Boy Scout Jamboree
my father pissing in a hole he dug
while his troop formed a circle
around him and Lana Turner drove by
breaking every boy's heart. He told me

old drunk stories
about the gallon of vodka a day
the DTs, snakes
falling out of the walls. We watched

two farm boys shooting baskets. Lean and hungry
they were "suicidally beautiful." *Jesus*
my father said. *I played ball like that.*
I looked into the sun and tears fell
without shame or honor. We got out of the car
in our basketball shoes. My father's belly
two hundred winter beers wide
and I've never been more afraid
of the fear in any man's eyes.

Fred Chappell

# The Overspill

Then there was one brief time when we didn't live in the big brick house with my grandmother but in a neat two-storey green-shingled white house in the holler below. It was two storeys if you stood at the front door; on the other side it was three storeys, the ground floor a tall basement.

The house was surrounded by hills to the north and east and south. Directly above us lay the family farm and my grandmother's house. Two miles behind the south hill was the town of Tipton, where the Challenger Paper and Fiber Corporation smoked eternally, smudging the Carolina mountain landscape for miles. A small creek ran through our side yard, out of the eastern hills. The volume of the creek flow was controlled by Challenger; they had placed a reservoir up there, and the creek water was regulated by means of the spillway.

At this time my mother was visiting her brother in California. Uncle Luden was in trouble again, with a whole different woman this time. Maybe my mother could help; it was only 5,000 miles round trip by train.

So my father and I had to fumble along as best we could.

Despite the extra chores, I found it exciting. Our friendship took a new and stronger turn, became something of a mild conspiracy. New sets of signals evolved between us. We met now on freshly neutral ground somewhere between my boyhood and his boyishness, and for me it was a heady rise in status. We were clumsy housekeepers, there were lots of minor mishaps, and the tagline we formulated soonest was: "Let's just not tell Mama about this one." I adored that thought.

He was always dreaming up new projects to please her and during her absence came up with one of masterful ambition.

Across the little creek, with its rows of tall willows, was a half-acre of fallow ground considered unusable because of marshiness and the impenetrable clot of blackberry vines in the south corner. My father now planned it as a garden, already planted before she returned.

We struggled heroically. I remember pleasantly the destruction of the vines and the cutting of the drainage ditch neat and straight into the field. The ground was so soft that we could slice down with our spades and bring up squares of dark blue mud and lay them along side by side. They gleamed like tile. Three long afternoons completed the ditch, and then my father brought out the big awkward shoulder scythe and whetted the blade until I could hear it sing on his thumb-ball when he tested it. And then he waded into the thicket of thorny vine and began slashing. For a long time nothing happened, but finally the vines began to fall back, rolling up in tangles like barbarous handwriting. With a pitchfork I worried these tangles into a heap. Best of all was the firing, the clear yellow flame and the sizzle and snap of the vine-ribs and thorns, and the thin black smoke rising above the new-green willows. The delicious smell of it.

After this we prepared the ground in the usual way and planted. Then we stood at the edge of our garden, admiring with a full tired pride the clean furrows and mounded rows of earth.

But this was only a part of the project. It was merely a vegetable garden, however arduously achieved, and we planted a garden every year. My father wanted something else, decorative, elegant in design, something guaranteed to please a lady.

The weather held good and we started next day, hauling two loads of scrap lumber from one of the barns. He measured and we sawed and planed. He hummed and whistled as he worked and I mostly stared at him when not scurrying to and fro, fetching and carrying. He wouldn't, of course, tell me what we were building.

On the second day it became clear. We were constructing a bridge. We were building a small but elaborate bridge across the little creek that divided the yard and the garden, a stream that even I could step over without lengthening my stride. It was ambitious: an arched bridge with handrails and a latticework arch on the garden side enclosing a little picket gate.

He must have been a handy carpenter. To me the completed bridge appeared marvelous. We had dug deep on both sides to sink the locust piers, and the arch above the stream, though not high, was unmistakably a rainbow. When I walked back and forth across the bridge I heard and

felt a satisfactory drumming. The gate latch made a solid cluck and the
gate arch, pinned together of old plaster lathe, made me feel that in
crossing the bridge I was entering a different world, not simply going
into the garden.

He had further plans for the latticework. "Right here," he said, "and
over here, I'll plant tea roses to climb up the lattice. Then you'll see."

We whitewashed it three times. The raw lumber sparkled. We walked
upstream to the road above the yard and looked at it, then walked
downstream to the edge of the garden and looked at it. We saw nothing
we weren't prideful about.

He went off in our old Pontiac and returned in a half hour. He parked
in the driveway and got out. "Come here," he said. We sat in the grass
on the shoulder of the culvert at the edge of the road. "I've been to the
store," he said. He pulled a brown paper sack from his pocket. Inside I
found ten thimble-shaped chocolate mints, my favorite. From another
pocket he produced a rolled band of bright red silk.

"Thank you," I said. "What's that?"

"We want her to know it's a present, don't we? So we've got to tie
a ribbon on it. We'll put it right there in the middle of the handrail." He
spooled off two yards of ribbon and cut it with his pocket knife. "Have
to make a big one so she can see it from up here in the road."

I chewed a mint and observed his thick horny fingers with the red
silk.

It was not to be. Though I was convinced that my father could design
and build whatever he wished—the Brooklyn Bridge, the Taj Mahal—he
could not tie a bow in the broad ribbon. The silk crinkled and knotted
and slipped loose; it simply would not behave. He growled in low tones
like a bear trying to dislodge a groundhog from its hole. "I don't know
what's the matter with this stuff," he said.

Over the low mumble of his words I heard a different rumble, a
gurgle as of pebbles pouring into a broad still pool. "What's that?" I
asked.

"What's what?"

"What's that noise?"

He stopped ruining the ribbon and sat still as the sound grew louder.
Then his face darkened and veins stood out in his neck and forehead. His
voice was quiet and level now. "Those bastards."

"Who?"

"Those Challenger Paper guys. They've opened the floodgates."

We scrambled up the shoulder into the road.

As the sound got louder it discomposed into many sounds: lappings, bubblings, rippings, undersucks, and splashovers. Almost as soon as we saw the gray-brown thrust of water emerge from beneath the overhanging plum tree, we felt the tremor as it slammed against the culvert, leaping up the shoulder and rolling back. On the yard side it shot out of the culvert as out of a hose. In a few seconds it had overflowed the low creek banks and streamed gray-green along the edge of the yard, furling white around the willow trunks. Debris—black sticks and leaves and grasses—spun on top of the water, and the gullet of the culvert rattled with rolling pebbles.

Our sparkling white bridge was soiled with mud and slimy grasses. The water driving into it reached a gray arm high into the air and slapped down. My father and I watched the hateful battering of our work, our hands in our pockets. He still held the red ribbon and it trickled out of his pocket down his trouser leg. The little bridge trembled and began to shake. There was one moment when it sat quite still, as if it had gathered resolve and was fighting back.

And then on the yard side it wrenched away from the log piers, and when that side headed downstream the other side tore away too, and we had a brief glimpse of the bridge parallel in the stream like a strange boat and saw the farthest advance of the floor framed in the quaint lattice arch. The bridge twirled about and the corners caught against both banks and it went over on its side, throwing up the naked underside of the plants like a barn door blown shut. Water piled up behind this damming and finally poured over and around it, eating at the borders of the garden and lawn.

My father kept saying over and over, "Bastards bastards bastards. It's against the law for them to do that."

Then he fell silent.

I don't know how long we stared downstream before we were aware that my mother had arrived. When he first saw her she had already got out of the taxi, which sat idling in the road. She looked good to me, wearing a dress I had never seen, and a strange expression—half amused, half vexed—crossed her face. She looked at us as if she'd caught us doing something naughty.

My father turned to her and tried to speak. "Bastards" was the only word he got out. He choked and his face and neck went dark again. He gestured toward the swamped bridge and the red ribbon fluttered in his fingers.

She looked where he pointed and, as I watched, understanding came into her face, little by little. When she turned again to face us she looked as if she were in pain. A single tear glistened on her cheek, silver in the cheerful light of midafternoon.

My father dropped his hand and the ribbon fluttered and trailed in the mud.

The tear on my mother's cheek got larger and larger. It detached from her face and became a shiny globe, widening outward like an inflating balloon. At first the tear floated in air between them, but as it expanded it took my mother and father into itself. I saw them suspended, separate but beginning to drift slowly toward one another. Then my mother looked past my father's shoulder, looked through the bright skin of the tear, at me. The tear enlarged until at last it took me in too. It was warm and salt. As soon as I got used to the strange light inside the tear, I began to swim clumsily toward my parents.

*Peter Oresick*
# My Father

My father was four years in the war,
and afterward, according to my mother,
had nothing to say. She says he trembled
in his sleep the next four years.
My father was twice the father of sons
miscarried, and afterward, said nothing.
My mother keeps his silence also.
Four times my father was on strike,
and according to my mother, had nothing
to say. She says the company didn't understand,
nor can her son, the meaning
of an extra 15 cents an hour in 1956
to a man tending a glass furnace in August.

I have always remembered him a tired man.
I have respected him like a guest
and expected nothing.
It is April now.
My life lies before me
enticing as the woman at my side.
Now, in April, I want him to speak.
I want to stand against the worn body
of his pain. I want to try it on
like a coat that does not fit.

*William Jay Smith*

# American Primitive

Look at him there in his stovepipe hat,
His high-top shoes, and his handsome collar;
Only my Daddy could look like that,
And I love my Daddy like he loves his Dollar.

The screen door bangs, and it sound so funny
There he is in a shower of gold;
His pockets are stuffed with folding money,
His lips are blue, and his hands feel cold.

He hangs in the hall by his black cravat,
The ladies faint, and the children holler:
Only my Daddy could look like that,
And I love my Daddy like he loves his Dollar.

*Guy de Maupassant*
# The Father

I

He was a clerk in the Bureau of Public Education, and lived at Batignolles. He took the omnibus to Paris every morning, and always sat opposite a girl, with whom he fell in love.

She was employed in a shop, and went in at the same time every day. She was a little brunette, one of those girls whose eyes are so dark that they look like black spots on a complexion like ivory. He always saw her coming at the corner of the same street, and she generally had to run to catch the heavy vehicle, and sprang upon the steps before the horses had quite stopped. Then she got inside, out of breath, and, sitting down, looked round her.

The first time that he saw her, Francois Tessier liked the face. One sometimes meets a woman whom one longs to clasp in one's arms without even knowing her. That girl seemed to respond to some chord in his being, to that sort of ideal love which one cherishes in the depths of the heart, without knowing it.

He looked at her intently, not meaning to be rude, and she became embarrassed, and blushed. He noticed it, and tried to turn away his eyes; but he involuntarily fixed them upon her again every moment, although he tried to look in another direction; and, in a few days they seemed to know each other without having spoken. He gave up his place to her when the omnibus was full, and got outside, though he was very sorry to do it. By this time, she had got so far as to greet him with a little smile; and, although she always dropped her eyes under his looks, which she felt were too ardent, yet she did not appear offended at being looked at in such a manner.

They ended by speaking. A kind of rapid friendship had become established between them, a daily free masonry of half an hour, and that was certainly one of the most charming half hours in his life, to him. He thought of her all the rest of the day, saw her image continually during the long office hours. He was haunted and bewitched by that form a beloved woman leaves in us, and it seemed to him that if he could win that little person it would be maddening happiness to him, almost above human realization.

Every morning she now shook hands with him, and he preserved the sense of that touch, and the recollection of the gentle pressure of her little fingers until the next day, and he almost fancied that he preserved the imprint on his palm. He anxiously waited for this short omnibus ride, while Sundays seemed to him heartbreaking days. However, there was no doubt that she loved him, for one Saturday, in spring, she promised to go and lunch with him at Maison-Lafitte the next day.

II

She was at the railway station first, which surprised him, but she said: "Before going, I want to speak to you. We have twenty minutes, and that is more than I shall take for what I have to say."

She trembled as she hung on his arm, and looked down, her cheeks pale, as she continued: "I do not want you to be deceived in me, and I shall not go there with you, unless you promise, unless you swear—not to do—not to do anything—that is at all improper."

She had suddenly become as red as a poppy, and said no more. He did not know what to reply, for he was happy and disappointed at the same time. He should love her less, certainly, if he knew that her conduct was light, and then it would be so charming, so delicious to have a little flirtation.

As he did not say anything, she began to speak again in an agitated voice, and with tears in her eyes. "If you do not promise to respect me altogether, I shall return home." And so he squeezed her arm tenderly and replied: "I promise, you shall only do what you like." She appeared relieved in mind, and asked, with a smile: "Do you really mean it?" And he looked into her eyes, and replied: "I swear it." "Now you may take the tickets," she said.

During the journey, they could hardly speak, as the carriage was full, and when they reached Maison-Lafitte they went toward the Seine. The sun, which shone full on the river, on the leaves and the grass, seemed to be reflected in their hearts, and they went, hand in hand, along the bank, looking at the shoals of little fish swimming near the bank, and they walked on, brimming over with happiness, as if they were walking on air.

At last she said: "How foolish you must think me!"

"Why?" he asked. "To come out like this, all alone with you." "Certainly not; it is quite natural." "No, no; it is not natural for me— because I do not wish to commit a fault, and yet this is how girls fall. But if you only knew how wretched it is, every day the same thing, every day in the month, and every month in the year. I live quite alone with mamma, and as she has had a great deal of trouble, she is not very cheerful. I do the best I can, and try to laugh in spite of everything, but I do not always succeed. But, all the same, it was wrong of me to come, though you, at any rate, will not be sorry."

By way of an answer, he kissed her ardently on the ear that was nearest him, but she moved from him with an abrupt movement, and, getting suddenly angry, exclaimed: "Oh! Monsieur Francois, after what you swore to me!" And they went back to Maison-Lafitte.

They had lunch at the Petit-Havre, a low house, buried under four enormous poplar trees, by the side of the river. The air, the heat, the weak white wine, and the sensation of being so close together, made them silent; their faces were flushed, and they had a feeling of oppression; but, after the coffee, they regained their high spirits, and, having crossed the Seine, started off along the bank, toward the village of La Frette. Suddenly he asked: "What is your name?" "Louise." "Louise," he repeated, and said nothing more.

The girl picked daisies, and made them into a great bunch, while he sang vigorously, as unrestrained as a colt that has been turned into a meadow. On their left, a vine-covered slope followed the river. Francois stopped motionless with astonishment: "Oh, look there!" he said.

The vines had come to an end, and the whole slope was covered with lilac bushes in flower. It was a purple wood! A kind of great carpet of flowers stretched over the earth, reaching as far as the village, more than two miles off. She also stood, surprised and delighted, and murmured: "Oh! how pretty!" And, crossing a meadow, they ran toward that curious low hill, which, every year, furnishes all the lilac that is drawn through Paris on the carts of the flower vendors.

There was a narrow path beneath the trees, so they took it, and when they came to a small clearing, sat down.

Swarms of flies were buzzing around them and making a continuous, gentle sound, and the sun, the bright sun of a perfectly still day, shone over the green slopes, and from that forest of blossoms a powerful fragrance was borne toward them, a breath of perfume, the breath of the flowers.

A church clock struck in the distance, and they embraced gently, then, without the knowledge of anything but that kiss, lay down on the grass. But she soon came to herself with the feeling of a great misfortune, and began to cry and sob with grief, with her face buried in her hands.

He tried to console her, but she wanted to start to return and to go home immediately; and she kept saying, as she walked along quickly: "Good heavens! good heavens!" He said to her: "Louise! Louise! Please let us stop here." But now her cheeks were red, and her eyes hollow, and, as soon as they got to the railway station in Paris, she left him, without even saying good-by.

III

When he met her in the omnibus, next day, she appeared to him to be changed and thinner, and she said to him: "I want to speak to you; we will get down at the Boulevard."

As soon as they were on the pavement, she said: "We must bid each other good-by; I cannot meet you again." "But why?" he asked. "Because I cannot; I have been culpable, and I will not be so again."

Then he implored her, tortured by his love; but she replied firmly: "No, I cannot, I cannot." He, however, only grew all the more excited, and promised to marry her, but she said again: "No," and left him.

For a week he did not see her. He could not manage to meet her, and, as he did not know her address, he thought that he had lost her alto- gether. On the ninth day, however, there was a ring at his bell, and when he opened the door, she was there. She threw herself into his arms, and did not resist any longer, and for three months they were close friends. He was beginning to grow tired of her, when she whispered to him; and then he had one idea and wish: to break with her at any price. As, however, he could not do that, not knowing how to begin, or what to say, full of anxiety through fear of the consequences of his rash indiscretion, he took a decisive step: one night he changed his lodgings, and disappeared.

The blow was so heavy that she did not look for the man who had abandoned her, but threw herself at her mother's knees, and confessed her misfortune; and, some months after, gave birth to a boy.


IV

Years passed, and Francois Tessier grew old, without there having been any alteration in his life. He led the dull, monotonous life of an office clerk, without hope and without expectation. Every day he got up at the same time, went through the same streets, went through the same door, past the same porter, went into the same office, sat in the same chair, and did the same work. He was alone in the world, alone during the day in the midst of his different colleagues, and alone at night in his bachelor's lodgings; and he laid by a hundred francs a month, against old age.

Every Sunday he went to the Champs-Elysees, to watch the elegant people, the carriages, and the pretty women; and the next day he used to say to one of his colleagues: "The return of the carriages from Bois du Boulogne was very brilliant yesterday." One fine Sunday morning, however, he went into the Parc Monceau, where the mothers and nurses, sitting on the sides of the walks, watched the children playing, and suddenly Francois Tessier started. A woman passed by, holding two children by the hand, a little boy of about ten and a little girl of four. It was she.

He walked another hundred yards, and then fell into a chair, choking with emotion. She had not recognized him, and so he came back, wishing to see her again. She was sitting down now, and the boy was standing by her side very quietly, while the little girl was making sand castles. It was she, it was certainly she, but she had the reserved appearance of a lady, was dressed simply, and looked self-possessed and dignified. He looked at her from a distance, for he did not venture to go near; but the little boy raised his head, and Francois Tessier felt himself tremble. And, as he looked at him, he thought he could recognize himself as he appeared in an old photograph taken years ago. He remained hidden behind a tree, waiting for her to go, that he might follow her.

He did not sleep that night. The idea of the child especially harassed him. His son! Oh! If he could only have known, have been sure! But what could he have done? However, he went to the house where she had lived, and asked about her. He was told that a neighbor, and honorable man of strict morals, had been touched by her distress, and had married her; he knew the fault she had committed and had married her, and had even recognized the child, his, Francois Tessier's child, as his own.

He returned to the Parc Monceau every Sunday, for then he always saw her, and each time he was seized with a mad, an irresistible longing to take his son into his arms, cover him with kisses, and to steal him, to carry him off.

He suffered horribly in his wretched isolation as an old bachelor, with nobody to care for him, and he also suffered atrocious mental torture, torn by paternal tenderness springing from remorse, longing, and jealousy, and from that need of loving one's own children which nature has implanted in all. At last, he determined to make a despairing attempt, and, going up to her, as she entered the park, he said, standing in the middle of the path, pale and with trembling lips: "You do not recognize me." She raised her eyes, looked at him, uttered an exclamation of horror, or terror, and, taking the two children by the hand, she rushed away, dragging them after her, while he went home and wept inconsolably.

Months passed without his seeing her again, but he suffered, day and night, for he was a prey to his paternal love. He would gladly have died, if he could only have kissed his son; he would have committed murder, performed any task, braved any danger, ventured anything. He wrote to her, but she did not reply, and, after writing her some twenty letters, he saw that there was no hope of altering her determination, and then he formed the desperate resolution of writing to her husband, being quite prepared to receive a bullet from a revolver, if need be. His letter only consisted of a few lines, as follows:

"*MONSIEUR: You must have a perfect horror of my name, but I am so wretched, so overcome by misery, that my only hope is in you, and,*

> *therefore, I venture to request you to grant me an interview of only five*
> *minutes.*
>
> *"I have the honor, etc."*

The next day he received the reply:

> *"MONSIEUR: I shall expect you to-morrow, Tuesday, at five o'clock."*

V

As he went up the staircase, Francois Tessier's heart beat so violently that he had to stop several times. There was a dull and violent thumping noise in his breast, as of some animal galloping; and he could breathe only with difficulty, and had to hold on to the banisters, in order not to fall.

He rang the bell on the third floor, and when a maidservant had opened the door, he asked: "Does Monsieur Flamel live here?" "Yes, Monsieur. Kindly come in."

He was shown into the drawing-room; he was alone, and waited, feeling bewildered, as in the midst of a catastrophe, until a door opened, and a man came in. He was tall, serious, and rather stout, and wore a black frock coat, and pointed to a chair with his hand. Francois Tessier sat down, and then said, with choking breath: "Monsieur—Monsieur—I do not know whether you know my name—whether you know—"

Monsieur Flamel interrupted him. "You need not tell it me, Monsieur, I know it. My wife has spoken to me about you." He spoke in the dignified tone of voice of a good man who wishes to be severe, and with the commonplace stateliness of an honorable man, and Francois Tessier continued: "Well, Monsieur, I want to say that: I am dying of grief, of remorse, of shame, and I would like once, only once to kiss—the child."

Monsieur Flamel got up and rang the bell, and when the servant came in, he said: "Will you bring Louis here." When she had gone out, they remained face to face, without speaking, as they had nothing more to say to one another, and waited. Then, suddenly, a little boy of ten rushed into the room, and ran up to the man whom he believed to be his father; but he stopped when he saw the stranger, and Monsieur

Flamel kissed him, and said: "Now, go and kiss that gentleman, my dear."
And the child went up to the stranger and looked at him.

Francois Tessier had risen. He let his hat fall, and was ready to fall
himself as he looked at his son, while Monsieur Flamel had turned away,
from a feeling of delicacy, and was looking out of the window.

The child waited in surprise, but he picked up the hat and gave it to
the stranger. Then Francois, taking the child up in his arms, began to kiss
him wildly all over his face; on his eyes, his cheeks, his mouth, his hair;
and the youngster, frightened at the shower of kisses, tried to avoid them,
turned away his head, and pushed away the man's face with his little
hands. But suddenly Francois Tessier put him down, and cried: "Good-
by! Good-by!" And he rushed out of the room as if he had been a thief.

*John Alexander Allen*
# Not an Elegy

By chance, over the angry years, I met
The father in the good physician twice
Before he died. In the day of the enemy,
The nation's gray disaster, like a prodigal
Patient bearing that disease, I came
To haunt him in his clinic, where the ill
Believed in miracles, and found the doctor,
Only in that moment, living alone,
Himself an invalid, and only then
Knew his poverty and knew my own.

Again, like strangers on the final evening,
We kept decorum in our ignorance;
I, as ever, stubbornly a ghost
In quest of an always missing person; he,
Matter-of-fact, admitting that his back
Was troubling him. I saw the doctor, rising,
Pit his disbelief against the fierce
Enemy; and only in that moment,
Only then, I took him into my care
And cured him homeward over the angry years.

*Louis Simpson*

# My Father in the Night Commanding No

My father in the night commanding No
Has work to do. Smoke issues from his lips;
      He reads in silence.
The frogs are croaking and the streetlamps glow.

And then my mother winds the gramophone;
The Bride of Lammermoor begins to shriek—
      Or reads a story
About a prince, a castle, and a dragon.

The moon is glimmering above the hill.
I stand before the gateposts of the King—
      So runs the story—
Of Thule, at midnight when the mice are still.

And I have been in Thule! It has come true—
The journey and the danger of the world,
      All that there is
To bear and to enjoy, endure and do.

Landscapes, seascapes . . . where have I been led?
The names of cities—Paris, Venice, Rome—
      Held out their arms.
A feathered god, seductive, went ahead.

Here is my house. Under a red rose tree
A child is swinging; another gravely plays.
      They are not surprised
That I am here; they were expecting me.

And yet my father sits and reads in silence,
My mother sheds a tear, the moon is still,
  And the dark wind
Is murmuring that nothing ever happens.

Beyond his jurisdiction as I move
Do I not prove him wrong? And yet, it's true
  They will not change
There, on the stage of terror and of love.

The actors in that playhouse always sit
In fixed positions—father, mother, child
  With painted eyes.
How sad it is to be a little puppet!

Their heads are wooden. And you once pretended
To understand them! Shake them as you will,
  They cannot speak.
Do what you will, the comedy is ended.

Father, why did you work? Why did you weep,
Mother? Was the story so important?
  "Listen!" the wind
Said to the children, and they fell asleep.

*Alan Cheuse*
# *from* Fall Out of Heaven

T he morning cold: early on a biting, windy November morning
filled with sunlight that lay on the skin like ice, the family piled
into the old Plymouth and drove into the city and parked on a side
street down which the wind rushed like water in a Western flash flood.
Off they marched to find Macy's Thanksgiving Day Parade. Within a few
minutes the two young brothers had spotted the giant helium balloons,
bears and moose and rabbits four stories high! Between the legs and
thighs of other onlookers they heard the marching bands and watched
the baton twirlers. Then Phil hoisted one and then the other onto his
shoulders—until he complained about their weight.

"Are you cold? Are you cold?" Tillie asked the boys over and over
again, but they did not tell her the truth since they were waiting for the
fabled Santa to appear on his sled.

"Are you cold?" Phil asked. "Listen to your mother. Tell the truth."

"They're cold," Tillie said over the raucous, blaring blast and wails
of the marching bands.

"They say no," Phil said for them.

"No-n-no!" said Alan.

"N-n-nooo," said the younger boy, echoing the older.

"You're cold," said their mother, but by that time the sled with the
white-bearded elf-man in red satin with white fringe came heaving into
view over the street-corner horizon.

"Santa!" shouted the older boy.

"S-s-s-anta!" echoed the younger.

"It's just a myth," said Phil. "I don't know why we waited in the cold
so long just to see a man in a costume."

"Don't tell them that," Tillie said.

"I just told them," Phil said, rubbing his hands against the icy air.
"They're smart boys, anyway. They know, they know," he said, his breath

coming out in great puffs of steam that rose up toward the streetlamps decked with green and wreaths. "Don't you, boys?"

"It's a myth," said Alan, watching the sled pass by and then turning his face to the nickel-cold coin of the sun.

"You're ruining it for them, Phil," Tillie said.

"Oh, Teel, ruining what?" The boy could see those incisors catching the light from that icelike orb up above. "They're Jews, what do they want to know from Santa Claus?" His voice brimmed over with derisiveness and disgust.

"I just wanted them to have a good time," said Tillie, her eyes turning liquid—which made at least one of the boys suddenly afraid that her eyes might freeze. But with a power he hadn't seen her use before she turned suddenly to his father and said, "Some Jew you are anyway."

With a few quick movements of her hands she turned and herded her boys away from the now rapidly disbanding crowd.

"Come on," she said. "Let's get out of the cold."

"Now what did you mean by that remark?" Phil asked as they walked along behind the children.

"Which remark?" Tillie asked.

"About my being a Jew."

"Well, you're not much of a Jew," she said.

"So, it's a myth, anyway," he said. "Santa Claus, the Jews, everything. Science shows that. This is the modern age, Teel. This . . ."

"Oh, Phil, please leave me alone."

They drove on for a while around the city, the parents silent, the boys gawking at the buildings, at the decorations that decked the streets full of shops. Around four o'clock Tillie began to ask if they were hungry. Yes, they were. Phil parked the car and they wandered through the midtown streets in search of a restaurant—only to find, everywhere they stopped, that all the tables had been reserved for the holiday meal.

Dark collapsed over them as though it were a balloon from which someone had pulled the plug.

"Let's go home, Phil," Tillie said.

"We're going to find a restaurant."

"I can fix something at home."

"Can we have turkey and stuffing at home?"

"You know we can't. You know that you told me you wanted to go to the parade and then eat out."

"You said the parade and the restaurant and I went along with it. That's what happened." He caught Alan's eye and made a movement with his head, something the boy had never seen before but the meaning of it was clear: the two of them against the mother.

"You agreed."

"Because I thought we could find a restaurant and now we can't."

"Let's go home," Tillie repeated.

"You have no turkey and the boys want turkey, don't you, boys?"

The boys nodded vigorously, they wanted turkey. They walked along together, Alan admiring his father's stubbornness and determination while at the same time wanting his mother to feel happier about the decision, as his brother clung to Tillie's coat sleeve and was buffeted by the argument like one of those balloons in high wind.

"I can fix something at home," Tillie said again.

"It's Thanksgiving," Phil said, "an American holiday, and we'll eat turkey."

"If it kills us," Tillie said.

It didn't, and it did. They wandered through the freezing streets for at least another half-hour, the sliver of sky between the high buildings above them turning dark blue, their fingers feeling like little stalks of icicles even within the confines of their mittens. Alan's stomach rumbled. Shel began to whimper.

"Shut that up," Phil said, "we'll find a place soon."

"Phil . . ."

"Teel . . ."

And just then they rounded yet another windy corner, the street-lights winked on, and they saw the festive, brightly illuminated storefront in the middle of the block. A restaurant! But what if it too was already filled to capacity with holiday diners? They rushed forward and entered the place. Success! There was a table waiting for them!

"Phil?"

"I can see, I have eyes," Phil said as he stared at the menu: vegetarian fare only. "Soybean turkey roast," he read from the listings. "That sounds interesting."

"What is it?" the boy asked.

"You'll find out," his father said.

"I don't want to," the boy said.

"You don't? Let me tell you a story. A man goes to the doctor and says, Doc, my upstairs neighbor keeps playing his radio day and night and it's driving me crazy. I want to go up there and throw it out the window. Do dot, the doctor tells him, Do dot."

Alan wasn't sure whether he was supposed to laugh at this story or listen carefully to hear more of it.

"What?" he said.

"Do dot," Phil said. "Do dot."

"Do what, Phil?" Tillie said.

"Oh, Teel," he said, "order the soybean turkey."

"But I don't want that," Tillie said, nearly in tears again.

"Order it," Phil said.

"Order it, Mommy," Shel said.

"You heard him," Phil said.

"Be quiet," Tillie said.

"Are you saying that to me?" Phil said.

"I'm saying that to all of you," Tillie said.

"I wasn't talking," Alan said.

"Be quiet," Tillie repeated.

"No, Teel, you be quiet," Phil said, slapping aside the menu.

"I want to go home," Shel said.

"Be quiet," Phil said.

"Don't talk to him like that," Tillie said.

"I'll talk to him," Phil said. "I'll talk to him any way I like."

"Not to them," Tillie said. "Maybe you talk that way to me but not to them."

"Who are they?" Phil said. "Are they a pair of princes? I want you to look at me. Teel? Teel?" He raised his hand in the air. "I want you to look at me," he said and brought his fist down on the plate before him with a crash, sending the other dishes and glasses and silverware flying across the table. Alan stared at the overturned water pitcher spilling liquid into his brother's lap, his brother the first one to cry.

*Theodore Roethke*
# My Papa's Waltz

The whiskey on your breath
Could make a small boy dizzy;
But I hung on like death:
Such waltzing was not easy.

We romped until the pans
Slid from the kitchen shelf;
My mother's countenance
Could not undrown itself.

The hand that held my wrist
Was battered on one knuckle;
At every step you missed
My right ear scraped a buckle.

You beat time on my head
With a palm caked hard by dirt,
Then waltzed me off to bed
Still clinging to your shirt.

*Richard Jones*
# Certain People

My father lives by the ocean
and drinks his morning coffee
in the full sun of his deck,
speaking to anyone
who walks by on the beach.
Afternoons he works
part-time at the golf course,
sailing the fairways like a sea captain
in a white golf cart.
My father must talk
to a hundred people a day,
yet we haven't spoken in weeks.
As I grow older, we hardly talk at all.
I wonder,
if I were a tourist on the beach
or a golfer lost in the woods
meeting him for the first time,
how his hand would feel in mine
as we introduced ourselves,
what we'd say to each other,
if we'd speak or if we'd *talk*,
and if, as sometimes happens
with certain people, I'd feel,
when I looked him in the eye,
I'd known him all my life.

# VII
# Great Loss

*Through weary life this lesson learn,*
*That man was made to mourn.*

Robert Burns

*Then, Time, let not a drop be spilt . . .*

Sidney Lanier

*Dylan Thomas*

# Do Not Go Gentle
# Into that Good Night

Do not go gentle into that good night,
Old age should burn and rave at close of day;
Rage, rage against the dying of the light.

Though wise men at their end know dark is right,
Because their words had forked no lightning they
Do not go gentle into that good night.

Good Men, the last wave by, crying how bright
Their frail deeds might have danced in a green bay,
Rage, rage against the dying of the light.

Wild men who caught and sang the sun in flight,
And learn, too late, they grieved it on its way,
Do not go gentle into that good night.

Grave men, near death, who see with blinding sight
Blind eyes could blaze like meteors and be gay,
Rage, rage against the dying of the light.

And you, my father, there on the sad height,
Curse, bless, me now with your fierce tears, I pray.
Do not go gentle into that good night.
Rage, rage against the dying of the light.

*Bill Henderson*

# Ceremonies

from   *His Son: A Child of the Fifties*

Mother and I sat at the kitchen table in Bryn Mawr and she told me about Pop's last night. With a Kleenex tucked in her dress pocket, she would tell the story over and over in the next few days.

Bob and I went to the barbershop to have my hair cut for the funeral.

It would be our first funeral. We didn't miss Pop as much as we imagined was appropriate. His death had become an embarrassment.

I remembered when Pop had asked Bob and me to help him trim the dead wood from the backyard trees. Dead wood only. Pop always refused to prune live wood because that would cause the trees to suffer. We protested that we had better things to do. But Pop insisted and produced his homemade pruning tool—a pair of clippers bolted to the end of a long pole and operated with a length of rope. It didn't work very well, and, bragging of my teenage strength, I said that I'd scramble up the trees and pluck out the dead limbs with my bare hands. But Pop kept poking at the trees, and we began to laugh at him, his two sons together. We left him in the yard alone. We walked away, laughing.

Bob and I left the barbershop and went home to dinner. Pop's chair sat empty at the end of the table. There were no other seats and I was still standing. Pop had sat in this chair since he was married. It was his, not mine.

But something was expected of me. A ceremony?

I sat down. "Is this where I sit now?" I attempted with a tight smile. An aunt glared at me. It had been a ceremony after all.

I lay on the den floor in front of the television set and watched for hours. I fell asleep and later woke to the dark house. I noticed that Mom's bedroom door was still open a crack as it always had been when we were children.

Whenever I woke I switched on the TV in order to sleep again. In the morning I watched children's cartoon shows. Others found comfort where they could.

Mom would tell her story of Pop's death. The guests would chatter about their children, grandchildren, and pets, and leave.

A typical sympathy card suggested "whatever thoughts sustain you in these moments I hope are with you."

"Wouldn't it be nice to imagine that Francis is with my mother now in heaven?" smiled twice-divorced Cousin Betty, the family scandal.

All the neighbors, friends, and relatives brought cakes, pies, and flowers. The house was filled with people eating and the scent of blossoms.

Nobody cried.

I drove the family to the church and we waited in a side room until the congregation had been seated in the chapel.

The minister arrived and took Mom's hand and said he was very sorry and shook hands with Bob, Ruth, and me before leaving for the altar.

As the door to the chapel closed behind him I noticed individuals sitting in the back by themselves, perhaps people Pop had worked with during his thirty-seven years at General Electric. Pop would have been abashed by their coming to honor him. He would have lowered his head and said "Aw."

He had been honored before, by the officials of the General Electric Company. They gave him a dinner, made speeches, handed him an inscribed wood and plastic plaque. Pop shoved the plaque in his bureau drawer under some underwear. Mom dug it out and hung it on the den wall. "For a quarter century of service to the company," it said over the signatures of Pop's boss and the president of GE.

I refused to view Pop's body and so did Bob and Ruth. To me it was just a body now.

But Mother went to say goodbye and covered him with a silk cloth. "I covered my father and mother and I will cover Daddy," she said.

When the casket was closed we assembled in the front pew. Behind us, Cousin Betty cried, "Francis, my baby. Francis."

The minister said a prayer. We sang a hymn. He said another prayer and read from Psalms. We left the casket for the undertaker's men, and lined up the cars for the trip to the cemetery.

At the cemetery, there were several funerals, at several striped tents. Pop's tent was green and white, and open on three sides.

We huddled next to the casket holding arms. I was determined that I wouldn't be the first to weep. I decided not to read my eulogy. This was Pop's funeral, his show not mine, and I would keep my mouth shut.

The minister seemed in a hurry. After a short prayer he read from Ecclesiastes. I knew the passage almost by heart. We had read it in high-school ceremonies because it was nondenominational, acceptable to Catholics, Jews, Protestants, and teenage atheists. "For everything there is a season, and a time for every matter under heaven: a time to be born, and a time to die . . ."

We left the coffin sitting on the electric jack and returned to the car.

I had let them bury Pop in a stock ceremony, like he was a stock character.

Nothing had been said of my Pop's renegade ideas like heaven and hell, and eternal life and the real Second Coming of Jesus. Unlike these Main Line Christians, he never doubted or equivocated. But we got rid of him, all of us, as if he were ordinary.

Back at the house, it was time to eat again. The mourners jammed the den and I couldn't get to the TV.

The tears slammed into me so hard and so suddenly that I didn't have time to escape. I hadn't cried for years, and didn't know what this was.

I ran upstairs, frantically looking for a hiding place. In the attic I sat on a rolled-up rug. "You know it all now, Pop. I thought I'd be such a hot shot telling you about Europe. But now you know it all. All there is to know."

My tears were a child's tears because his death had made me his child again.

*James Dickey*
# The Hospital Window

I have just come down from my father.
Higher and higher he lies
Above me in a blue light
Shed by a tinted window.
I drop through six white floors
And then step out onto pavement.

Still feeling my father ascend,
I start to cross the firm street,
My shoulder blades shining with all
The glass the huge building can raise.
Now I must turn round and face it,
And know his one pane from the others.

Each window possesses the sun
As though it burned there on a wick.
I wave, like a man catching fire.
All the deep-dyed windowpanes flash,
And, behind them, all the white rooms
They turn to the color of Heaven.

Ceremoniously, gravely, and weakly,
Dozens of pale hands are waving
Back, from inside their flames.
Yet one pure pane among these
Is the bright, erased blankness of nothing.
I know that my father is there,

In the shape of his death still living.
The traffic increases around me
Like a madness called down on my head.
The horns blast at me like shotguns,
And drivers lean out, driven crazy—
But now my propped-up father

Lifts his arm out of stillness at last.
The light from the window strikes me
And I turn as blue as a soul,
As the moment when I was born.
I am not afraid for my father—
Look! He is grinning; he is not

Afraid for my life, either
As the wild engines stand at my knees
Shredding their gears and roaring,
And I hold each car in its place
For miles, inciting its horn
To blow down the walls of the world

That the dying may float without fear
In the bold blue gaze of my father.
Slowly I move to the sidewalk
With my pin-tingling hand half dead
At the end of my bloodless arm.
I carry it off in amazement,

Higher, still higher, still waving,
My recognized face fully mortal,
Yet not; not at all, in the pale,
Drained, otherworldly, stricken,
Created hue of stained glass.
I have just come down from my father.

*Donald Hall*

# White Apples

when my father had been dead a week
I woke
with his voice in my ear

                             I sat up in bed
and held my breath
and stared at the pale closed door

white apples and the taste of stone

if he called again
I would put on my coat and galoshes

*W. S. Merwin*
# Strawberries

When my father died I saw        a narrow valley

it looked as though it began        across the river
from the landing where he was born      but there was no river

I was hoeing the sand        of a small vegetable plot
for my mother       in deepening twilight
and looked up in time       to see a farm wagon
dry and gray       horse already hidden
and no driver       going into the valley
carrying a casket

              and another wagon
coming out of the valley       behind a gray horse
with a boy driving       and a high load
of two kinds of berries       one of them strawberries

        that night when I slept       I dreamed of things
wrong in the house       all of them signs
the water of the shower       running brackish
and an insect of a kind       I had seen him kill
climbing around       the walls of his bathroom
        up in the morning       I stopped on the stairs
my mother was awake       already and asked me
if I wanted a shower       before breakfast
and for breakfast she said       we have strawberries

*Robert Gibb*

# Fox Grapes

I missed them last year.
My father traveling north as ashes,
my mind was on something other
than the light. Curved in its sides,
I think I might only have glimpsed
the hard lip of the chalice coming
my way, dribbling holy communion.
I'd have dwelled in the withered stems.
This year, the summer still with me,
I found them growing wild up the hill—
purple, dusky, dime-diametered grapes
clustered on the climbing vine.
Not cloudy like frost grapes,
nor as small.
The air was heavy with their scent.
Bees swung drunkenly around me
and doves drank that cool slide of music,
the tonic of their song.
And though I had been brooding on
darkness, the seed's slow suction
further into the fruit, I was kindled,
flashed through with a new ferment.
And so make of those grapes a sacrament,
saying *autumn, father,*
unclouding the wine of the heart.

*John Hall Wheelock*

# Together

*(In Memory of My Father)*

On the old garden-seat that fronts the grove
His hands had planted, years gone by,
At dusk I sat, remembering one I love—
We had sat there together often, he and I;
And were together now, although no word was said—
I looked away into the quiet air,
Knowing that if I did not turn my head
I still might have him there.

*Thomas Reiter*
# Handholds

After the long flow of things outward, on the last day of closing up the house, I went back into the basement. Pantry, furnace room, workshop—I found nothing. Then the swaying bulb drew shadows from something I had missed, toothed and moon-pale behind the workbench: a handsaw, balanced on one end and bent slightly upon itself, as though some gag musician had just left off playing. I steadied the bulb to plumb and went down to my knees. Behind that light I found another saw, lying in the seam of wall and floor. Those upright handles on their long blades, yes; I lifted out my father's crosscut saw. I felt a disappointment. I set the surprising mirror of the saw on the benchtop, where he once oiled and sharpened that spring steel before putting it up on hooks, safe and high. He hadn't spoken of tools or the workshop in his last letters, only cobalt and the tracking patterns drawn on his chest. No matter that the crosscut had gone out of sight in the dark and light of the basement, for I had discovered it and, to my surprise, it was moving between us again.

We resumed. "Don't push on the handle," he said. "Just pull." Father drew back the saw, doing all the work, as I leaned and followed the supple path of the instrument. The pear tree had come down, he said on the last visit before his death; yellowjackets got drunk on the windfall, then territorial.

He wanted to leave only a short stump, so we dropped to our knees and began work. Two-handed grip, a quick grooving through bark for the full stroke, then we took up the reaching rhythm that makes a crosscut work. Less than half its depth in, the gloss remaining from the whetstone, he made it flex and halt. Then he ran his scallop-shell thumb across the blade to assure me of the cause.

He asked if I remembered the gypsy moths, how I helped him hold a broomstick wrapped with kerosene rags to kindle their already bright tents, and enable us to save a precious tree. "That was the spring of '34,"

he said, not waiting for me to speak. He and his father had just been laid
off by the Milwaukee Railroad. They put away their tools of woodwork-
ing, the fine teeth and specialized edges with which they had finished
pullman cars until they took up crosscut, axe, and wedge for the W.P.A.,
and in a single day corded a dozen trees this size. *Yes*, I wanted to tell
him: *Those flaming webs of larvae are raining down again.*

When would we come through? I felt the handle's grain, darkly
stained, enter my palms. Then father stopped to blame the honing. From
time to time I'd push, buckling the blade, but he didn't seem surprised
and he didn't correct me. As I shifted my knee off of a surface root and
into a bed of moss, I saw my father, his head bowed; I remembered the
air raid blackout some 30 years ago.

My mind followed father's clomping footsteps into the solid ground
of the basement. Light from a passing car turned loose, danced on the
wall. I looked about: I wanted to save my father. Nineteen forty-three and
I crossed myself at the vigil candle he lit. On the kitchen wall I faced he
had taped up a newspaper cartoon: lights, bright as dogwood, caught in
the crosshairs of goggled mice. Those bombardiers, I knew, could lock
in on the Mississippi and ride its reflected moon to the munitions plant
if town lights gave them bearings. Our lights. Later, while my father
patrolled in his grey block warden's helmet, alert for any light that might
roll through with the fog, I rocketed angels from my rosary—all the
decades and mysteries I knew—sending up prayers like flak. Until the all
clear. "I thought I was helping you," I told him after thirty years. He
smiled and studied me easily but said nothing, then sure as memory,
brought us back cleanly, effortlessly, gracefully to a handhold.

*James Tate*
# The Lost Pilot

*For My Father, 1922–1944*


Your face did not rot
like the others—the co-pilot,
for example, I saw him

yesterday. His face is corn-
mush; his wife and daughter,
the poor ignorant people, stare

as if he will compose soon.
He was more wronged than Job.
But your face did not rot

like the others—it grew dark,
and hard like ebony;
the features progressed in their

distinction. If I could cajole
you to come back for an evening,
down from your compulsive

orbiting, I would touch you,
read your face as Dallas,
your hoodlum gunner, now,

with the blistered eyes, reads
his braille editions. I would
touch your face as a disinterested

scholar touches an original page.
However frightening, I would
discover you, and I would not

turn you in; I would not make
you face your wife, or Dallas,
or the co-pilot, Jim. You

could return to your crazy
orbiting, and I would not try
to fully understand what

it means to you. All I know
is this: when I see you,
as I have seen you at least

once every year of my life,
spin across the wilds of the sky
like a tiny, African god,

I feel dead. I feel as if I were
the residue of a stranger's life,
that I should pursue you.

My head cocked toward the sky,
I cannot get off the ground,
and, you, passing over again,

fast, perfect, and unwilling
to tell me that you are doing
well, or that it was mistake

that placed you in that world,
and me in this; or that misfortune
placed these worlds in us.

Keith Orchard
# A Bigger Boy Remembers

The grey Gothic cathedral was crowded, standing room only for the funeral. Hundreds of civilians merged down the aisles and into the pews. Uniformed law enforcement officers from the city, county, state stood in formation on the sides and around the front. The sight of all this should have made a small boy pause in wonder. There, Americans in their blue and dark blue, stood out against the contingent of Canadian mounties dressed in red, who had also come to pay their respects to a man whom most didn't even know. I thought of a royal wedding. I could hear the media—reporters and photographers peeking, protruding, and jockeying about in strategic locations, hoping to catch all the angles and not miss anything. It was the death of a policeman. It was the death of my father.

I stood there with all that before me. I couldn't cry. I wanted to, and I tried, but I couldn't. I promise, I couldn't. I was trying to cry because I thought it was the right thing to do. No one said, "You didn't cry," and I didn't tell anyone about it except my best friend, until now, as I write this.

My father was being buried that day and I couldn't cry! Looking back, maybe people thought I was being a brave little trooper. I wasn't being brave. I just didn't feel much emotion over the death of my father. I felt bad for that; down inside I felt guilty. I mean, what kind of son does not feel terrible about losing his father? What kind of son cannot cry?

My father and I were never very close. By close, I mean we never became friends. I didn't know that fourteen-year-old boys were supposed to be friends with their father. I grew to spend most of my childhood afraid of my father and his temper. Though he was a loving and fun dad at times, when he entered the house a silence knotted the place. It even rounded corners where a child would hide. In fact, the whole family walked softly in order not to make him angry—in order to keep the silence.

A few years after my parents got divorced, however, I noticed a change had come over my dad. He was happier and more patient. His physical presence changed too. He quit smoking. He was taking care. A thirty-eight-year-old man could change for the better. Maybe that paved the way for improved self-concept, maybe not, but he and I actually started to get along a little. I wouldn't say it was perfect, but there was a will to change, readable on his strong face.

I wasn't old enough to realize that my dad had a life too, that before he died he had dreams. (I have just come to that.) At that time he was finding himself. He bought property in the country and wanted to make a house. He developed more disciplined eating habits and reduced his slight paunch. The lines of his uniform unbent and aligned. Indeed the horizon was opening, and then it snapped closed.

My Dad's death happened while staking out two men involved in an illegal arms sale. When he approached the car and got near, they shot and killed him. They escaped for a short time and were captured, sentenced to life after an interminably long trial, and I was left without him.

At the time of my dad's death, I didn't think his loss would affect my life very much. I guess that's why I sit now remembering the funeral, the shuffle of the police, the stiff corners to their turns. I guess I figured since I only saw my father on every other weekend and I never really relied on him for support or advice, it wouldn't matter. I was wrong. How wrong!

It is now that I'm a little older, and more mature and experienced, that I understand what I have missed out on. There are, of course, the obvious things, such as learning how to hunt or fish or work on cars. My dad liked these things and I cannot do them. I also missed out on the opportunity to truly please my dad. Since he died, I have accomplished some good things. Some people say that I have, anyway. I was valedictorian in high school and I got to give the valedictory speech at graduation. In my valedictory speech, I wished my grandmother a happy birthday; it made Grandmother cry. It might have made my father cry. It might have even caused him to say he was proud of me. I felt sad to think that I couldn't remember graduation with Dad, side by side in the receiving line, beaming and light-hearted.

As I try to access my memories, there's no denying I'm my dad's son. He was six foot two with big shoulders and very green eyes—like me. The same laugh lines etch the corner of my eyes. A track athlete, my father would have loved to see me play my sport in college basketball. I played for Whitman College, a twelve hundred-student, Division 3 school. I averaged eighteen points a game on slashing drives to the basket and long, quick release jumpers. I even made All-Conference.

I remember one time I went to see *Field of Dreams* with my best buddy. We sat there camouflaged in the dark and in the quiet. There is this scene where Kevin Costner is able to say everything he needed to say to his dad by asking him to play catch. Costner gets a second chance to say, "I'm sorry and I love you." After all those years he gets his say.

I came to this with my buddy and we were swept away with the scene. After all these years I wanted my say. We were sitting next to one another and he was right next to his father—who is an aloof man, who didn't do things like that with his son. And my dad was dead. I gripped my buddy's hand tightly and tears rolled down our unmeasured faces. I wouldn't have believed it when my father was here, but somebody recently told me that he cried in movies, too. It doesn't matter, I suppose, that they couldn't name the movie or movies where they saw him cry.

I guess I am lucky that I have come to understand him over the years. Now and then I still feel the guilt from the funeral, but I do feel better about myself. The past dredges itself up one way or another and it has with me, in spades. Today, my father is here in my mind and heart. Today I have a relationship with my father.

In case you think this is my imagination doffing a hat only to cover an eternal sadness, think again. There are times when I spend quality times—a sunny afternoon or balmy evening or lonesome night—with Dad. I talk to him and miss him, and sometimes even cry for him. I show off. I pull up, leap in the air, and loft a shot for him. I finger-roll the ball against the glass and kiss takes on new meaning—all for him.

It's nice to be close to him. But it's also hard to think that I am closer to him now than I ever was when he was alive. I'm asking with my heart for him to come back at this moment—and he does.

*Pablo Neruda*
# Father

The brusque father comes back
from his trains:
we could pick out
his train whistle
cutting the rain,
a locomotive's
nocturnal lament
an unplaceable howl
in the dark.
Later,
the door started trembling.
Wind entered
in gusts with my father;
and between the two advents, footfalls and tensions,
the house
staggered,
a panic of doorways
exploded with a dry
sound of pistols,
stairs groaned
and a shrill voice
nagged hatefully on
in the turbulent
dark. Rain
flooded the roof tops,
the world drowned
by degrees, there
was only the wind's sound
trading blows with the rain.

Still, he was punctual.
Commanding his train in the freeze of the morning,
the sun barely
aloft in the sky, he was there with his beard
and his green and red
signal flags, lanterns ready,
the engine-coal blazing like hellfire,
the Station House showing coach after coach through the fog—
to settle his debt with geography.

Railroader, land-sailor
touching ports with no seacoasts
—whistle stops in the woods—the train races on
brakeless as nature
in its terrestrial voyage.
Not till it rests all
its length of the rails and friends greet
and come in, do the doors of my infancy open:
the table is shaken again
by a railroader's fist
knocking thick glass together, a brotherhood
glowing,
flashing sparks
from the eyes in the wine.

Poor, durable father,
there on the axle of life,
virile in friendships, your cup overflowing:
the whole of your life was a headlong militia;
between daybreaks and roadbeds,
comings and goings, you lived on the double.
Then, on the rainiest day of them all,
the conductor, José del Carmen Reyes,
boarded his death train and has not come back to us since.

*William Shakespeare*

# Full Fathom Five
# Thy Father Lies

*(The Tempest I, ii)*

Full fathom five thy father lies;
  Of his bones are coral made;
Those are pearls that were his eyes:
  Nothing of him that doth fade,
But doth suffer a sea-change
Into something rich and strange.
Sea-nymphs hourly ring his knell:
  Ding-dong.
Hark! now I hear them—Ding-dong bell.

*Ben Jonson*

# On My First Son

Farewell, thou child of my right hand, and joy;
  My sin was too much hope of thee, loved boy.
Seven years thou wert lent to me, and I thee pay,
  Exacted by thy fate, on the just day.
O, could I lose all father, now! For why
  Will man lament the state he should envy?
To have so soon 'scaped world's and flesh's rage,
  And, if no other misery, yet age!
Rest in soft peace; and, asked, say: Here doth lie
  Ben Jonson his best piece of poetry—
For whose sake, henceforth, all his vows be such,
  As what he loves may never like too much.

*W. S. Merwin*
# Yesterday

My friend says I was not a good son
you understand
I say yes I understand

he says I did not go
to see my parents very often you know
and I say yes I know

even when I was living in the same city he says
maybe I would go there once
a month or maybe even less
I say oh yes

he says the last time I went to see my father
I say the last time I saw my father

he says the last time I saw my father
he was asking me about my life
how I was making out and he
went into the next room
to get something to give me

oh I say
feeling again the cold
of my father's hand the last time

he says and my father turned
in the doorway and saw me
look at my wristwatch and he
said you know I would like you to stay
and talk with me

oh yes I say

but if you are busy he said
I don't want you to feel that you
have to
just because I'm here

I say nothing

he says my father
said maybe
you have important work you are doing
or maybe you should be seeing
somebody I don't want to keep you

I look out the window
my friend is older than I am
he says and I told my father it was so
and I got up and left him then
you know

though there was nowhere I had to go
and nothing I had to do

*George Garrett*
# Abraham's Knife

Where hills are hard and bare,
rocks like thrown dice, heat
and glare that's clean and pitiless,
a shadow dogs my heels, limp
as a drowned man washed ashore.
True sacrifice is secret, none
to applaud the ceremony, nor
writers to be moved to tears.
No one to see. God alone
knows, whose great eye winks not,
from whom no secrets are hid.

My father, I have loved you,
loved you now, dead twenty years.
Your ghost shadows me home.
Your laughter and your anger still
trouble my scarecrow head like wings.
My own children, sons and daughters,
study my stranger's face. Their flesh,
bones frail as a small bird's,
is strange, too, in my hands.
What will become of us,
I read my murder in their eyes.

And you, old father, Abraham,
my judge and executioner, I pray
bear witness for me now. I ask
a measure of your faith. Forgive
us, Jew and gentile, all
your children, all your victims.

In the naked country of no shadow
you raise your hand in shining arc.
And we are fountains of foolish tears
to flood and green the world again.
Strike for my heart. Your blade is light.

*Greg Kuzma*
# Funeral Poem for My Father

I have one hammer. It is somewhere.
My other one, made in China I think,
with a black rubber handle
I loaned my daughter for her new
apartment. The rule is—when you
don't know how to use things, give them
away. She doesn't know how
to fix things either. She and her
roommates have a kitten. It is a joy
to hold it, and to play with it.
Its favorite thing is crumpled
paper on the floor, balled up and
rolled. With crumpled paper and
a kitten we can play all day,
and go to bed tired at night, tired
and fulfilled. Let the house fall in
around us, let the roof fall in,
our hammer is missing or we can't
find it. I think I saw it
on the porch, or it was in the
drawer last week, last year.
Where did I see it last? Or
in a dream? I don't know how
to fix things. All I know is how
to break them, or wear them out.
My pleasure is to wear my shoes
right down to the threads, and
then, when they're exhausted,
let them rest. My father's
pleasure was a different thing.

Equipped with every kind of tool,
he waited for the world to break,
He knew it would. He had seen it
before. He had buried a son.
Friends would come from here and
there, as they have come today,
and ask of Harry for his expertise.
Mike told me—or was it Sue?—
you could always rely on Harry—
just bring him your problem—
give him time—and he would
have an answer. Toward the end
he liked being so treated.
Don't we all like being relied on—
somebody with an answer—
amidst the million questions of
our lives. Can it be bolted?
he would ask, and answer. Can it be
tapped or threaded? Can it be filed down
if it is too big, or hardened
if it is too soft. We are all
too soft, I guess, in need of
proper tempering in the furnace
of life. Put a wire on the back
and we can hang it on the wall,
and look at it. We have a picture!
Check to see by scraping with a
penknife through layers and layers
of paint—to see what sort of wood
it is, and if it is cherry, like this
casket here, or pine, the way we
used to bury men on the frontier—
mountain men—whose stories my
father knew—if it was wood like
that, but not oak!—he did not
quite approve of oak—presto
in six months or maybe in a

jiffy of a year—we'd have
a piece of furniture—a night
stand or a dresser or commode—
standing startled in its own raw
wood, bright beneath a window sill.
My father knew how to do things—
he knew things, and how to do things,
in order that I could idle myself
and worry endlessly on how to say things.
His house is full of things
done, but not done with. Touched
into life, where the hand passing
over the wood over and over
discloses and brings out the grain—
so that you look at it and it offers
itself as it is, without disguises.
So a tree lived and grew and stretched
to grow in the light, which now
encloses my father's socks, safe
in a drawer.
And which will serve
my feet, now his socks are mine.
So have his tools passed to me.
More hammers than I have ever
seen, except in a store. A dozen
different shapes. All manner of
handle and head. For tapping, for
nudging, for setting, for pounding
nails, for pulling out the ones I
can't pound straight. Can there be
so many jobs to do, I ask, so many which
might be done exactly right, precisely,
the way he knows. So many things
that need to be persuaded. Now these
hammers fall into my hands. The rule
is—the tools set down by those
who know their use fall always

to those less competent. Just as
the rule seems to be that all this
steel that lasts forever would mock
our lives for being so brief. I
know that I will never know
the things he knew. I know
that I can never live long
enough to know the
secrets kept by the metal,
or held in the grain of the
wood, disclosed as it is
by his hand, revealed in his
eye. Father, your work is
done. We will all pick up
where you leave off, the
fisherman to fish, my son
to carry your rod and
reel, or bang his knuckles
on a bolt fixing his car with
your wrench. The poets
to write. My daughter sits
at the table in your house
tonight as I write this,
and writes her poems. My
wife consults the undercarriage
of a chair to see how you
joined fabric to wood, and
how your placed your tacks,
and plans how she will keep
your memory.

*Geoffrey Wolff*
*from* The Duke of Deception

*Geoffrey Wolff writes compellingly in his autobiographical book,* The Duke of
Deception, *about his life and relationship with his father who was a con-man and
petty criminal. In the following Wolff commiserates with his wife's grandmother Kay
over her husband's death by suicide and likewise she over his father's death.*

The morning with Kay changed me. She spoke of her dead husband
and I told of my dead father; we traded scandal for scandal, and
soon we were laughing. I told how my father despised prudence,
savings accounts, the *idea* of savings accounts, the *fact* of savings accounts, looks before leaps. Yes, her husband too, hobbling along the
itching deck of a sailboat he had chartered to sail solo before he taught
himself to sail. It had been fun to be her husband's wife, and my father's
son. This was important to understand.

Kay led me through my father's history, let me begin to apprehend
him as a critic of the conventions, a man who caricatured what he
despised. *Is it Yale men you like? Okay, I'm a Yale man, see how easy it is?
Nothing to it but will and nerve.* My friend led me to understand how lucky
I was to be free, that there was a benign side to my father's dishonor, that
I had never had to explain or apologize to him any more than he had had
to explain or apologize to me. Much of this, of course, was casuistry. I
don't believe now that my father was truly a critic of society, or that his
life was any more happy than it was defiant.

Never mind. I had come into that night alienated. I was becoming
handy with repudiations of every kind, and learning to nurture anger
solicitously. I had felt betrayed by my father, and wanted to betray him.
Kay turned my course. She had the authority of someone who had passed
through the worst of fires. I listened to her. I saw again what I had seen
when I was a child, in love with my father as no one else. He had never
repudiated me or seen in my face intimations of his own mortality. He
had never let me think he wished to be rid of me or the burden of my

judgment, even when I had hounded him about his history, had quibbled with its details like a small-print artist, like a reviewer, for God's sake! He didn't try to form me in his own image. How could he? Which image to choose? He had wanted me to be happier than he had been, to do better. He had taught me many things, some of which were important, some of which he meant, some of which were true. The things he told me were the right thing to tell a son, usually, and by the time I understood their source in mendacity they had done what good they could. I had been estranged from my father by my apprehension of other people's opinions of him, and by a compulsion to be free of his chaos and destructions. I had forgotten I loved him, mostly, and mostly now I missed him. I miss him.

When I finally left Kay's house I felt these things, some for the first time. I drove home slowly, and stopped at stop signs. The door to the room I shared with Priscilla was open when I came in, but I didn't go through that door that night. I went to my children's room. I stood above Justin, looking down at him. And then my son Nicholas began to moan, quietly at first. They did not know their grandfather was dead; they knew nothing about their grandfather. There would be time for that. I resolved to tell them what I could, and hoped they would want to know as much as I could tell. Nicholas cried out in his sleep, as he had so many times before, dragging me out of nightmares about his death with his own nightmares about his death, his dreams of cats with broken legs, broken-winged screaming birds, deer caught in traps, little boys hurt and crying, beyond the range of their parents' hearing. Sometimes I dreamt of my son bleeding to death from some simple wound I had neglected to learn to mend.

Now I smoothed his forehead as my father had smoothed mine when I was feverish. Justin breathed deeply. I crawled in bed beside my sweet Nicholas and took him in my arms and began to rock him in time to Justin's regular breaths. I stunk of whiskey and there was blood on my face from a fall leaving Kay's house, but I knew I couldn't frighten my son. He ceased moaning, and I rocked him in my arms till light came down on us, and he stirred awake in my arms as I, in his, fell into a sleep free of dreams.

*Paul Zimmer*

# The Persistence of Fatherhood

Yesterday the autumn finished.
I began raking it into piles
Around the house. Sue came out
And called from the distance.
I cupped my ears but could not hear
Through bare winds and branches rattling.

I thought she said,
"Your father's on the phone,"
And started walking toward
The house, until I remembered
He's been dead for five years.

Then last night this dream:
Suddenly leaves were children's clothing,
Blue jeans, caps and flannel shirts.
I raked them up, bent over by sadness,
Fatherhood all used up and gone,
Playthings and storytimes gone,
I swept and piled, doing my duties,
Only this caretaking left to do.

*Miller Williams*
# Vision in Black and White

leaning back in a Naugahyde
covered recliner
reading proofs

I flash on my father stepping carefully
in hightop shoes
in nineteen hundred and twelve

across a road
all wagon tracks and mud
alive in the sun

to someone waiting on the other side
I think a woman

I give my attention to him
and the image breaks
I go back to my proofs
and he starts across again

The problem is not to notice
The problem is to let him go

# VIII
# Conversations

*Do not flee conversation, nor let your door always be shut.*

Ovid

*Gary Gildner*
# Prayer for My Father

That gleaming boat they took the time and grief
to christen with carnations and the shakes
of holy water,
let it go.
And let the pain go with it.
Let it stay down there below the roots intact,
a tribute to the undertaker.
Let him join it.
And let my father stand
as in this photograph—
planted to his hips in current, holding up a bucketful of smelt
and beaming, as if any second he might fly!

Let him fly—
and let that blur, a child's hand that fluttered into view
when he looked up,
fly with him.

*Raymond Carver*

# Photograph of My Father in His Twenty-second Year

*October.* Here in this dank, unfamiliar kitchen
I study my father's embarrassed young man's face.
Sheepish grin, he holds in one hand a string
Of spiny yellow perch, in the other
A bottle of Carlsbad beer.

In jeans and denim shirt, he leans
Against the front fender of a Ford *circa* 1934.
He would like to pose bluff and hearty for his posterity,
Wear his old hat cocked over his ear, stick out his tongue . . .
All his life my father wanted to be bold.

But the eyes gave him away, and the hands
That limply offer a string of dead perch
And the bottle of beer. Father, I loved you,
Yet how can I say thank you, I who cannot hold my liquor either
And do not even know the places to fish?

*Brewster Ghiselin*

# For My Children
# and Their Children

Vikings blown from the mist and the smokey spume of the sea
Nine centuries past,
The oak of their black boats hard with ocean salt,
Rounding the river reaches inland
To burn and to build:
On the Lys, Busbecq—of Flanders and France.

Six hundred years:
Knights and burghers, seigneurs, and one a saint,
One a musician,
Master of countersong, shaper
Of madrigal, mass, motet,
Of the North and the court of Ferra,
One an ambassador,
Man of tongues,
Bringer out of the East of tidings and tokens,
Peace and its bloom,
Green of antiquity lifted up from the dust,
A flowering tree,
Coin and codex and flower,
Tulip to astonish and craze the west
And lilac to scent the world.

Six hundred years—and then—
The long flight north to the freedom of God,
And west:
The worker in silver and gold that crossed from England,
Artist and founder, father of artificers,
Men of the land and shores—
Philadelphia, Annapolis, Norfolk;

The Captain fighting long to unking;
The diver from the high rigging of ships in Hampton Roads,
Deaf in his old age from the smash and press of waters,
He whose horse pistol, ironblue, tooled and balanced for use,
Lay after use in war, honor and loss,
In my childhood, beautifully useless
Pointing toward his death, beyond us all.

To the white mist and deep of the ocean past
And the mist before us that ravels and clears and moves
Away and away
As we move.

*Norman Hindley*
# Wood Butcher
*(for my father)*


After the Navy and war,
You drafted big prints and started a summer house
In Bay Springs. I was your helper, and that first year
We worked weekends through most of the winter,
The wind, your cold immaculate tools, the hole
In the floor of the Ford we traveled in . . .
I hated it all. Especially my carpentry. I ruined doors,
My tape never returned,
I couldn't saw for shit. "Measure twice, cut once."
You said it a hundred times.
I tried everything to please you,
You my ex-flyboy, the perfectionist.
Even your smile was mitered. You hands cool and silky
On the tools, brown as the lining
Of your flight jacket. Mine were white,
Mitts of a wood butcher.
You never said that,
But when you came across the scarred paneling,
The wrong nail, the split grain,
Doughnut grease on the new glass,
I'd watch your eyes, the drained bluebirds
That flew your face.
I fucked some screens up once,
Wrinkles, wavy frames;
You broke them out with a chair.
My best day I spent hauling dry wall,
Holding while you fitted and tacked.
For years I would devote myself
To carrying and fetching.

Strong, good with mortar, but squirrely,
A world class gofer.

I want you to know
That today I finished a boat, designed it,
22 feet, foredeck, wheel,
A transom you could hang a Pratt & Whitney on.
But none of this is a way of speaking, a tongue
Saying I still want to please you,
That it's your disappointment that drives me.

*Howard Moss*
# Elegy for My Father

Father, whom I murdered every night but one,
That one, when your death murdered me,
Your body waits within the wasting sod.
Clutching at the straw-face of your God,
Do you remember me, your morbid son,
Curled in a death, all motive unbegun,
Continuum of flesh, who never thought to be
The mourning mirror of your potency?

All you had battled for the nightmare took
Away, as dropping from your eyes, the sea-
Salt tears, with messages that none could read,
Impotent, pellucid, were the final seeds
You sowed. Above you, the white night nurse shook
His head, and, moaning on the moods of luck,
We knew the double-dealing enemy:
From pain you suffered, pain had set you free.

Down from the ceiling, father, circles came:
Angels, perhaps, to bear your soul away.
But tasting the persisting salt of pain,
I think my tears created them, though, in vain,
Like yours, they fell. All losses link: the same
Creature marred us both to stake his claim.
Shutting my eyelids, barring night and day,
I saw, and see, your body borne away.

Two months dead, I wrestle with your name
Whose separate letters make a paltry sum
That is not you. If still you harbor mine,

Think of the house we had in the summertime
When in the sea-light every early game
Was played with love and, if death's waters came,
You'd rescue me. How I would take you from,
Now, if I could, its whirling vacuum.

*Philip Levine*
# 1933

My father entered the kingdom of roots
    his head as still as a stone
    (Laid out in black with a white tie
    he blinked
    and told no one
    except himself over and over)
    laid out long and gray

The hands that stroked my head
    the voice in the dark asking
    he drove the car all the way to the river
        where the ships burned
    he rang with keys and coins
    he knew the animals and their names
        touched the nose of the horse
        and kicked the German dog away
he brought Ray Estrada from Mexico in his 16th year
    scolded him like a boy, gave him beer money
    and commanded him to lift and push
he answered to the name father
he left in October without his hat
who my mother later said was not much at love
who answered to the name Father

Father, the world is different in many places
    the old Ford Trimotors are gone to scrap
    the Terraplane turned to snow
    four armies passed over your birthplace
        your house is gone
        all your tall sisters gone

> your fathers
> everyone
Roosevelt ran again
you would still be afraid

You would not know me now, I have a son taller than you
> I feel the first night winds catch in the almond
>> the plum bend
>> and I go in afraid of the death you are
> I climb the tree in the vacant lot
>> and leave the fruit untasted
>> I stare at the secrets, the small new breasts
>> this sparse muff where no one lives
> I blink the cold winds in from the sea
>> walking with Teddy, my little one
>> squeezing his hand I feel his death
> I find a glacier and wash my face in Arctic dust
> I shit handfuls of earth
> I stand in the spring river pissing at stars
> I see the diamondback at the end of the path
>> hissing and rattling
>> and will not shoot

The sun is gone, the moon is a slice of hope
> the stars are burned eyes that see
> the wind is the breath of the ocean
> the death of the fish is the allegory
>> you slice it open and spill the entrails
>> you remove the spine
>> the architecture of the breast
>> you slap it home
>> the oils snap and sizzle
>> you live in the world
> you eat all the unknown deeps
> the great sea oaks rise from the floor
> the bears dip their paws in clear streams
>> they hug their great matted coats

and laugh in the voices of girls
a man drops slowly like brandy or glue

In the cities of the world
    the streets darken with flies
    all the dead fathers fall out of heaven
        and begin again
    the angel of creation is a sparrow in the roadway
    a million ducks out of Ecuador with the names of cities
        settle on the wires
    storks rise slowly pulling the house after them
    butterflies eat away at the eyes of the sun
    the last ashes off the fire of the brain
    the last leavening of snow
    grains of dirt torn from under fingernails and eyes
    you drink these

There is the last darkness burning itself to death
    there are nine women come in the dawn with pitchers
    there is my mother
        a dark child in the schoolyard
        miles from anyone
        she has begun to bleed as her mother did
    there is my brother, the first born, the mild one
        his cold breath fogging the bombsight
    there is the other in his LTD
        he talks to the phone, he strokes his thighs
        he dismisses me
    my mother waits for the horsecart to pass
    my mother prays to become fat and wise
        she becomes fat and wise
    the cat dies and it rains
    the dog groans by the side door
    the old hen flies up in a spasm of gold

My woman gets out of bed in the dark and washes her face
    she goes to the kitchen before we waken

she picks up a skillet, an egg
(I dream:
a man sets out in an inner-tube to Paris
coming back from dying "the ride aint bad a tall")
the kids go off to school without socks
in the rain the worms come out to live
my father opens the telegram under the moon
     Cousin Philip is dead
       my father stands on the porch in his last summer
       he holds back his tears
       he holds back his tears


Once in childhood the stars held still all night
       the moon swelled like a plum but white and silken
       the last train from Chicago howled through the ghetto
       I came downstairs
       my father sat writing in a great black book
       a pile of letters
       a pile of checks
       (he would pay his debts)
       the moon would die
       the stars jelly
       the sea freeze
       I would be a boy in worn shoes splashing through rain

*James J. McAuley*
# The Shirt

From a drawer somewhere upstairs I stole
A shirt of my father's and got past the kitchen
Into the garden without being stopped.
The big white shirt of heavy cotton
Covered my knees when I put it on
Over my head, over my clothes, as I'd seen
The priest through the sacristy door one time
Getting ready for Mass. I lifted my arms
The way he lifted the chalice for consecration,
And the sleeves fell back to my elbows; raised
The right hand in blessing, and genuflected.

A backless chair thrown out of the kitchen
Against the wall that brought the sky
Down to the apple-trees and the hen-run:
This was my altar. A leaf for the Host,
A jar for the Chalice; a mumbled offering,
And Mass was over. All that holiness I carried
Between my steepled fingers back into the house.
The maid and my mother in the flagstone kitchen
Laughed and scolded and laughed, could not be cross
Though my father's one good shirt was stained,
And he needed it for work; and shirts
That good were hard to get with a war on.

Fifty years later, I'm convinced I said
A true Mass by the old wall,
The crumbling mortar, the grey stones,
The broken chair seat weathered grey,
The apple-boughs breaking into bud.

Yet even in priestly prayer, I knew
It was my father's fine white shirt I wore.
Child, when you have a mind to raise your hand
To bless the transubstantiated world,
Take anything of mine you need to change
Body and blood to spirit, yet keep its beloved form.

*Sir Walter Raleigh*

# To His Son

Three things there be that prosper up apace
And flourish, whilst they grow asunder far,
But on a day, they meet all in one place,
And when they meet, they one another mar;
And they be these: the wood, the weed, the wag.
The wood is that which makes the gallow tree;
The weed is that which strings the hangman's bag;
The wag, my pretty knave, betokeneth thee.
Mark well, my boy, whilst these assemble not,
Green springs the tree, hemp grows, the wag is wild,
But when they meet, it makes the timber rot;
It frets the halter, and it chokes the child.
Then bless thee, and beware, and let us pray
We part not with thee at this meeting day.

Paul Zimmer
# The Ritual

As my father had done with me,
Once when my infant son
Woke crying from his sleep,
I carried him out to the yard
To show him the full moon
Rising branch by branch through
The trees, a vision strong enough
To settle him.
          "Moon!" I said,
"Moon!"
          He was dazzled,
Struggled with the word until
He croaked, "Moo, moo!"

Next day when I came home
From work I went to his crib.
He was playing with his toes,
Brightened when he saw me.
"Moo!" he said, the memory
Rising behind his eyes, "Moo!"
Our first secret together,
An ancient confidence he has kept
To share now with his own son.

*for Aaron Paul Zimmer*
*May 14, 1987*

Richard Shelton
# Letting Go

you walk down the road
my young and only son
as if everything
were there for your pleasure
and you are right

you pause to touch a tree
and say *alligator juniper*
and again you are right

why should I be surprised
that you have learned
what I have forgotten
and more than I ever knew

my tall bright son
nothing I can do now
will alter the length
of your shadow
as you leave the desert
which has been your home

when you look back
the moon will set
over your shoulder
and the sun will rise
each morning to meet you

turn then
turn away and walk on
nothing I can give you
will forestall
the moment of your death
nor determine how long
how much you will suffer
between this point of light
and that point of light

you have learned
to accept your life
as if it were music
played with great skill
and would last forever
and you are right again
my son my only son
it will last long enough

*Robert Olen Butler*

# In the Clearing

T hough I have never seen you, my son, do not think that I am unable to love you. You were in your mother's womb when the North of our country took over the South and some of those who fought the war found themselves running away. I did not choose to run, not with you ready to enter this world. I did not choose to leave my homeland and become an American. I have chosen so few of the things of my life, really. I was eighteen when Saigon was falling and you were dreaming on in your little sea inside your mother in the thatched house in An Khe. Your mother loved me then and I loved her and I would not have left except I had no choice. This has always been a strange thing to me, though I have met several others here where I live in New Orleans, Louisiana, who are in the same condition. It is strange because I know how desperately many others wanted to get out, even hiding in the landing gears of the departing airplanes. I myself had not thought of running away, did not choose to, but it happened to me anyway.

I am sorry. And I write you now not to distract you from your duty to your new father, as I am sure your mother would fear. I write with a full heart for you because I must tell you a few things about being a person who is somewhere between a boy and a man. I was just such a person when I held a rifle in my hands. It was a black thing, the M16 rifle, black like a charcoal cricket, and surprisingly light, with a terrible voice, a terrible quick voice like the river demons my own father told stories about when it was dark and nighttime in our village and I wanted to be frightened.

That is one thing I must tell you. As a boy you wish to be frightened. You like the night; you like the quickness inside you as you and your friends speak of mysterious things, ghosts and spirits, and you wish to go out into the dark and go as far down the forest path as you can without turning back. You and your friends go down the path together and no one dares to say that you have gone too far even though you hear every

tiny sound from the darkness around you and these sounds make you
quake inside. Am I right about this? I dream of you often and I can see
you in this way with your friends and it is the same as it was with me
and my friends.

This is all right, to embrace the things you fear. It is natural and it
will help build the courage you must have as a man. But when you are
a man, don't become confused. Do not seek out the darkness, the things
you fear, as you have done as a boy. This is not a part of you that you
should hold on to. I myself did not hold on to it for more than a few
minutes once the rifle in my hand heard the cries of other rifles calling
it. I no longer dream of those few minutes. I dream only of you.

I cannot remember clearly now any of the specific moments of my
real fear, of my man's fear with no delight in it at all, no happiness, no
sense of power or of my really deep down controlling it, of being able
to turn back with my friends and walk out of the forest. I can only
remember a wide rice paddy and the air leaning against me like a
drunken man who says he knows me and I remember my boots full of
water and always my thought to check to see if I was wrong, if there was
really blood in my boots, if I had somehow stepped on a mine and been
too scared to even realize it and I was walking with my boots filled with
blood. But this memory is the sum of many moments like these. All the
particular rice paddies and tarmac highways and hacked jungle paths—
the exact, specific ones—are gone from me.

Only this remains. A clearing in a triple-canopy mahogany forest in
the highlands. The trees were almost a perfect circle around us and in the
center of the clearing was a large tree that had been down for a long time.
We were a patrol and we were sitting in a row against the dead trunk,
our legs stuck out flat or tucked up to our chests. We were all young and
none of us knew what he was doing. Maybe we were stupid for stopping
where we did. I don't know about that.

But our lieutenant let us do it. He was sitting on the tree trunk, his
elbows on his knees, leaning forward smoking a cigarette. He was right
next to me and I knew he wanted to be somewhere else. He was pretty
new, but he seemed to know what he was doing. His name was Binh and
he was maybe twenty-one, but I was eighteen and he seemed like a man
and I was a private and he was our officer, our platoon leader. I wanted
to speak to him because I was feeling the fear pretty bad, like it was a river

catfish with the sharp gills and it was just now pulled out of the water and into the boat, thrashing, with the hook still in its mouth, and my chest was the bottom of the boat.

I sat trying to think what to say to Lieutenant Binh, but there was only a little nattering in my head, no real words at all. Then another private sitting next to me spoke. I do not remember his name. I can't shape his face in my mind anymore. Not even a single feature. But I remember his words. He lifted off his helmet and placed it on the ground beside him and he said, "I bet no man has ever set his foot in this place before."

I heard Lieutenant Binh make a little snoring sound at this, but I didn't pick up on the contempt of it or the bitterness. I probably would've kept silent if I had. But instead, I said to the other privates, "Not since the other dragon came south."

Lieutenant Binh snorted again. This time it was clear to both the other soldier and me that the lieutenant was responding to us. We looked at him and he said to the other, "You're dead meat if you keep thinking like that. It's probably too late for you already. There've been men in this place before, and you better hope it was a couple of days ago instead of a couple of hours."

We both turned our faces away from the rebuke and my cheeks were hotter than the sun could ever make them, even though the lieutenant had spoken to the other private. But I was not to be spared. The lieutenant tapped me on the shoulder with iron fingertips. I looked back to him and he bent near with his face hard, like what I'd said was far worse than the other.

He said, "And what was that about the dragon?"

I was too frightened now to make my mind work. I could only repeat, "The dragon?"

"The dragon," he said, his face coming nearer still. "The thing about the dragon going south."

For a moment I felt relieved. I don't know how the lieutenant sensed this about me, but somehow he knew that when I spoke of the dragon going south, it was not just a familiar phrase meant to refer to a long time ago. He knew that I actually believed. But at that moment I did not understand how foolish this made me seem to him. I said, "The dragon. You know, the gentle dragon who was the father of Vietnam."

The story my father told of the gentle dragon and the fairy princess had always been different from the ones about ghosts that I sought in the candlelight to chill me, though my father did believe in ghosts, as do many Vietnamese people and even some Americans. But the story of how our country began was always told in the daylight and with many of our family members gathered together, and no one ever said to me that this was just a made-up story, that this was just a lovely little lie. When I studied American history to become a citizen here, there was a story of a man named George Washington and he cut down a little tree and then told the truth. And the teacher immediately explained that this was just a made-up story. He made this very clear for even something like that. Just cutting down a tree and telling the truth about it. We had to keep that story separate from the stories that were actual true history.

This makes me sad about this country that was chosen for me, makes me sad for a whole world of adults. It makes me sad even for Lieutenant Binh as I remember his questions that followed, all with a clenched face and a voice as quick and furious as the rifles at our sides. "Is this the dragon who slept with the fairy?" he demanded, though the actual words he used at that moment of my own true history were much harder.

"He married a fairy princess," I said.

"Who married them?" the lieutenant said.

I couldn't answer the question. It was a simple question and it was, I see now, an unimportant question, but sitting in that clearing in the middle of a forest full of men who would kill me, having already fired my rifle at their shapes on several occasions and felt the rush of their bullets past my face and seen already two men die, though I turned my face from that, but having seen two men splashed with their own blood and me sitting now in a forest with the fear clawing at my chest, I faced that simple little question and I realized how foolish I was, how much a child.

The lieutenant cried, "Is this the fairy princess who's going to *lay eggs*?"

And in a moment as terrible as when I first felt the fear of my adult self, I now turned my face from the lieutenant and I looked across the clearing at the tree line and I knew that someone out there was coming near and I knew that dragons and fairies do not have children and the lieutenant's voice was very close to me and it said, "Save your hide."

I don't know if some time passed with me sitting there feeling as crumbly and dry as the tree trunk I leaned against. Maybe only a few seconds, maybe no seconds at all. But very soon, from the tree line before me, there was a flash of light and another and I could only barely shift my eyes to the private sitting next to me and his head was a blur of red and gray and I was as quick as my rifle and over the trunk and beside my lieutenant and we were very quiet together, firing, and all of the rest is very distant from me now. Half of our platoon was dead in those first few seconds, I think. When air support arrived, there was only the lieutenant and me and another private who would soon die from the wounds he received in those few minutes in the clearing.

Not many months later the lieutenant came to me where we were trying to dig in on the rim of Saigon and he said, "It's time," and all the troops of the Army of the Republic of Vietnam were streaming past us into the city, without leaders now, without hope, and so I followed Lieutenant Binh, I and a couple of other soldiers in his platoon that he knew were good fighters, and I did not understand exactly what he meant about its being time until we were in the motorboat of a friend of his and we were racing down the Saigon River. This was the last little bit of my childhood. I was holding my rifle across my chest, ready to fight wherever the lieutenant was leading me. But the lieutenant said, "You won't need that now."

He was talking me and the others into the South China Sea and when I realized I was leaving my country and my wife and my unborn son, I was only able to turn my face to him, for I knew there was no going back. He looked at me with a quick little smile, a warm smile, one man to another, and a nod of the head like he thought I was a good fighter, a good man, a man he respected, and all of that was true, and he thought he was helping me save my life, and maybe that was true, but maybe it wasn't true at all. You must understand, though, that I did not choose to leave.

My son, I love you. Your mother does not love me now and you have a new father. Has she told you about me? Are you reading this? I pray you are; with all the little shiny pebbles of my childhood faith that I can find in the dust, I pray it. And I am writing to tell you this. Thousands of years ago a gentle and kindly dragon grew lonely in the harsh wide plains of China and he wandered south. He found a land full of beautiful mountains and green valleys and fresh, clear rivers that ran so fast in their banks that they made a singing sound.

But even though the land was beautiful, he was still lonely. He traveled through this new country of his and at last he met a beautiful fairy princess. She, too, was lonely and the two of them fell in love and they decided to live together in the beautiful land and one day the princess found that she had laid a hundred eggs in a beautiful silk pouch and these eggs hatched and they were children of the dragon and the princess.

These children were very wonderful, inheriting bravery and gentleness from their father and beauty and charm and delicacy of feeling from their mother. They grew and grew and they were fine, loving children, but finally the dragon had to make a difficult decision. He realized that the family was too large for them all to live together in one place. So he called his family to him and told them that even though he loved them all very much, he would have to divide the family into two parts. His wife would take fifty of the children and travel to the east. He would take the other fifty children and travel to the south. Everyone was very sad about having to do this, but they all understood that there was no other way.

So the princess took fifty of the children and went far away to the east, where she became Queen of the Ocean. And the dragon took fifty children far away to the south, where he became the King of the Land. The dragon and the princess remained with the children until they were adults, wise and strong and able to take care of themselves. Then the dragon and the princess vanished and were reunited in the spirit world, where they lived happily together for the rest of eternity. The children married and prospered and they created Vietnam from the far north to the southern tip and they are the ancestors of all of us. Of you, my son, and of me.

From a time in my life, the part of me that could believe in this story was dead. I often think, here in my new home, that it is dead still. But now, at least, I do not wish it to be dead and it does not make me feel foolish, so perhaps my belief is still part of me. I love you, my son, and all I wish for you is that you save your life. Tell this story that I have told you. Try to think of it as true.

*Stanley Kunitz*
# Father and Son

Now in the suburbs and the falling light
I followed him, and now down sandy road
Whiter than bone-dust, through the sweet
Curdle of fields, where the plums
Dropped with their load of ripeness, one by one.
Mile after mile I followed, with skimming feet,
After the secret master of my blood,
Him, seeped in the odor of ponds, whose indomitable love
Kept me in chains. Strode years; stretched into bird;
Raced through the sleeping country where I was young,
The silence unrolling before me as I came,
The night nailed like an orange to my brow.

How should I tell him my fable and the fears,
How bridge the chasm in a casual tone,
Saying, "The house, the stucco one you built,
We lost. Sister married and went back home,
And nothing comes back, it's strange, from where she goes.
I lived on a hill that had too many rooms:
Light we could make, but not enough warmth,
And when the light failed, I climbed under the hill.
The papers are delivered every day;
I am alone and never shed a tear."

At the water's edge, where the smothering ferns lifted
Their arms, "Father!" I cried, "Return! You know
The way. I'll wipe the mudstains from your clothes;
No trace, I promise, will remain. Instruct
Your son, whirling between two wars,
In the Gemara of your gentleness,

For I would be a child to those who mourn
And brother to the foundlings of the field
And friend of innocence and all bright eyes.
O teach me how to work and keep me kind."

Among the turtles and the lilies he turned to me
The white ignorant hollow of his face.

Paul S. George
# Latecomers

The Fourth of July come and gone, the streets still hugged a a few old, wet banners. In the classroom high above, Professor L. Dary, a short, distinguished-looking man in a Brooks Brothers no pocket dress shirt, rose from the desk. Anybody there would squint hard to read the green surface of the chalk board and, in cramped handwriting, the words: "Marriage and Family 101. If I have to call you down two times, you're out of the class." Those words, that threat, could have been intimidating and account for the unusual low register of sound. After all, Miami is Miami, and silence, when represented, is usually an unreal silence—the kind you find only where an accident nips a jaywalker, or worse.

The professor stepped forward, as if years of knowledge had welled up in him, and he spoke or—one might say—burst.

"You don't know, but Zangara was an Italian immigrant—anarchist. He learned Roosevelt would be coming to stay at the J.C. Penney's estate. Roosevelt had agreed to go to Bayfront Park in Miami to speak and that's where he—Zangara—would make his move.

"So he bought a gun the same day Roosevelt arrives. This was February 15, 1933—Roosevelt was to be sworn in as president in three weeks!

"That's where we are—we're on the site of the apartment that housed Guiseppe Zangara when he was stalking Franklin D. Roosevelt. This place has history!

"I had a girlfriend once who said I was pretty good in history, but I was great on dates." The professor slapped his knee in delight like he hadn't in years.

Outside the window, sparrows scattered like clouds in the windy sky. The professor watched them web off and caught the direction of thought he intended.

"You know the atomic family consists of mother, father, and child.

That's what my family was like in the fifties. It was idyllic. My childhood was a much simpler time."

A body shifted out of a presumed boredom; the door to the classroom opened a crack and a bespeckled young man leaned in.

"I thought this was Marriage," he said, turning before the professor could answer. The professor rustled in his chair until the door had closed all the way.

"My parents were typical, in many ways, of the families of the times. I should tell you, though, they were married *three* times!

"Yes . . . three times." He laughed. "One was by the justice of the peace for the sake of the institution; one was before the minister to satisfy Dad's family; one was before the priest to satisfy Mom's family. Is that three times or one?"

The professor chortled by himself.

"Today, the rate of divorce is one out of two. Back in their day—or at the turn of the century anyway—it was one in sixteen.

"Ostracism and pressure kept people together in those days. Yet it's interesting. Studies show people are not any happier today in their marriages than at the turn of the century—though the divorce rate is eight to ten times as much. Strange.

"I'm happy I married. I started feeling funny in my mid-twenties when all my friends got married. I started thinking, 'Would I grow old alone?' People would remind you of it, too. And I don't mean just mothers."

A face squinted painfully as if taking medicine.

"Three years ago I started thinking—I'm a sport—but I have this fear. At times in the course of the day or night—even with people around me—I felt so isolated—so alone—even though there were people around me! Sometimes beautiful people.

"I heard a wonderful voice within that said, 'You've got to settle down.' I was forty-nine years old and I wanted life with a wife and child. Then I met the right woman." He paused for a splitsecond. "She had wonderful, almond-shaped brown eyes." As light danced across the wall like snow flurries, he looked out across the classroom.

"They're your eyes," he said, gesturing to a small face in front of him.

"I think my fears illustrate some myths about the process. First, there's a myth that you must get married young if you intend to sire a child. Proved that one wrong," he said, smiling. "Second, there's the idea that you won't have the patience for a child if you marry late—or you're too set in your ways for it. All of above? None of above?"

No response, though the professor expected none.

Down the tile-lined hall, a door puffed out a hydraulic sound, and the voices of the faithful latecomers, some of whom had skipped class altogether, boomed off the blue ledge of the stairwell. Hearing footsteps, soft as hellos, he spoke rapidly, more rapidly. In no manner would he be expungable in his effort to complete something deemed important. L. Dary would tell you that.

"Oh, during the assassination attempt on Roosevelt—I'll quickly finish this—a woman in the audience grabbed onto Zangara's arm and he shot the mayor of Chicago, Anton Cirmak, not Roosevelt.

"So Cirmak is lying there, wounded, about to die, and he whispers to Roosevelt, 'I'm glad it was me, instead of you.'

"I guess this could be appropriate for a Marriage and Family discussion. What do you think?

"That's the line I believe any father would say—would want to say—having the opportunity and being in the position to act in a situation like that." He paused, his voice almost floating from the tears that sprung from his now reddened eyes.

"I'd say that to you—if it ever came to that, I'd say, 'I'm glad it was me, instead of you.'"

Before him his eight-month-old child half-slept, his suspenders tight over his shoulders and the white T-shirt blooming over the blue sailor suit. The professor didn't believe the child understood a word spoken there, but he wanted to tell him all he had—and more—as indeed he had whispered words, foreign languages, codes and sayings into his wife's pregnant belly. He wanted to go on and say more, but he heard what had to be his wife's steps closing.

"Class dismissed," L. Dary said, affectionately gesturing to the empty room and greeting an almond-eyed woman at the door, her arms full of Christmas packages.

*Robert Penn Warren*

# XII Lullaby: Smile in Sleep

Sleep, my son, and smile in sleep.
You will dream the world anew.
Watching you now sleep,
I feel the world's depleted force renew,
Feel the nerve expand and knit,
Feel the rustle in the blood,
Feel wink of warmth and stir of spirit,
As though spring woke in the heart's cold underwood.
The vernal work is now begun.
Sleep, my son.
Sleep, son.

You will see the nestling fall.
Blood flecks grass of the rabbit form.
You will, of course, see all
The world's brute ox-heel wrong, and shrewd hand-harm.
Throats are soft to invite the blade.
Truth invites the journalist's lie.
Love bestowed mourns trust betrayed,
But the heart most mourns its own infidelity.
The greater, then, your obligation.
Dream perfection.
Dream, son.

When the diver leaves the board
To hang at gleam-height against the sky,
Trajectory is toward
An image hung perfect as light in his mind's wide eye.
So your dream will later serve you.
So now, dreaming, you serve me,

And give our hope new patent to
Enfranchise human possibility.
Grace undreamed is grace forgone.
Dream grace, son.
Sleep on.

Dream that sleep is a sunlit meadow
Drowsy with a dream of bees
Threading sun, and the shadow
Where you lie lulled by their sunlit industries.
Let the murmurous bees of sleep
Tread down honey in the honeycomb.
Heart-deep now, your dream will keep
Sweet in that deep comb for time to come.
Dream the sweetness coming on.
Dream, sweet son.
Sleep on.

What if angry vectors veer
Around your sleeping head, and form?
There's never need to fear
Violence of the poor world's abstract storm.
For now you dream Reality.
Matter groans to touch your hand.
Matter lifts now like the sea
Toward the cold moon that is your dream's command.
Dream the power coming on.
Dream, strong son.
Sleep on.

*George Garrett*
# For My Sons

This world that you are just beginning
now to touch, taste, feel, smell, hear and see,
to have and to hold, and daily more and more
finding sound in your throats, tremors of tongue
to play with, words (some like a ripe plum
or an orange to daze the whole mouth
with sweetness, so that in speaking
you seem to kiss, some like a bitter phlegm
to be coughed up and spit out clean), this world
is all I would claim for you, save you from.

I am a foolish father like all the rest,
would put my flesh, my shadow in between
you and the light that wounds and blesses.
I would throw a cloak over your heads
and carry you home, warm and close, to keep
you from the dark that chills to the bone.
Foolish (I said) I would teach you only words
that sing on the lips. Still, you have to learn
to spit in my face and save your souls.
Still you must curse with fever and desire.

Nothing of earned wisdom I can give you,
nothing save the old words like rock candy
to kill the taste of dust on the tongue.
Nothing stings like the serpent, no pain greater.
Bear it. If a bush should burn and cry out,
bow down. If a stranger wrestles, learn his name.
and if after long tossing and sickness you find
a continent, plant your flags, send forth a dove.
Rarely the fruit you reach for returns your love.

Richard Blessing
# Calling Home

I call about my father's business.
Mother takes the hard route, the climb
upstairs to the bedroom, where the bed
used to be. Father stays where he is.

*How goes it?* I say to him, and it does.
Mother says, *Don't expect him to say too much.*

Suddenly I hear everything he is saying:
His knees have forgotten to go up stairs or down.
His eyes have forgotten there is light to let be.
My mother and I are talking about snow, the terrible snow.

When he goes to the mirror, Father says, one face
cries out loud, but the other is still. He forgets
buckling and unbuckling, the complexities of buttonholes.
Sometimes he forgets the boy across the street
who shovels their snow, and sometimes remembers him
but calls him by our secret name that was mine.

*Don't worry about us,* says Mother. *Don't worry, don't worry.*
*Never,* I promise, again and again. *What's to worry?*

My father is trying to say one thing, something so terrible
it must be said out loud. *Be careful,* he says, *driving after dark.*
He thinks again I am coming to get him, to take him away.
*Darlin',* my mother says to him then, *he's in Seattle,*
*remember? He won't be in today.* There is so much love
in the touch of her voice, if the phone company heard,
it would charge night rates. *I forgot,* says my father,
but he says it again: *Be careful driving after dark.*

For days after I hang up, I hear him. He names over and over
all he has forgotten. How old he is. How old I am. His dead father.
He has forgotten any women he ever knew. When have we ever
talked on so long? *Father,* I write him here, *father, it's all right
to be old.* What do I know? What does he know? For the first time
I am afraid of the dark. *Sing me a sleep-song,* I ask him,
from a poem. He is seventy now, and this is his business.
*Be careful,* he tells me. *Be careful driving after dark.*

*Lewis Carroll*

# You Are Old, Father William

"You are old, Father William," the young man said,
    "And your hair has become very white;
And yet you incessantly stand on your head—
    Do you think, at your age, it is right?"

"In my youth," Father William replied to his son,
    "I feared it might injure my brain;
But now that I'm perfectly sure I have none,
    I do it again and again."

"You are old," said the youth, "as I mentioned before,
    And have grown most uncommonly fat;
Yet you turned a back-somersault in at the door—
    Pray what is the reason for that?"

"In my youth," said the sage, as he shook his gray locks,
    "I kept all my limbs very supple
By the use of this ointment—one shilling the box—
    Allow me to sell you a couple."

"You are old," said the youth, "and your jaws are too weak
    For anything tougher than suet;
Yet you finished the goose, with the bones and the beak:
    Pray, how did you manage to do it?"

"In my youth," said his father, "I took to the law,
    And argued each case with my wife;
And the muscular strength which it gave to my jaw
    Has lasted the rest of my life."

"You are old," said the youth; "one would hardly suppose
    That your eye was as steady as ever:
Yet you balanced an eel on the end of your nose—
    What made you so awfully clever?"

"I have answered three questions, and that is enough,"
    Said his father; "don't give yourself airs!
Do you think I can listen all day to such stuff?
    Be off, or I'll kick you downstairs!"

*Peter Davison*

# Words for My Father

> *If God chooses you to have a son, tremble:*
> *For just twelve years you may remain his father.*
> *From twelve to twenty, try to be his teacher.*
> *Thereafter you may hope to die his friend.*
>                                        A Mexican villager

### 1. VOICE

Your gorgeous voice soared
down the flumes
of the trembling canyons.
Sentences and judgments rang out
with the clarity of air that knows little rain.
Giver, trainer of tongues,
even cottonwoods do not grow without water.
Your voice's notes were poetry, pity, war.
It restored bodies to the dead.
It taunted my mother, turning you into her child.
It sharpened the duellers' blades of long-forgotten rages.
It yearned for the doting and the pity of your children.

### 2. VOYAGE

I, Telemachus, came to the sea after twenty years
and sailed to inquire
through all the trafficked harbors of the world
for news of my father's victories.
The voyage brought home little but pain,
messages garbled in transmission.
The air was dirty and silent still.
My father's eyes turned away
from the knowledge-swollen face of his son.

3. DEAD

Later, when death began paying
its visits,
we were manacled by the knowledge
of how Penelope, infuriatingly patient,
had us bound together.
On the voyages since, another ten years,
we have kept silence like Greeks
"carrying heavy urns full of the ashes of our ancestors."
We have not forgotten
your mother's rectitude, her shabby flirtatious plumage,
nor your father, whose testament
was leaner than you desired—as every father's is.
His blood has scalded you
but you need not share his blame.
Give him your blessing.


4. ROAD

I walk forward in the afternoon of dying
along the road of words, cruel to the feet.
The dry tawny hills below your orchard
stretch away without shade or the sound of water.
Not yet in sight of you, Laertes, I hear your
cough, your parched and grating throat.
Shall I answer the question you are sure to ask?
*If you are Odysseus, my son, come back,*
*give me some proof, a sign to make me sure.*
I have three signs: the scar, the trees, the words.
The trees you planted, felled, buried under rubble.
The love we shared, carried by words only.
Deeds overwhelmed us.

5. WORDS

Words need not always fail.
No matter how seldom
we gather ourselves
to gather our hopes
into flocks, herding them before us
to huddle in their pens,
they are our dearest gift from this sparse soil,
the locked and grudging earth. They are
our servants, our sacrifice, our pledges.

Your gift to me
is my gift to you . . .

*John Hall Wheelock*
# The Gardener
*(In Memory of my Father)*

Father, whom I knew well for forty years
Yet never knew, I have come to know you now—
In age, make good at last those old arrears.

Though time, that snows the hair and lines the brow,
Has equalled us, it was not time alone
That brought me to the knowledge I here avow.

Some profound divination of your own,
In all the natural effects you sought
Planted a secret that is now made known.

These woodland ways, with your heart's labor bought,
Trees that you nurtured, gardens that you planned,
Surround me here, mute symbols of your thought.

Your meaning beckons me on every hand,
Grave aisles and vistas, in their silence, speak
A language that I now can understand.

In all you did, as in yourself, unique—
Servant of beauty, whom I seek to know,
Discovering here the clue to what I seek.

When down the nave of your great elms I go
That soar their Gothic arches where the sky,
Nevertheless, with all its stars will show,

Or when the moon of summer, riding high,
Spills through the leaves her light from far away,
I feel we share the secret, you and I.

All these you loved and left. We may not stay
Long with the joy our hearts are set upon:
This is a thing that here you tried to say.

The night has fallen; the day's work is done;
Your groves, your lawns, the passions of this place,
Cry out your love of them—but you are gone.

O father, whom I may no more embrace
In childish fervor, but, standing far apart,
Look on your spirit rather than your face,

Time now has touched me also, and my heart
Has learned a sadness that yours earlier knew,
Who labored here, though with the greater art.

The truth is on me now that was with you:
How life is sweet, even its very pain,
The years how fleeting and the days how few.

Truly, your labors have not been in vain:
These woods, these walks, these gardens—everywhere
I look, the glories of your love remain.

Therefore, for you, now beyond praise or prayer,
Before the night falls that shall make us one,
In which neither of us will know to care,

This kiss, father, from him who was your son.

*Donald Justice*

# Sonnet to My Father

Father, since always now the death to come
Looks naked out from your eyes into mine,
Almost it seems the death to come is mine
And that I also shall be overcome,
Father, and call for breath when you succumb,
And struggle for your hand as you for mine
In hope of comfort that shall not be mine
Till for this last of me the angel come.
But, father, though with you in part I die
And glimpse beforehand that eternal place
Where we forget the pain that brought us there,
Father, and though you go before me there,
Leaving but this poor likeness in your place,
Yet while I live, you cannot wholly die.

# PERMISSIONS ACKNOWLEDGMENTS

Peter Oresick, "My Father." From *Definitions*, published by West End Press. Copyright © 1990 by Peter Oresick.

Simon J. Ortiz, "My Father's Song." Copyright © 1976 by Simon J. Ortiz. Reprinted by permission of author.

Tom Reiter, "Handholds." Copyright © 1992 by Tom Reiter. Used by permission of author.

Theodore Roethke, "My Papa's Waltz," copyright © 1942 by Hearst Magazines, Inc. From *The Collected Poems of Theodore Roethke* by Theodore Roethke. Used by permission of Doubleday, a division of Bantam Doubleday Dell Publishing Group, Inc.

Gamble Rogers, "My Father Was a Voyager," Copyright © 1991 by Gamble Rogers. Used by permission of Nancy Lee Rogers.

Stephen Sandy, "Expecting Fathers." From *Man in the Open Air*. Copyright © 1977 by Stephen Sandy. Reprinted by permission of Alfred A. Knopf, Inc.

Jonathan Schwartz, "Over the Purple Hills." *From The Man Who Knew Cary Grant.* Copyright © 1988 by Jonathan Schwartz. Reprinted by permission of Random House, Inc.

Steven Schwartz, "Madagascar." From *Lives of the Fathers*. Copyright © 1991 by Steven Schwartz. By permission of University of Illinois Press.

Richard Shelton, "Letting Go." From *Selected Poems: 1969–1981*, University of Pittsburgh Press, 1982. Copyright © 1982 by Richard Shelton. By permission of Richard Shelton.

Louis Simpson, "My Father in the Night Commanding No." From *At the End of the Open Road*. Copyright © 1963 by Louis Simpson. Wesleyan University Press by permission of University Press of New England.

William Jay Smith, "American Primitive." Reprinted with permission of Charles Scribner's Sons, an imprint of Macmillan Publishing Company, from *Collected Poems 1939–1989* by William Jay Smith. Copyright © 1957, 1990 by William Jay Smith.

Matthew J. Spireng, "The Snake" by Matthew J. Spireng. Copyright © 1992 by Matthew Spireng. Used by permission of the author.

William Stafford, "Listening." From *Stories That Could Be True*, Harper & Row, 1977. Copyright © 1977 by William Stafford. Used by permission of the author.

Lucien Stryk, "Rites of Passage." From *Collected Poems, 1953–1983*, published by Swallow Press/The Ohio University Press, 1984. Reprinted with the permission of The Ohio University Press/Swallow Press, Athens.

James Tate, "The Lost Pilot." From *The Lost Pilot* by James Tate. Copyright © 1967 by Yale University. Reprinted by permission of the James Tate.

Henry Taylor, "Green Springs the Tree." From *The Flying Change: Poems* by Henry Taylor. Copyright © 1985 by Henry Taylor. Reprinted by permission of Louisiana State University Press.

Dylan Thomas, "Do Not Go Gentle Into that Good Night." From *Poems of Dylan Thomas*. Copyright © 1952 by Dylan Thomas. Reprinted by permission of New Directions Publishing and David Higham Associates.

John Updike, "Son." From *Problems and Other Stories* by John Updike. Copyright © 1973 by John Updike. Reprinted by permission of Alfred A. Knopf, Inc.

Robert Penn Warren, "XII Lullaby: Smile in Sleep." From *Selected Poems: 1923–1975*. Copyright © 1957 by Robert Penn Warren. Reprinted by permission of Random House, Inc.

Jerome Weidman, "My Father Sits in the Dark." From *My Father Sits in the Dark and Other Stories* by Jerome Weidman. Copyright 1934, copyright renewed © 1961. Reprinted by permission of Brandt & Brandt Literary Agents, Inc.

Tom Whalen, "The Missing Part." Copyright © 1989 *Timbuktu*. Reprinted by permission of author.

John Hall Wheelock, "The Gardener." Reprinted with permission of Charles Scribner's Sons, an imprint of Macmillan Publishing Company, from *By Daylight and in Dream: New and Collected Poems, 1904–1970* by John Hall Wheelock. Copyright © 1957 by John Hall Wheelock. Originally appeared in *The New Yorker*.

John Hall Wheelock, "Together." Reprinted with permission of Charles Scribners' Sons, an imprint of Macmillan Publishing Company, from *By Daylight and in Dream: New and Collected Poems, 1904–1970*. Copyright © 1929, 1936 by Charles Scribner's Sons; renewal copyrights © 1957, 1964 by John Hall Wheelock.

Miller Williams, "Vision in Black and White." From *Halfway to Hoxie: New and Selected Poems*. Copyright © 1964, 1968, 1971, 1973 by Miller Williams. By permission of Louisiana State University Press.

Clive Wilmer, "The Sparking of the Forge." From *The Dwelling Place* by Clive Wilmer. Copyright © 1977 by Clive Wilmer. By permission of Carcanet Press Limited.

Thomas Wolfe, from *The Face of a Nation: Poetical Passages from the Writings of Thomas Wolfe*. Reprinted with the permission of Charles Scribner's Sons, an imprint of MacMillan Publishing Company. Copyright © 1935 by Charles Scribner's Sons, renewed © 1963 by Paul Gitlin, Administrator, C.T.A.

Geoffrey Wolff, from *The Duke of Deception*. Copyright © 1979 by Geoffrey Wolff. Reprinted by permission of Random House, Inc.

Charles David Wright, "Shaving." Reprinted, by permission of the publisher, from *Early Rising* by Charles David Wright. Copyright © 1968 by the University of North Carolina Press.